Of His Bones

Tracey Scott-Townsend

Inspired
Quill

Published by Inspired Quill: March 2017

First Edition

Contact the author through her website:
traceyscotttownsend.com

Chief Editor: Sara-Jayne Slack
Cover Design: Jane Dixon-Smith
Typeset in Adobe Garamond Pro

Paperback ISBN: 978-1-908600-55-4
eBook ISBN: 978-1-908600-56-1
Print Edition

Printed in the United Kingdom
1 2 3 4 5 6 7 8 9 10

Inspired Quill Publishing, UK
Business Reg. No. 7592847
www.inspired-quill.com

Praise for Tracey Scott-Townsend

If you are looking for a book that will take you along on an emotional family journey, grab you down deep and keep you guessing – look no further. Ms. Townsend has crafted a lovely tale here [in The Last Time We Saw Marion] that will fully immerse you. The author has done a fine job of creating a cast of characters that are as multi-faceted as every human being with both good qualities and bad. There is no down-time in this novel. The writing is crisply and richly detailed.

– Louise Caiola,
author of *The Making Of Nebraska Brown*

When I had to put [Another Rebecca] down, I felt disoriented, confused; so involved was I in the lives of these fictional characters, so skillfully created by the author. Tracey cleverly describes unearthly events – fleeting glimpses of something the reader cannot see, whispers we cannot fully hear, a brush of something not quite real against our skin – yet at the same time, she pulls no punches in her earthy descriptions of the all-too-human protagonists.

– Sharon Booth,
Goodreads author

Tracey Scott-Townsend has done it again. Of His Bones surpassed my very high expectations. It's a glorious, melodic, haunting and beautiful book, exploring themes of family, choice, destiny and love. While the language was so exquisite I longed to read slowly, the page-turning plot had me steaming ahead. The characters are gorgeously painted, pulsating and real. And the

To my mother, Margaret McCall Wilson, my grandmother, Agnes McCall and my great-grandmother, Frances Wildy: female marrow of my bones.

Full fathom five thy father lies, of his bones are coral made;
Those are pearls that were his eyes: Nothing of him that doth fade,
But doth suffer a sea-change
Into something rich and strange.
Sea-nymphs hourly ring his knell: Ding-dong.
Hark! Now I hear them, – ding-dong bell.

The Tempest
Act One Scene Two
William Shakespeare

1

Mariana Rivers, February 2009

YOU KNOW WHEN you wake up the day after some momentous event and you don't even remember it happened? This morning, my first thoughts were that my feet were cold and what the hell had happened to my quilt because it didn't snuggle around me like I'm used to – it felt thin and sort of stretched over the top of my shoulders, letting the air in. Too much light penetrated my eyelids. I didn't open them straight away. There were unfamiliar sounds going on; something clinking, and there was snoring and an unusual smell and – the atmosphere around me just felt *different*. I knew without even opening my eyes.

It felt sore between my legs as well, like that time me and Damon… No, I won't. It's too private. Also, my boobs felt heavier than normal, even with me being – and then it hit me like a blow to the head. *I've had the baby.*

I've had a baby. I'm in the postnatal ward. There are

three other women and their babies in this side room with me, and loads of others out there in the other rooms off the main ward. The place is buzzing with us. Mothers, I mean, and babies. *Sweet Jesus*, can you believe it? I gave birth to an actual, real-life baby: a wee boy. There he is, lying in the see-through plastic crib next to my bed.

The memories slowly came back as I lay, still waking up. My mam brought me to hospital yesterday when the pains got too bad to stay at home. Dad would've taken us here because Mam doesn't really like driving but he was too far away on a gardening job, so she had to do it. The next person to arrive was Damon, my baby's daddy – *ha-ha, his friends are going to take the piss out of him now* – and then, would you believe it? Bloody Aunty Geraldine turned up. *What the…?* You'd think she could've at least waited until I'd had the ruddy baby but no, she had to get herself in on the action. Wherever you look, she seems to be there. As if she thinks my mam can't cope or something; it's really getting on my rag. Just because she's had some daughters of her own and Mam 'only' adopted me.

I hated seeing Mam's face when one of the nurses let Geraldine into the room. It kind of fell, like she was thinking *not her again*. I've always called her Aunty but she's a cousin or something of Mam. Maybe once-removed. But I did hear Dad on the phone once to his work partner. "A close family friend would be more accurate." And then, *get this*, "I've had to bite my tongue on many an occasion, but we *are* stuck with her. It's in the contract."

In. The. Contract. What the bloody hell does that mean?

I'd forgotten all about it. Except now I'm mad at her for muscling in on the birth of Mam's first grandchild. Why doesn't she get some bloody grandkids of her own?

Ah, look, my new little baby has opened his eyes. *My baby*, I can't believe it.

I'M EIGHTEEN YEARS old and a mother. My son's birthday will always be exactly a week after mine. *Always*. I hold him in my arms and look down into his searching, blue-green eyes and wonder why I can't stop crying. It's as if I can see the future, and my boy's already grown up and gone away. *You'd better take your time, my boy.* This baby is the first true relative I've ever had of my very own. Mam and Dad are wonderful – really, truly wonderful, but for the first time I can't help considering the woman who gave birth to me. Did she ever hold me in her arms like this?

I never realised how much having a baby would hurt and I don't mean inside my stomach and between my legs and my nipples from letting this little one suck on them (yeah, Damon read something about how good it is for the baby so he agreed it was the right thing to do.) It hurts in my heart though, and I wasn't expecting that. Nor had I expected the raging anger that comes flooding into me at my birth mother for giving me away.

DAMON SUGGESTS NAMES. "Donal?" Tapping his fingers

on the arms of the orange-coloured bedside chair, frowning with what…? Disgust, awe, puzzlement? The sight of me and our child. The baby tugging at my nipple. A shock of lust powers through me as Damon catches my eye. It takes my breath away, but then it's gone again just as quickly. Possibly I imagined it. I'm woozy and alert all at the same time. I'm ecstatically happy but also mournfully sad. I'm all over the place, in other words.

"No, I don't like that." Our son doesn't look like a Donal. The baby closes his eyes and loosens his grip, his head lolling on my arm. With my spare hand I pull my vest back over my boob.

"Babe," Damon whistles. "You make me so horny." He wiggles his hand in a rude gesture.

"Shhhh, they'll hear you!"

I giggle and glance at the other mothers, all older than me. They have their husbands and children with them. None of their new babies looks as beautiful as mine. I know – new mothers always think their baby's the most gorgeous, but it's really true in the case of the little lad Damon's reaching his arms out for now. Our kid has round cheeks and feathery blonde eyebrows, he has these intense greenish eyes. *Look*, I can't really explain what makes him look bonnier than the others but he honestly does.

I pass him over with a feeling of actual reverence. Damon comes across proper confident, holding our boy upright against his chest. He kisses the top of the baby's head.

"Are those tears?" I kind of hope the way his eyes are brimming is only a joke. He needs to stay the same because of this swelling feeling in my chest, I'm scared I'll burst. He sniffs and wipes his eyes on his sweatshirt sleeve.

"Might be. What if they are? Look at what we made though, babe."

Yeah.

"He's like an angel." With his hand under the baby's head, Damon lowers him backwards until he's resting him on his knees. Our boy curls his tiny hands into fists. Looking at him from a different angle like this my stomach caves in. *What if I lose him?* I want to reach out and grab him back. For a second my ears go muffled, then the sound returns and Damon's saying, "…in the school play, you know, the Nativity?"

"Yeah." I felt like the Virgin Mary with my huge belly when I went with Damon to see his little sister's performance at Christmas. "What about it?"

"We should call him Gabriel. Gabe for short."

➤➤➤❮❮❮

AUNTY GERALDINE'S SHOWING me something in a newspaper – the posh one she always reads. Before opening it on my bed she insisted on taking Gabriel out of my arms and tucking him under the blanket in the plastic crib. "It doesn't do to spoil them," she said in her prim-and-proper voice. *Bog off,* is what I thought in my head, but I didn't say. You have to pick your arguments with that woman and this one wasn't worth it. He was fine, anyway – still fast asleep. Probably bored of hearing her harping voice.

It's a review of some sort, I don't know what she's

showing *me* for. A play in a theatre in London. "Yeah, and…?"

"Mariana. No need to be so rude. It's about a mother who had to give up her baby and now wants to make contact with her lost daughter. I thought you might be interested in seeing it with me?"

"Why?" I span out my fingers, tip my hand towards the baby in the crib, like, *have you forgotten something?*

"You could bring the baby along. We could get a babysitter while we went to see the play."

I glance at the writing on the page and it dawns on me what she's saying. "You mean go to London?" *To. See. A. Play.* "Why would I?"

The woman's in a world of her own. Seriously, I've just given birth and she wants me to go gallivanting off to London. Her lips disappear – it's as if they've moved up to her forehead, the horizontal frown there's so deep. Her skin, normally dead white, is now red.

"Don't you see? It's entirely appropriate. You're eighteen now, the age when most adopted children begin searching for their birth parents. This play might help you understand what it was like for your mother. It's important that you know, dear."

I keep staring at her. Since I got pregnant she's never stopped going on about me finding my birth mother. *What. The…?*

"You're a mother yourself now, Mariana. Your own mother might be waiting for you to make contact with her…"

"I'm not being rude, Aunty Geraldine, but what

business is it of… I mean, why do you even care? Surely you should be on Mam's side – you know how sensitive she is about stuff like that."

"I'm not on anybody's *side*." But it doesn't ring true. Red earrings sway against her neck as she starts messing about with a handkerchief in her bag. Damon calls her a classy bird for her age but she looks like she's struggling to hold it together at the moment. *What is up with her?* She dabs the end of her nose with the hanky then puts it away again. It looks odd, the way she smooths her hand over the page of newspaper, glancing at me again before beginning to fold it, slowly. Like something's really bugging her. "I do think you should see this play, dear."

My baby stirs in his crib, flinging his hands out from under the blankets. Gushing between my legs and I need to go to the bathroom. Hot prickling breaks out all over me. The hospital lights suddenly feel too bright and I want Aunty Geraldine to go away. She finally notices.

"Why are you crying, dear?"

"I'm not. I'm just… I can't deal with this right now, Aunty Geraldine. I'm not going with you to see the play, ok? Just accept it. Please."

She looks so disappointed. But it's not my fault. Everything's gone blurry through the water in my eyes and at the periphery of my vision I see those small pink hands flailing. *He needs me.* It's a physical pull. But I need to get to the bathroom and back before he begins screaming the place down. It's not my job to do what Aunty Geraldine wants – I've got my baby to think of now.

2

Maria Child, January 2013

I WIPED MY chin on the back of my hand, hoping Alice hadn't noticed me dribbling. Maybe I'd been snoring too. No-one, apart from occasional lovers, had ever seen me in the vulnerability of sleep. Except in hospital – and that was different. Impersonal. Then, I was so detached I barely existed. Now, in the car, I struggled to rise from the clinging cobwebs of my dark pit, the sweet unconsciousness that had threatened to cocoon me indefinitely so many times.

Bleary eyed, I pulled myself into a more upright position, extracted a soft mint from a packet I found in my handbag and offered one to Alice. She refused with a sideways smile, taking her eyes only briefly from the road.

The mint freshened my mouth enough to speak and restored me, at least outwardly, to the realms of the awake.

"It's got dark since I dozed off. What time is it?"

"Almost five o'clock," her eyes flickered to the

dashboard clock and back to the unlit strip of road in front of us. "You've been asleep most of the trip."

"I've no energy at the moment."

That was an understatement. I didn't even know the name of the place we were heading, and I hadn't been interested enough to ask. Alice had taken me by surprise, turning up at my mother's house and demanding that I accompany her on a weekend break by the sea. And of course my mother encouraged it – she would try anything to get me well.

I trusted Alice, both as an actress and as a friend. She reminded me of my youngest sister and as such, I'd allowed myself to get closer to Alice than I had to most other people.

During the time I'd known her, Alice had probably chattered on about some idyll by the sea where she'd grown up, referring to it by various pet names, but I couldn't remember where she'd said it was. Lincolnshire? Anyway, within driving distance of Leeds, where my family lived.

"Mum'll be pleased to have some female company. She was good friends with our next door neighbour, but she died last year." We held a respectful silence for a few moments. "And Mum misses my brother. He only comes home for a couple of weeks at a time."

"What about your dad?"

"My step-dad. Well, he's ok but he has these dark moods." She lifted a hand from the wheel. "Maybe we women can arrange an evening out together."

Ha. She was nothing if not an eternal optimist. *Me, on a night out?* "I'm not much of a drinker, Alice."

I didn't like crowds either. *She knows that.* I peered

ahead at the black road. With no streetlights, I could see nothing beyond the tarmac surface with its white lines.

"Where are we?"

"We're just coming up to Restingham."

Alice steered the car carefully around a bend. "If you look over there, you'll see the gas terminal, all lit up. I used to think it magical when my father drove me back on Sunday nights after I stayed the weekend with him."

I couldn't see anything at first. But the name rang a bell. *Restingham.* Where had I heard it before?

A door slamming shut inside me.

"What's your village called?" The air around my lips was cold – preposterous that I hadn't asked already, I could see that now.

"It's called Pottersea. Oh yeah, I once told you it was Weepot, didn't I? A joke me and my brother made up when Mum was toilet-training my sister – get it? We'd be in the car, little Sis with her legs crossed and my brother and me chanting, *hurry back home to Weepot.*" Typical Alice. She can't ever have told me the actual name. I would never have agreed… oh no…

My muscles were tingling. My jaw becoming numb. No.

I need to tell Alice something. Something very important.

I can't go back to this place.

"Maria, Maria…" Alice's voice filtered through to me. "We're here. Are you ok? I think you just had one of your…you know."

I flexed my fingers. Alice leaned over me. "Don't worry, we're here now. Let's go inside and get you a drink. I'll carry your bag in for you. Can you move properly yet?"

No, I wanted to shout. *I can't go in there. I can't go into that house.* But my voice was no more than a croak. She handed me a bottle of water. I took a sip, not knowing how to ask her to take me straight home.

Perhaps his family had left a long time ago. Somebody else lived at Blackberry House now. But her name carried the answer. Alice. I had a fleeting mental image of a golden-haired child.

What have I done? How have I ended up back where I started?

All those years of careful work.

Alice came around to my side of the car, opened the passenger door and extended a hand. She obviously didn't remember we had met once before, decades ago. If she had, she wouldn't have worked in my theatre company. Would have avoided me like the plague.

"Alice, I…"

The neatly packaged boxes in my memory had been rattled, their contents shaken. I took a deep breath.

Get a grip, Maria.

"Out you get. You'll feel better once we're out of the car and inside. There'll be a fire in the kitchen. Cal will offer you a whiskey."

With one hand clutching the back of the seat I managed to swing my feet outwards, but the movement was too sudden; I vomited onto the gravel. With her previous knowledge of my illness, Alice had already stepped out of the way, anticipating what would happen. Then she moved forward again and grasped my arm.

"Come on. Step around it carefully." It was only mucus anyway. I'd barely eaten for two days. With deft movements, Alice reached into the back seat for my holdall and kicked both the front and back doors shut, still holding onto me with one hand.

A cold wind buffeted us as she propelled me to the front door of her home, a three storey white house with the windows of the top floor set back from the rest of the façade. Just as we stepped into the stone-flagged porch, a woman pulled open the heavy wooden door.

"Alice!" Her mother's greedy hands snatched the girl and enveloped her in a hug.

"Mum!" Alice reproved, pulling away at last. "We need to get Maria inside, she's not very well."

"Oh, I *am* sorry, hello!"

Lisa. She beckoned us through the hallway and into her huge kitchen. Lamps set into the walls cast a homely glow. The long table in the centre of the room sat on red floor tiles which looked as if they'd been polished. I saw that Lisa, always full-figured, had thickened around the waist. She'd be nearly fifty-seven, my stirred brain calculated. *I would have been, too, if…* I pressed a hand against my mouth at the sight of the quarry tiles. This kitchen had played such a significant part in my story.

"There's a cloakroom to your right, if you need to freshen up." Lisa had hardly looked at me. "Can I get you a drink?"

It used to be called the downstairs toilet. I took unsteady breaths. Lisa stared at me.

"Sorry, you look familiar." She took a few steps backwards, turning my name over in her mouth. Her icy distrust blew through my clothes. "Maria Child. Have we met before?"

If Alice hadn't been there I would have explained, but I didn't want to awaken bad memories. The colour drained from Lisa's face. Quite clearly she shared my concern for her daughter and hid her shock well.

"What can I get you?" Her voice was like water cracking ice.

Alice didn't notice, bending to stroke a tortoiseshell cat. "Get her a whisky, Mum. And one for me as well, please. Look, Maria, isn't this woodstove cosy? We had it installed after Christmas last year. Well, I mean the year before." She laughed. "I keep forgetting last week was technically last year. Anyway, come and sit down by the stove." She took my arm and pulled me with her to the other end of the kitchen to a sofa, strategically placed to catch the immediate warmth from the wood-burning stove.

Lisa had her back to us, but I could sense the trembling in her long cotton skirt. A girl with dyed black hair thumped down the open, antique-carpeted staircase behind us. The girl scanned me with green eyes, causing my empty stomach to lurch. *His* daughter, his other daughter.

"Who's that?" the girl muttered to her mother at the counter.

"Don't be rude, Angel," Alice jumped up and pulled her unwilling sister into a hug. "Maria," she said. "This is my delightfully named sister."

Alice seemed pleased to be home. *It would have been so much better for her to have arrived without me.* Angel barely glanced my way. "How's your boyfriend?" she asked her sister.

A smile warmed my protégé's face. She'd spent Christmas in Spain. Angel rolled her eyes, went over to a different counter and opened a wooden bread bin. She cut herself a hunk of bread which, once she'd spread it with butter she carried in two hands back up the stairs. There was something animal-like about her. Above us a door slammed and the footsteps continued upwards. *The attic,* I thought. *She has her room in the attic.*

Lisa handed Alice and me our whiskies. She stood uncertainly for a moment, and then perched on the arm of a chair. She met my eyes briefly. The antique sofa I sat on had once nestled under the stairs, the new woodstove had replaced the old Aga and in place of the Aga a black metal cooker sat to one side of the alcove. Lisa saw me looking.

"What do you think?"

There was no warmth in her tone. She looked as sick as I felt. We were two restless animals trapped in a cage.

"It's lovely." I pushed my trembling hands between my knees, wishing I could make myself disappear. Alice shifted uncomfortably.

"Do you two know each other?"

"From a long time ago; it doesn't matter now." Lisa made an effort to smile. "Can I get you another whisky?"

I'd downed the first one too quickly. I declined with a shake of my head. Lisa swallowed hard. "So *you* wrote the play that gave Alice her big break."

A flat statement. But she followed it with a loaded question. "Is it autobiographical?"

Alice rested her hand on my shoulder before I could answer. She had been in the office with me at work when I learned that my daughter had, for the second time, rejected my request for contact. Her empathy in that circumstance was what had led to her become one of my few friends.

"Leave it, Mum," she prompted softly. "Maria's had a rough time. And she's not been well."

"Your stepfather will be home shortly."

Lisa pricked out each word, hung lights around it so I couldn't fail to notice what she was saying. It was me she looked at with her piercing blue eyes. Neither of us knew what to do. I couldn't be there when Cal Wilde arrived home. I started to rise shakily from my seat, feeling sick.

"Is there a B&B I could stay at near here?"

Alice's mouth dropped open. She looked at me, and then at Lisa with confusion in her eyes. Grabbing my wrist, none too gently, she pulled me back down into the embroidered sofa cushions.

"You're not going to a B&B, Maria, of course you're not. What are you thinking of? You're here as our guest. Oh my God, why would you suggest such a thing?" Tears gathered in her big blue eyes, so like her mother's.

"Perhaps you could do with an early night, though," Lisa butted in. "Alice, why don't you show Maria to her room? She looks exhausted." She turned to me. "Alice could bring you up some food on a tray."

Yes. Let me go. I stood up again and felt my way around

the back of the sofa, longing to escape up the stairs. Lisa defended herself against her daughter's cold stare. "You said Maria wasn't feeling well."

I gripped the polished dome on the banister post. It seemed the only solution. Keep me hidden away from Cal. Perhaps I'd be able to sneak out of there in the morning. I wondered if the bus I'd caught to the village so long ago still ran or whether recent public service cuts had rendered it extinct. I'd just have to hope for the best, stay out of Cal's way at any cost. My long-term illness threatened me with every shaking breath; every tingle and ache in my muscles. Alice raised her hands in a helpless gesture, glancing from one of us to the other as if we'd both gone mad.

"Well if you insist… But I thought we could have a lovely evening together. Mum, I thought Maria might be company. But you obviously…"

She looked about to cry, shoulders slumping as if all the air had gone out of her. Giving up the fight, she followed me to the staircase.

"It's the room at the far end of the landing."

Sliding the strap of my holdall more firmly onto her shoulder, she guided me in a U-turn around the top banister. She flicked a switch, bathing the landing in a soft glow. I noticed straight away the carpet up here was new, well: new to me. I experienced a flash of the compulsion I once had for this home, exploring it as a girl of seventeen.

"It used to be Angel's room," Alice said. "But she's moved into my old room, that's the attic. I still sleep up there when I'm home. It's divided into two."

Oh, I know the attic, alright.

She opened the bedroom door at the end of the corridor.

"Sorry, it's still got one black wall, Angel was supposed to repaint it fully before she moved upstairs but she never got round to finishing it. It does have its own tiny bathroom, though."

Three of the walls were painted a rich butterscotch, with darker patches where the black showed through. We both sat on the edge of the bed. It had a dark blue quilt cover, decorated with gold stars. Alice searched my eyes.

"That was pretty weird, you know, you and my mum. Where have you met before?"

I was silent, picking at the edges of my fingernails.

"Tell me." She held my gaze steadily.

"It doesn't matter, really," I said, the same as her mother. Standing up I pushed at the curtain, nudging the top pane of the window open. Darkness glared in. I could smell the sea and hear the wind blowing through the trees at the side of the house. My stomach hurt. "It was a lifetime ago, but we'll talk about it another time, ok? Please. I can't face it now." I sat down again, rubbed my eyes.

"You're really not very well, are you? I'm sorry for pushing you. Hopefully you'll feel better in the morning."

Alice gave me an anxious glance and drew the curtains against the black night, but I tugged a narrow gap open again. I wanted to tilt my face and sniff the air like a dog. A long-ago memory came back to me of Jude, the collie that once lived in this house.

"I'll bring you a sandwich and a cup of tea. Promise me you'll try and eat something?"

Alice peered into my eyes again and I had a brief recollection of the child she was, probing me with questions. What if she discovered me?

"You're very kind."

"Are you sure you want to be up here on your own? It's still early. You could come down and eat with us, if you change your mind."

"No, honestly, I'd rather stay up here. I'm not very good at coping with new situations. I shouldn't have come…"

I rubbed the side of my face with one hand, pinched a corner of quilt with the other.

Let me go. "It's so thoughtful of you to offer… but I'm really very tired."

She stared a moment longer. Then she switched on a little bedside lamp, and moved to turn off the overhead light.

"There should be a clean towel in the bathroom if you want to have a shower or anything. Oh, and there's a bookshelf over there if you're looking for something to read, but not much variety, I'm afraid."

She gave a small grin and I followed her glance. A row of Callum Wilde's novels filled one whole shelf, his name writ large on each book spine. Nausea charged me again. Why had she never mentioned him? I wouldn't have come here. She saw my face.

"Callum Wilde's my step-dad. I guess you must have heard of him? He's been on telly and stuff." Now she looked down at her fingernails.

"You never said…"

"I hardly ever tell people. All the girls at school and

University used to plague me for his autograph, you know he was on the English curriculum? I happen to have a father of my own and I felt defensive for him. When I went to London it was a new start. I decided to be known just for myself."

Twenty years of defences crumbled like chalk. *Maybe this was all meant to happen.* Alice didn't seem to notice me shivering.

"We'll go for a bracing walk on the beach in the morning. It'll do you the world of good. I'm sure Mum will be friendlier towards you tomorrow. I think she had a shock, seeing someone from her past. She's a bit isolated out here, you see."

The headlights of a car swung slices of light around the walls of the room and outside, tires crunched on gravel. A car horn tooted, the engine went dead. Cold washed through the inside of my body. I wanted to hide under the covers.

"That'll be Cal." Alice brightened. "I'd better go down and say hello. You can meet him in the morning. If you're in the shower when I get back up, I'll just leave your sandwich on the desk over there. Try and get a good night's sleep."

I gazed wistfully at the closed door. Unless I avoided Cal in the morning, it was possible that this moment signified the end of my four-and-a-half year friendship with Alice.

3

OCCASIONALLY I LOOKED in a mirror, but not often. I still found it hard to identify myself as a physical body. I kept my anorexia under control with a series of strict routines and low-level antidepressants and I did my best to avoid situations that might induce my other ailment, the one that rendered me immobile.

After showering I opened the box of tablets I'd slipped into my overnight case and took one with a bite of the sandwich Alice had left on the desk. I forced myself to consume a further three bites of sandwich, the first food I'd eaten in thirty hours. But I'd promised Alice I would eat, and I didn't want to disappoint her after all the trouble she'd gone to. I wondered if, despite the relative closeness of our age, I was beginning to substitute her for the daughter I so badly wanted to see.

I dried my hair and forced myself to look.

My hair, once the colour of fresh conkers, had faded as if it had been left out in the sun too long. My sister tried to get me to apply highlights. She offered me complimentary treatments at her Knightsbridge salon, but I didn't accept. And I never wore make up. She said my thick eyelashes and clearly defined eyebrows were lucky, since she was never going to persuade me to pluck them. I forced myself to look into amber coloured cat eyes that sometimes appeared green, feeling the bitterness in my stomach. I hated my eyes because I didn't consider them truly mine. They were *her* eyes, exactly the same as his, Callum Wilde's.

I couldn't look any longer. I hung the towel over the mirror, obscuring the image that stared at me. *Mine now*, because Marion Wilde had never reached the age I'd achieved. I turned away and climbed into the bed. I wanted to be silent. I wanted to be invisible.

THE TIMBRE OF his voice came up through the floorboards, punctuated by Alice's laugh and Lisa's quiet tones. I could only imagine the tension Lisa must be feeling, her concern that the life she shared with Cal was about to be blown apart again. *Cal.* My arrival here was a cruel prank of fate. I didn't blame Lisa for her coldness. We were both in an impossible position. To distract myself, I pressed the switch on the radio-alarm clock next to the bed but I couldn't bear to listen to the news report about the civil war in Syria.

In silence again, I drifted off to sleep.

The sound of the bedroom door scraping open awoke me some time later. Lisa stood in the frame, wearing a thick jumper and velvety trousers, silhouetted by light from the hallway. She put a finger to her lips. I pulled myself up on the pillows. Lisa slid into the room, clicked the door shut quietly. I'd fallen asleep with the lamp on and the glow lit her profile as she leaned towards me. She pulled over a chair from the desk and I brought myself fully upright in bed, feeling strangely relaxed, as if my reckoning had come.

The first words she whispered were, "Did you know?"

I met her eyes in the low light. "I didn't know who Alice was."

"Why did you come to Pottersea, then," she asked. "To this house?"

"I didn't know I was coming here. She's only ever referred to the place she grew up as 'the back of beyond', or 'the East Coast'. I'm sorry. For some reason I thought her family lived in Lincolnshire, not Yorkshire."

Lisa paused to think. "She must have been talking about her father; he lives on the Lincolnshire coast. But didn't you realise when she started driving in the opposite direction?"

"I fell asleep. I'm sorry, I wasn't taking any notice."

"Oh Lord." Lisa regarded me steadily.

She still says 'oh Lord'… An epoch hasn't changed her.

"Alice sets a lot of store by you," she finally said. "I know you looked after her when she first went down to London."

I pinched the bridge of my nose. Alice had been determined but somewhat overawed by the capital. I told Lisa, "You raised a daughter to be proud of."

Years slipped away. We recognised each other from a lifetime ago – two lifetimes, since I'd reinvented myself in my current one. We'd been so close; or rather, Lisa had been to *the other me*. Lisa leaned forward. Her hair was still mainly blonde, but now cut in a short bob. She used to wear it long, thick and honey-coloured. The silver strands in her older-woman hairstyle glinted in the lamplight.

"So from your play... I guess you had a baby...?"

"A girl." I had to bite hard on my lower lip. "I called her Mariana, after..."

"After Tennyson, Cal's favourite," Lisa clenched her hands. "Is she?" She meant, *is she Cal's*? I nodded, holding her gaze. Her face was inscrutable. "When was she born?"

The tears I'd been fighting rose in my eyes. "Her birthday is the ninth of February. She'll be twenty-two."

Lisa let out a choking sound. "The same age as Aiden, he was born the following day. So you were pregnant when..."

"Aiden is your son?"

"Mine and Cal's, he was born in the early morning of February tenth, 1990. So you were pregnant when you came here."

Her voice was rough. I nodded and we both shuddered as if someone had walked across our graves. Then her eyes widened.

"Oh *Lord*." She bit on a thumbnail. "It all makes sense now. He's seen her, a girl called Mariana. Cal has, and Sarah as well. From what they said, it *must* have been her."

Her father and her aunt have seen her.

But I hadn't.

"It was in a café in Scarborough," Lisa said, nodding. "About three years ago. Cal was convinced it was you. Well, *Marion*. The girl he saw looks just like you. He's been in a depression ever since. He's obsessed with seeing her again."

She turned her gaze on me and I saw she had wrinkles around her eyes. "He thought you were dead. I never believed him until Sarah told me how like you the girl was. Then I thought, how could it happen again?"

My mouth dried up. I reached out and sipped water from the glass on the bedside cabinet. My pulse pounded in my ears.

"Cal and Sarah have seen my daughter? She looks like me?"

She looks like me, not Marion. Ha. Lisa's face softened.

"Sarah said she has your eyes."

She has my eyes, not Cal's or Marion's. But they could have been any of ours. But it was me who grew that girl in my own body, fed her my own milk. Not Marion's.

"She had a baby with her. A little boy."

I couldn't speak. Lisa was obviously thinking back to what she had heard. Did I have a grandson? My mother had kept the promise she made to me when Mariana was adopted. She hadn't told me anything.

"Cal's grandson…" Lisa breathed softly. "But you… This is all so weird."

He's my grandson. We looked at each other. "Oh Lord," she repeated. "Everything's so different from what I thought."

She made a decisive movement with her hands on her velvet-covered knees, and stood up. "Would you like to come down to the kitchen for a drink? It'll be warmer down there."

It was easy to slip back into the familiarity of that other

life, the one before mine. When I brushed hair away from my face, the sleeve of my nightshirt fell away to my elbow. Lisa's eyes were drawn to the sight of the silvery scar on my wrist. I pulled the sleeve down and curled my fingers inside it.

"I can't go downstairs," I said after a pause. "What if he sees me?"

"He never wakes up at night. But he *is* going to have to know about you, now."

I thought my heart was going to stop. But despite my misgivings I pushed back the quilt and swung my legs over the side of the bed. She handed me my dressing gown and held open the door. I slipped my feet into the slippers I had arranged at the side of the bed and stood up, peering out into the hallway. Memories of an excited teenager admiring every crevice of this house flitted by again. *That had been me.*

I hadn't had *her* memories for a long time.

"Come on," Lisa whispered. She turned at the kitchen staircase to beckon me down. But I lingered at the open door of the attic staircase, compelled to look up.

"Come on," she said again.

I felt cold as I made my way carefully downstairs. In the kitchen Lisa balanced a piece of wood on the glowing embers in the stove and I watched it catch light.

"I often get up in the middle of the night." Her voice was soft. "He wouldn't think anything of it if he woke up and found me gone."

Cal. "What's he like now?"

Lisa didn't answer. Instead she put in a question of her own, "Do you remember that day?"

My eyes automatically searched the quarry tiles. *Over there*. We probably both thought it. *Just on that spot*. Everything had been moved but it stayed the same in my mind. A girl who couldn't stand the fight with herself any longer – two personalities didn't fit inside one body.

"That day was when it first sank in, who I was – *what* I was. It all fell into place and I couldn't cope. She wanted to leave. I just wanted to escape."

The bird fluttered in my chest as it had then. Lisa handed me a cup of tea.

"Do you take milk now?"

I examined my palms in a memory-response to the day I'd blistered them on the mug, in this same kitchen, then I reached over the table for the milk jug and poured some in, an act of defiance. Our eyes met. I understood that she'd accepted me.

"What is it *like?*"

I couldn't say anything, struggled for words. She tried again. "Do you remember things from…before?"

I felt the breaths travelling in and out of my lungs. Lisa's presence was soothing, familiar. Only Cal's could destroy me.

"My life isn't Marion's."

I examined my hands again, confirmed the physical presence of me to my own eyes. *Maria is real*. Me. I flexed my fingers.

"I've struggled to retain my identity in the present. I can't be two people at once. I understand now that I *was* Marion, in a different body, a different life. But this body is me, Maria."

I saw her mouth open to speak again but I held up a hand, went through the remaining breathing exercises I'd been taught in therapy. Lisa waited. When she judged I was ready she asked, "What happened after, you know," she indicated my scarred wrists.

"I spent a week in a coma. Afterwards I remembered everything, being Marion and all the people in her life. But at the same time I wanted to make a go of being Marianne Fairchild. It was me who was pregnant with Cal's baby."

I paused, took a sip of tea; curved my hands around the mug in an echo of that resurrected day. "I had a family of my own, people to support me. They were great. But I discovered I couldn't maintain my identity as Marianne Fairchild when I had such a physical connection to Cal, and so to his twin sister." I looked up to see if she'd understood. "The connection was his baby."

Lisa topped her tea up, proffering the teapot but I shook my head. She reached over and placed it on the flat top of the woodstove. Wrapped in a hand-knitted cosy it looked snug. I stared at it a minute, imagining a life filled with the comforts of home and family; the security of knowing exactly who you were.

"I had to give Mariana up because I feared I'd be driven to another suicide attempt. I was having recurrent fits."

Absences from my body, filled with scenes from Marion's life.

"It wasn't safe for her, being my daughter."

The top of my nose prickled with a fresh gathering of tears. I pinched it angrily, reached into my dressing gown pocket for a tissue. Lisa hadn't said anything but her face, the flesh beginning to sag now she was in her late fifties, showed signs of strain. I remembered her from twenty-two and a half years before, in her prime, and further back than that, when we were both – *when she and Marion,* were teenagers.

"I kept her with me for six months."

A normal person would cry. The recollection of handing her to the social worker was still a raw gash, a chasm into which I could fall. But my life was a constant battle for control, and I'd been winning for the past few years. I couldn't let go even for a moment.

"That's when I changed my name to Maria Child."

Lisa's eyes filled with tears. "I'm so sorry. I can't imagine how awful that must have been. None of it was your fault. It seems so unfair."

Silence fell over us, two minutes for the memory of my lost motherhood.

"I didn't know anything about you until that day you turned up in our kitchen," she said. "I'm sorry I wasn't able to help you."

"It wasn't your fault either," I said. "When it comes down to it, Callum Wilde was a weak man. And he and I should never have done what we did."

"He's still weak, Mari…Maria." She'd been about to call me Marianne, or maybe Marion. "He's a weak man," she continued. "But I've always loved him, ever since we were children."

I had to repeat my breathing exercises. This was tougher than therapy. But it was a relief to finally be able to talk about it with somebody who remembered Marion, who understood the thread of my life, *my lives.*

4

WE'D BEEN TALKING quietly but it must have disturbed someone, because there were footsteps overhead. Lisa and I froze. The faintest suggestion of light came into the kitchen from outside, edging a tub on the windowsill with silver.

Oh God, don't let it be Cal.

If I kept still long enough I'd be invisible.

Water trickled through pipes somewhere in the house; a floorboard creaked. I heard the distant bark of a fox. My muscles coiled as if ready to spring, but I forced myself to withdraw my hands from under my arms. Footsteps approached along the landing. We turned to look behind us and saw a figure at the top of the stairs: Alice. She trod slowly down.

"What are you two doing?"

Her voice was a hoarse whisper. Lisa chuckled. I remained silent. Alice looked confused.

"I was just thinking," Lisa said, "How you wanted Maria

and me to have a lovely evening together."

Alice and I looked at each other. I pressed my hand against the table edge.

"Tell me," she said in her husky voice. Alice sighed heavily and grabbed the teapot from the stove. She sat next to Lisa and removed a cup from a carved stand in the centre of the table, poured herself some tea. The older woman smoothed her daughter's heavy blonde hair away from her face. I felt at home, but knew it couldn't last. I was being sucked back into a life that would spit me out, battered and bruised. My eyes found Lisa's and I dipped my head. It was easy to communicate wordlessly with her. Marion had been selectively mute for the last two years of the seventeen she'd lived, and Lisa had been her best friend.

Lisa coughed.

"This is going to be a shock for you," she told Alice. She placed her hand over Alice's and curved her fingers around it. I looked away, jealous of that little act of motherhood.

"Maria *has* been here before."

I had to laugh.

"In this kitchen, when you were seven," Lisa clarified.

"I didn't know who you were when you joined our theatre company," I swore to Alice. "Honestly. I didn't realise until we pulled up outside this house."

"What do you mean, who I was? Maria, Mum, what are you talking about?"

I worried Cal would wake up at the sound of his stepdaughter's voice, felt my shoulders hunching protectively. I glanced back towards the stairs.

"Don't worry, he'd sleep through an earthquake." Lisa

could still read my thoughts.

I tried to tell Alice. "You're the little girl who watched me..." Vivid lights danced at the corners of my eyes. I smelt burning. "You came home to this kitchen one day with your mum and Cal..."

I tried to continue but my muscles were tingling. My jaw went numb; I couldn't force out another word or move my lips.

Oh no.

"MARIA."

Alice made her way out of the cloakroom with a wad of toilet roll, pressing it to her eyes. Lisa handed me a mug. "Warm water with Rescue Remedy, sip it slowly, it'll help."

A slight spasm remained in my jaw. I also had pins and needles in my hands and feet, but I managed to make my voice work.

"Two in two days..."

Lisa looked at me questioningly.

"Fits," I explained. "It will only get worse now."

Lisa hugged herself. "I'm sorry," she said. "I've told Alice everything. She hadn't remembered much about that day. She had to have counselling afterwards, and eventually she just seemed to block it out."

Alice came over to the table. She spread out her hands. "I called you the funny girl, I do remember that."

Shock swished through me, the terror of the things the child had said about seeing me standing in her room, frozen and silent, when I couldn't possibly have been there. Similar to what my own sister had told me.

"You were sitting here when we got back from our picnic on the moors." Alice dabbed her eyes. "You'd got in through that little window."

We all looked up at the small window above the sink, grown women of varying ages now. I forced my eyes back to meet Alice's. She gave her nose another blow.

"I was shocked because you smoked a cigarette in the kitchen. Mum sent me upstairs, and then you… I was still watching through the banisters. Mum screamed at me not to look."

The knife.

She moved closer to me. Gently she pulled back the sleeves of my dressing gown and examined my wrists. This simple act of acknowledgement took my breath away.

"Why did you do it?"

My muscles thudded with weariness but I only cared about one thing. "Are we still friends, Alice?"

"Of course." She looked surprised. "But I want to know why you did that."

"It's a long and very complicated story."

How could I even begin to explain? But she was thirty years old now, an adult. Not the seven year-old who watched a girl of seventeen slit her wrists. She deserved to know some of the truth. "I had a very brief affair with Cal, before he got back together with Lisa. I'd just come out of a psychiatric unit and I thought Cal would be happy to see me. I didn't know it at the time, but I was pregnant with his baby."

She sighed. "Cal has never taken responsibility for his

own actions. Why the hell wasn't he in the kitchen with you and Mum, stopping you from doing that?" The penny dropped. "Oh my God, so the baby girl you gave up for adoption…?"

I finished her sentence. "She's Cal's."

"She's the same age as Aiden," Lisa put in, "Born just a few hours apart."

It probably occurred to us at the same moment that we'd created another set of twins, like Cal and Marion. I felt nauseous and shaky. Alice pushed up from her chair, hands flat on the table.

"Maria needs to go back to bed, Mum. She always feels unwell after one of her turns." She stood, looking from one of us to the other for a moment. "You know, when all's said and done, it feels great to know you survived that horrible day, Maria. I blocked it out. I had to."

She gave me a quick kiss on the cheek. "Maybe we were meant to end up working together."

Lisa flicked the switch on the kettle. "I'm going to stay down here for a bit. I need to think how to deal with this, how we should tell Cal."

5

Cal Wilde

MY EAR WENT deaf, like a plug had been shoved in it. Lisa kept telling me I should get them syringed, but I hate going to the doctors. They try to make me take anti-depressants. *Bloody idiots.* Why can't they understand? I need the rocket-roar of anger to keep me alive. Spending my existence as a drugged-up zombie would render it pointless. What the hell would I write? I may as well just die.

I tilted to one side and let off a satisfying fart. Lisa wasn't in bed to complain. She always gets up in the night, says it's her best time for thinking, with nothing to distract her. I stretched out, flung my legs and arms wide, a bed-angel. Inevitably my hand found its way to my dick and I fiddled with it, a comfort object.

I'd woken from a dream about the girl named Mariana again. *The spitting image of my twin sister.* On several occasions, I'd returned to the café in which I saw her but never found her again. I should have been satisfied – she must have gone safely back to another life, and I wasn't around to ruin it. *Still, it makes no sense.*

I clutched my dick more forcefully, angry at the memory of the waitress who'd threatened to call the police if I kept pestering her. My hand squeezed reflexively and I was seized by an unexpected, bitter climax. *Fuck.* Overtaken by a coughing fit, I had to breach the warm waves of quilt to emerge into the cold room; sort around in the bedside drawer for a tissue. When I'd cleaned the sticky mess from the hair on my belly I tossed the tissue into the dust under the bed. Then I snuggled back down, pulling the covers tightly around me, eager to return to my familiar obsession.

Ma-ri-a-na. *She only said 'my life is dreary, he cometh not, she said'. She said, 'I am aweary, aweary, I would that I were dead'.* I'd quoted that to her in the café but she hadn't appreciated it.

Turning over I pushed my head deeper into the pillow, thinking about my twin. What perversity made me write *The Shell* in secret, while we spent all that time clacking away on our typewriters together, ostensibly writing our 'first' novels concurrently? For forty years I'd been asking myself that question, but I'd never managed to come up with an answer.

I concocted the plot of *The Shell* alone in my room, a teenaged boy writing feverishly at night. She knew nothing about it. And I admit the viciousness of my story; it ran away with itself. But it *was* just a story; Marion should have understood that.

Still working secretly, a publisher accepted my

manuscript. The era of the 'angry young man' was not long over and *The Shell* became an instant hit. For the first time, I'd done something by myself, *for* myself.

Why do I always go back to this? What's done is done. But it was never done. Marion played the trump card. Her own death. Immortalised, she was so much more special than me and not only that, despite my ongoing success as a novelist, she still steered my writing. Each heroine of every novel I turned out was a version of Marion, and always a heroine, I never created a hero. And finally she came back to haunt me in the flesh, as a girl named Marianne Fairchild. The nightmare trapped me completely.

Interrupting my confused thoughts, Lisa slipped into the bedroom in the pre-dawn light. She shed her bulky jumper and the loose trousers she always pulled on for her nocturnal wanderings. A draught crept in when she lifted the quilt and slid into bed. She lined herself up against my back. Lisa has an uncanny ability to read my body with her hands.

"Cal, you've been crying again…" She put an arm over me and stroked the hair off my forehead. "What is it this time sweetheart, a nightmare?"

I turned, allowed her to take me in her arms, buried my face in her breasts, still large but much softer than they used to be. I grasped a handful of fat at her hip; she cradled my balls. I lifted my head and looked into her face. A wisp of hair lit up silver in the light from the window.

She ought to say something to make me feel better, but she didn't, and I couldn't help my anger at her for it. She stroked my hair, soothing.

"It won't help to get angry at me Cal, you know that."

Her hand slowed its stroking. "I love you, silly old man."

Her voice slurred with tiredness. I pulled her in closer, jealous of the sleep about to claim her. I moved my hand from her hip to her breast and she stirred irritably.

"Not now Cal, too tired, darling."

I hadn't really wanted sex anyway, but it didn't stop my resentment at her rejection.

Lisa's relationship with sleep is at its best around dawn. I considered an argument but decided against it. She was right; it wouldn't help to be angry at her, it never had. So I let her slip into sleep. I extricated myself from the bed, the cold hitting my skin and prickling me with goose-bumps, and went to one of the two windows, treading carefully on morning-stiff feet, straightening my clicking old knees. When I stepped off the thick rug onto the floorboards under the window I hissed through my teeth, but the discomfort at least made me feel real. The bedroom had once been dark, rich reds and browns, heavily-lined curtains at the windows. But Lisa had lightened and brightened it many years ago. She'd done the same to my life, despite me being a grumpy old bastard.

From our bedroom we had a view of the river and, when the tide was out, of an endless stretch of mudflats. Through the haze on the horizon, I could barely distinguish the far bank from the silver gleam of water in the distance. The tide had pulled the river out of sight. I watched fishermen in waders walking across the mud carrying buckets, looking for worms. I imagined being out there under that limitless sky, with only my task of collecting worms to focus on. Sometimes I wished I could cut out my own mind, let it float free. It'd been Marion's main goal in her short life to escape her body and experience one-ness with nature.

Why did she leave me behind?

Lisa lay in our four-poster bed with the cream lace canopy and snored like she complained I did. I pulled on my boxers and jeans, not sparing the noise dragging my boots out of the cupboard, hoping I'd wake her. It wasn't fair that she now slept soundly after waking *me* up with her absence. But nothing worked; she was dead to the world. I tugged a t-shirt over my head, then Lisa's oversized jumper. I jerked my heavy wool jacket out of the wardrobe, leaving the hangers clattering, and shrugged myself into it, then banged my way out of the bedroom.

I missed having a dog and I'd been thinking more and more of getting another. Aiden's old terrier Jet had died over a year ago and before him there was Alice's Labrador, Bonzo. A dog makes sense of a morning walk, why didn't we have one now? *Cats*, Lisa said.

If Lisa was the night insomniac; I'd become the early-hours one.

As if in answer to my thoughts a black cat startled me by running across my path when I opened the back door: Angel's kitten. Clouds of steam billowed from my nose and mouth. My feet crunched on gravel as I made my way down the garden, past Lisa's fenced-off vegetable patch. Chickens rustled and clucked sleepily as I stamped past their enclosure. Ivy smothered the brick walls of my sister Sarah's old painting studio, these twenty-three years my writing haven. I proceeded out through the gate in our boundary wall. It hung now on rusted hinges, creaking when I pushed it open. *I ought to do something about that.*

The cold made my throat hurt. I threaded my fingers into the loopy wool of Lisa's jumper sleeves. Melancholia hollowed me. I felt weary, so weary, fed up with searching endlessly for something, someone who could heal the pain. I felt like roaring at the sky.

I picked my way across a strip of bedraggled grass, slippery with frost. From the low bank, I could look out on the estuary. Lit up by the sharp morning light, the colours were intense, vivid green patches of marsh grass spiked across dark sand like lime marmalade over toast. With the light hurting my eyes, I scanned the familiar curve of the sandbank, protecting farmland from the sea. The ghost of Bonzo galloped towards me with his tongue lolling and I wished again that I still had a dog.

I looked to my left and began walking. My neighbour, Jim, already leaned on the fence at the end of his garden, smoking a pipe; dressed in scarf and dressing gown and wellington boots. He'd got rid of his recently late wife's beloved ponies and let the paddocks overgrow. *She would hate to see the mess things have got into.* I couldn't imagine living without Lisa. I nodded but kept walking. We never said much to each other but I'd play a game of Dominos with him later down at the Rose and Crown. Lisa was the one he'd have his heart-to-heart with. Most days she popped over with a covered plate of dinner or persuaded him to join us in our kitchen. Sometimes Angel took him a loaf of bread she'd baked herself; the only time she seemed a little girl again to me.

Angel. With her dyed-black hair and angry looks, I

couldn't make head nor tail of her. She liked to go next door and pet the one remaining horse in the stable, Dodger, the old pony that had belonged to our neighbour's absent son. A donkey, recently retired from seaside duties up the coast at Wittersea, had come to live in the stables as company for Dodger. Having to look after them was probably the only thing that kept Jim going. For a minute I felt jealous that my intransigent daughter would run so happily to the man next door whereas she would barely speak to me. And yet, I knew the fault lay on my shoulders.

I walked along the bank for a while. I'd forgotten my gloves and hat and cursed the freezing wind that howled in my ears and took bites out of them. It forced me to pull my coat collar up as high as I could and hold it around the bottom of my face with fingers that felt like frozen sausages. But I pushed on, wanting to work the dream out of me. Maybe the cold would do it. I knew I should fix myself permanently into the life I was living now; the past could never be rekindled. The start of a new year is a fitting time to make a resolution to move on, for good.

6

GRASS MADE BRITTLE by frost crunched under my feet. I half walked, half slid down the bank onto the cold sand, keeping my eyes on the ground and not on the icy blue sky, avoiding treacherous seaweed, picking my way over slimy rocks. *Jesus*, the cold was like something physical, a wall in the air in front of me. A splintery wall you'd rip your hands on if you tried to climb it. I wished I had my long johns on under my jeans. I should consider flouncing out a lesson; my balls were freezing while Lisa slept snug and warm in our bed.

I cupped frozen hands around my mouth, shouted into the bitter wind; words that meant nothing. It only mattered that I put my cry out there, rivalling the gulls' screams in its intensity. But even my howl was sabotaged, snatched away by that wicked wind, and thrown back in my face. Head hung, I marched doggedly on; followed the marsh path as far as a road which dissected the salt lands in two. The road led out to a point, demarking a boundary between river and sea.

My path continued across the marshes on the other side of the thin road, towards the wide, open ocean. I needed more punishment to break my melancholy. I needed the roar of angry waves to deafen me; an even more bitter blast of cold to scour my skin, clean out my soul.

AFTER ALL THE years of living in Pottersea, I still got a thrill of anticipation climbing the rise above the salt marsh. You could hear the sonic bellow of ocean before you reached the breath-taking view of the sea, still protected by the green arm of bank until you reached the top. I was panting by the time I stood and watched battalions of grey waves thrashing the beach. They sang in a million voices, cymballic and tinkling, a cacophonous symphony. The red-muddied cliffs were low enough to climb down at that point but I picked my way carefully; even in big boots my feet were numb. *One foot at a time…*

When I reached the stones at the top of the beach I planted my feet and stood with spread-out arms, mouth opened wide, gasping the crisp salt air. A band of thick white clouds hung over the horizon, and a tattered ribbon of seabirds streamed across the sky, screaming. I closed my eyes and lost all sense of self in the assault of sound and sensation.

When I opened them again I saw a woman walking up the beach from the opposite direction, she must have come from the caravan park. Who else would be mad enough to be out here at this time of the morning? The hood of a woollen jacket covered her bowed head, but strips of hair had escaped and whipped wildly like seaweed in a current. Her hands were plunged deep in her pockets. She wore ankle boots and had a hold-all over one shoulder. Precisely, my mind noted these details as if writing them. She kept walking towards me, but hadn't seemed to notice I was there.

A ringing started in my ears. An internal sound unrelated to the seashore orchestra which had suddenly gone silent.

I felt something in me, moving around, pressing my ribs from the inside. *What the...?*

Of their own accord, nothing to do with me, my feet started moving. I seemed to be left behind on the stones as my feet made their way towards the sandy part of the beach, standing outside myself, watching the impending encounter between this woman and this man. She still had her head down; the sound of the wind and waves must have deafened her to my approach.

I see him stop in front of her, see the depressions in the sand made by their halting feet, see her head jerk up; he has grabbed her arm. He shouldn't have touched her like that. She flies backwards, stumbling on a rock spiking up under her heel, falling onto the cold sand, her knee catching on the rock. She lets out a little cry. Her open mouth looks ugly in her twisted face. The bag has slipped off her shoulder, landing halfway into a rock pool. He takes her thin arm again in his big hand, dragging her back to her feet. I see blood blooming

through the knee of her jeans. His mouth is also open
in a scream of words but I can't hear what he's saying.
Everything is silent: a silent movie.

"I am not dead," she repeated again. Her voice sliced
into me and I re-joined myself, realising I'd been screeching
at her.

She is not dead. Why would she be dead anyway? Because I
needed her to be dead, so that the girl I saw in the café could be
my sister, come back to life whole and new.

Jesus. Everything had turned upside down. I could only
understand my anger, pure and molten, fury like boiling
lava. She'd ruined everything by turning up here again.

The stark reality of her made the world frightening,
mockingly attacked the meaning I'd constructed from the
past and created an unknown trajectory for the future. The
forces had misaligned.

She was supposed to come back again new and
undamaged – not still be here, older, with all the scars of the
bygone; reminding me of the mistake she and I made.

She dangled from my grasp of her ridiculously thin
wrist. I plucked unsuccessfully at the sleeve of her jacket
with unpliant fingers and perversely, she helped me. She
folded her sleeve back and I saw the evidence offered by the
jagged white line. Her bones rattled in my hands, she'd
broken into uncontrollable shivering. I looked down at the
blood on the leg of her jeans and sweat sprang to the surface
of my face.

"You've come back."

Even as it cracked out of my throat I wondered what the

fuck could come of her resurrection. Staring into me, her amber cat-eyes seared my heart. Her nose was red, her lips split and dry. I picked up her bag, which dribbled a spout of water from one corner. A roar still built inside me, an injured animal temporarily paralysed, threatening to burst through layers of skin and clothes. My confused mind wondered if I'd imagined that other girl I saw in Scarborough, young, just as I wanted Marion to be. Just believing she was back fresh and new, undamaged, had been enough.

Now she, this devil of an older, faded Marianne, limped and slipped beside me up the grassy slope, not protesting at my grip on her arm. The risen sun crowned her exposed hair with highlights of gold. But the hair was faded, greyish. She was cracked and broken, old before her time.

I hated her.

7

Maria

I COULD HEAR Cal's ranting voice, at times snatched out of earshot by the wind, at others blown right into my face with his fury. It washed over me like a bucket of hot water, but it couldn't touch me in the safe place where I hid. Instead, I felt the utmost tenderness welling up, feelings I'd tried so hard to bury. It came as a surprising relief; at last I could stop fighting my own fate.

I've managed to keep away from you for so long. I wish this could have waited until I'd seen my baby, our daughter. Then it wouldn't have mattered what happens.

Too late, what's done is done.

In a last effort at avoiding Cal I had sneaked out of the house the moment I heard Lisa enter her bedroom. Slipping out through the front door, I had walked along the main road in the direction of the beach. That way I could check the bus timetable at the stop by the caravan park. But there were no buses leaving the village for more than an hour and a half, so I decided to take a stroll towards the salt marshes. I had done my best to avoid him, but still Fate intervened.

I could hardly keep up with Cal as he dragged me along. I stumbled behind him across the salt marsh, heading for the river beach. Several times I tripped on half-submerged hunks of wood or slipped on the green slime of seaweed plastered to a rock, but he only jerked roughly on my arm, his hard fingers burning through my jacket. I felt exposed, exhilarated: almost truly myself.

Cal. It was really him, the same headstrong boy he had always been. I remembered his shouted arguments with our mother, her cowering under his escalating height. *No, that was Marion, not me.* I seemed to be losing myself already. What would he do if I had an episode out here in the icy wind, sand blowing into my fixed-open eyes? Probably nothing, keep trying to drag me along, asleep to anything but his own pain.

Poor Cal, *silly boy.*

MY TREMBLING RATTLED the mugs on the table. Alice sat on a chair opposite me; so familiar now. Light filled the kitchen, making everything brighter than I remembered it. The colour of the walls had changed to primrose-pale. In my memory the kitchen had a tangerine shade. Lisa pushed the mugs across the table to both me and Cal. Her hair had been rubbed into a rosette on one side of her head, like a baby lifted out of its cot moments before. Her eyes looked heavy with sleep, or a form of weariness much deeper. In the unforgiving light of morning she looked old, which scared me. Through layers of time I saw her as a child, as a teenager, and then as the thirty-four-year old woman *I'd* met in this kitchen, her own golden-haired child clinging to her waist. Now that child was a grown woman and Lisa was in her late fifties.

She stood behind Cal, her fingers massaging his shoulders. She smiled sadly at me. I sensed Cal relax infinitesimally. But he kept his watchful gaze on me, or rather slightly to my left. I could see his hurt and confusion like an aura of boiling colours. *Don't be disappointed in him,* I said to myself. *We'll be forced to play our parts, just as we were in the past.*

But it was tiring. I felt a deep empathy for Lisa; she must have spent her life with Cal working to keep the tumult within him tempered. Even then, his was merely a shadow of the elemental intensity of Marion, perhaps imbibed from her in the womb.

Foggy shapes crowd my mind: darkness, the push and pull, tangle and separation of limbs, the awareness, always, of an 'other'. I shuddered, flexed my fingers; jammed them between my legs to keep them still.

"How's your knee, Maria?" Alice had come downstairs shortly after Cal pushed me through the kitchen door, throwing my bag down onto the tiles, still ranting. Alice had run towards us, pulled me away from Cal, crying out in shock at the blood seeping through the leg of my jeans.

"It's ok, Alice," I managed through chattering teeth. "He's had a shock, that's all. I'm all right, I promise you."

"We need to get this cleaned up. Maria, you look terrible."

"Can you get me a bowl of water and some cotton wool or something?"

"Yes, yes of course." She sprang into action. "Go and sit down by the woodstove."

She brought the water; helped me roll up my jeans leg, glancing at her stepfather. "Cal. You need to come over and get warm as well, you look white as death." Her familiar, husky voice soothed us both. By the time Lisa came downstairs, we must have seemed calm.

⟫⟫✕⟪⟪

"YOU NEED TO get your head around this, Cal," Lisa was still massaging his shoulders. "Don't blame her."

"I could have had a life." Cal suddenly said, wresting himself out of Lisa's grip. His eyes were glazed over. "If it hadn't been for you, if you'd never come back." He pointed a shaking finger at me. "You messed things up for me and Sarah. You always had to be the one, didn't you? You sucked up all the emotion. You got all the attention because you were so thin, so quiet, the cleverest of us all. Everybody always noticed you, *Marion*."

"I am NOT Marion." I half-stood but my sore knee gave way under me and I sat back down again, gripping the edges of the seat. "My name is Maria Child. I've worked hard to be that. I'm a successful playwright, just as you're a successful author. It's not fair to blame me for how you feel. You *do* have a life, you always have." I blurted out the next bit. "At least you've only had one to concentrate on!"

"Not one that's good enough for him."

The feminine voice was rich, but not husky like Alice's. She would be the spitting image of her father if not for her black-dyed hair. Her eyes were similar to mine, but more green than amber. She fascinated me, this daughter of Cal's. Alice had told me her half-sister's name was Angel, although I couldn't think of a less apt description for the recalcitrant creature standing at the bottom of the stairs wearing long purple socks and a striped nighty. But she was my own daughter's half-sister too, and I took in her image hungrily, wondering what similarities and differences the two girls shared.

"Nothing is ever good enough for him," Angel said.

"All right, Angel," Lisa warned, but the girl pushed on.

"Certainly not his children, when he even notices he has them. Of course you don't have a life, Dad, poor you."

Cal put his cup down hard but he didn't say anything. Out of the corner of my eye I saw Lisa's fingers curl protectively into his shoulders again. The girl turned to glare at me, her lip curling. "Who the hell *are* you anyway?"

This daughter of Cal makes my heart jolt painfully. My baby is just a few years older; does she possess a similar spirit?

"I'm…"

"She's my boss, Angel. I told you she was coming."

"She's an old friend of mine. Someone I knew a long time ago."

Alice and Lisa had spoken together. But Cal still didn't speak, staring at nothing. Angel held her gaze on me a moment longer, puzzled.

"Yeah right, whatever."

She walked to the bread bin and pulled out an irregularly sawn loaf. Cal's head had sunk into his hands.

"So what's the matter with him?" Angel mumbled through a mouthful of bread, which she had spread thickly with butter. Nobody answered and she started rummaging in a cupboard, shuffling jars and tins. Lisa got up from the table and moved her daughter gently to one side while she reached for a packet of oats. "You need some proper breakfast, Angel. I'll make a pan of porridge, and then we can all have some."

It was as incongruous a suggestion as on the evening she had tried to persuade me to eat pasta just before I slit my wrists. We all remained at the table nevertheless, I with my hands between my knees again, the cut throbbing with welcome pain: I'd always appreciated any reminder of my corporeal existence. This body was my own; something *she* had never inhabited. But it was also an object of confusion between Cal and me. The body that carried *me* around was Maria. But Cal's compulsion focussed towards his dead twin sister. He hunched over at the table, his arms clenched around himself, his chin deep in a thick woollen jumper. Though his hair had gone greyer there were still hints of the conker-colour it had been, a thick hunk still falling over his forehead in a way that made me yearn to sweep it back. He didn't look up. Every now and then he muttered something under his breath. I got the impression his family was used to this kind of behaviour.

Lisa poured milk onto oats in a saucepan, lit the gas and placed the pan on the cooker. Alice got up and walked across to add a couple of logs to the woodstove. Angel leaned against the wooden counter, her arms folded across her stomach in the loose nightdress. A ray of sunshine filtered through the small window above the sink, lighting up the silver streaks in Lisa's hair, glancing off the kettle's metal surface. A flap in the outer door rattled and a sinewy cream and brown cat entered, stretching each leg as it sniffed the air, before wandering to the rug in front of the newly-blazing woodstove. Shortly afterwards came a smaller black cat. That one headed without hesitation to a place on the other side of the stove. We all watched the animals, avoiding each other's gazes.

"Go and put some warmer clothes on before you eat, Angel."

Lisa reached into another cupboard and started lifting out bowls. *She remains so calm.* Right from the first time I'd seen her in this kitchen she had occupied it so comfortably, in a way Cal and his sister Sarah never seemed to.

With a huffing sound, Angel turned and stomped up the stairs.

This kitchen had such a pull of home, and yet I could never really belong here. Though I would like to sink into the embroidered cushions on the sofa in front of the stove, I must repeat my attempt to leave, straight after breakfast. I hadn't wanted to come back, but I'd never have thought it would be so hard to leave again, all these years later.

CAL WATCHED ME like a hawk. His anger was still palpable

and yet I really didn't think he wanted me to go. I'd gone up to the room Alice put me in the previous evening to have a shower. When I came out again Cal was waiting outside the door, his back curved away from the wall, fists under his chin. The tension in his body reminded me of a quivering cat. When he opened his hands I could see they were shaking. I saw the boy he had once been, his need for control but I, *she*, had always been stronger. Age had softened the sharp curve of his jaw, but it still delineated the outline of the boy and the man I'd known. I wished I could free him from his demons.

"Why have you come back?" His eyes had darkened to the colour of treacle.

"Cal." It was obvious the slightest provocation could tip him over the edge. "I didn't come here on purpose. I'm so sorry; Alice invited me. I didn't know where she lived. This was the last thing I wanted."

I counted my breaths the way I'd been taught in therapy. *Live one moment at a time.* Cal straightened, burnt-sugar eyes brushing over me. He thumped the wall behind him with both fists.

"I can't *continue* like this. Every day I have to remind my fucking heart to beat. Who was she then, that girl I saw, if not you?"

I didn't think he wanted an answer. He pushed himself away from the wall and took a few steps along the corridor. At the end of the landing he turned and came back towards me.

"Living is too much of an effort."

He flexed his fingers, making the joints click. *Here you*

are, I was thinking, looking at him. I felt peaceful at last.

"You'll never allow me to escape from this torment, will you?" I saw his big hand coming up towards my face just as the tingling in my jaw began. He must have thought my rigid expression was defiance, because he took my chin in his hand, trying to force me to look at him. But I was already on my way out, head swirling with mist.

8

Mariana Rivers, January 2013

GABE WAS PERFECTLY capable of dressing himself, but he'd refused to; he couldn't cope with being rushed. I'd got him out of bed too late because my bloody alarm clock hadn't gone off.

I was having one of those *stop the world I want to get off* moments. Gabe stood in his pyjama bottoms, arms rigid around his waist. The dim light in the hall enhanced his scowl. I almost screamed with frustration, again wondering if I was fit to be a mother.

Mam told me I should have stayed close to her and Dad so they could help me look after Gabe. But it felt important to get away, even if just up the coast. On the whole, Gabe had settled in well at his new nursery, and we were happy in our two-bedroomed flat on the third floor of a townhouse in Whitby. It had an iron-railed balcony with wood around the bottom so that Gabriel could safely play out with his toy cars.

Oh, fuckit. So what if I'm going to be late?

Gabe was more important than work or college, more important than nursery. I sat on the floor in front of him and pulled him close.

"I'm sorry, baby."

He stared at me a moment longer then hiccupped and went limp. I rocked him, singing his favourite nursery rhyme, *Little Boy Blue,* croaky from shouting. After a while I held him away from me so I could look at him properly, hands on his shoulders. His face stretched tight with tension. I stroked his red-gold hair, like Mam used to with mine when I was little.

Now I have Gabriel my memories of Mam are always tinged with sadness. I wish she was my birth mother.

It was hard for me to accept that someone else had been pregnant with me, someone other than Mam. A woman had given birth to me and then handed me over for adoption. I'd have been happier if my parents had never said anything about it. *If it wasn't for bloody Geraldine, always on the case…*

Nothing would have made me give away my own baby, *nothing*, however hard things might have been, and they *did* get hard when Damon and me split up.

The pressure wasn't fair. Aunty Geraldine had encouraged me to meet my birth mother from the time I was pregnant, but it was my choice not to. First of all she tried the angle that it would help to build a genetic family background for my son. That's one of the problems of being adopted. When you're pregnant they ask you all sorts of questions about inherited diseases and all that. But I didn't need to actually meet my birth mother to find out most of those things. When I asked Mam why Aunty Geraldine was so keen for me to find my birth mother, she said it was only because she had been in touch with the adoption agency and she'd got a surprising amount of information already. "She only cares about you, love," Mam said, but she couldn't hide the anger behind her eyes.

So I asked her to pass the relevant information on to the GP. Then last year Geraldine said my birth mother had made another request for contact and by that time I was curious, I've got to admit. It was my twenty-first birthday and my little boy was almost three – shouldn't he have the chance to be a part of a wider family? I would have agreed if it hadn't been for Mam. She's never tried to stop me doing anything before but she was adamant about this. My curiosity had only grown since then, though, and I couldn't stop it.

Gabe finally allowed me to dress him. I decided not to embark on another argument about the grubby blue hoody he insisted on wearing. I'd just have to explain at nursery he was going through a phase. Aunty Geraldine once attempted to persuade me that I should convince my boy that '*my will is stronger than yours.*' She said I should never let him win. Mam laughed. "It's just her way, don't let it upset you, pet. You bring up your baby the way *you* see fit." I love the way Mam trusts me to be a good mother.

At the nursery gates he clung to my gloved hand.

"This isn't like you, Gabe." I took off my glove and brushed a finger under his eye, wiping away a tear ready to either fall off or freeze on his face.

"What's the matter?"

But he only stared fixedly at me, green eyes sullen; bottom lip trembling. He shivered, despite being bundled up in a down jacket and a hat and scarf. I stood up straight, hair whipped into my face by the wind, so cold it felt like spikes; I could have sworn icicles were forming in it.

Mam's easy-going parenting and Geraldine's rigid rules fought a battle in my head. *I'll take him to work with me, Mrs Bingham won't mind.*

"Come on then Gabe, just this once."

We climbed onto the bus that went up to West cliff. Gabe had none of his usual excitement for the sea, whipping itself in frenzy onto the beach far below. This worried me. I dragged my shivering child round the corner to Hudson Street where Mrs Bingham had lived her whole life. I loved cleaning the three-storey house.

"I'm afraid he's not very well," I apologised as soon as she opened the door.

"Eh, love." She creaked down onto one knee to fumble with Gabriel's zip and divest him of his weatherproof layers. I had to help her get up again. I hoped Gabe wouldn't pass anything on to her; I'd have the guilt of that added to dragging my unwell child out in the cold. But she loved children, had brought up five of her own, and was happy I'd brought him with me. I installed the old woman and my little boy in the front room with the blazing open fire I finally got going with only the tiniest amount of kindling, then I began my cleaning routine. I started in the kitchen, washing up the old lady's pots, wiping down all the surfaces, emptying and cleaning out the fridge before replacing all the viable contents and chucking the out-of-date ones away. Next I mopped the floor. I calculated how I'd manage if Gabriel didn't improve. I'd have to miss college the next day, miss work the following two days if he was still ill. It depressed me, the thought of being trapped in the flat with a sick Gabe, unable to get out for shopping or any other company. We'd have to get a taxi home from Mrs Bingham's as it was; that would eat into my weekly budget. But I couldn't make him go on the bus again. The *looks* you get when your child is sniffing and coughing, not to mention the thoughtless comments.

While I vacuumed the hall, for once keeping my eyes on the carpet instead of examining all the interesting little ornaments Mrs Bingham had on the ledge that ran along the wall at eye level, my worries built up. For the first time I heeded Mam's concerns about me moving up to Whitby. Living in the bedsit round the corner from her had meant she'd always been on hand to look after her grandson.

I dragged the hoover up the two flights of stairs, knocking the nozzle into corners; making sure I picked up all the cat hairs. Once Mrs Bingham's oldest daughter had complained I hadn't done the job properly and I'd had to be a lot more careful since then. Mrs Bingham defended me but the daughter made me follow her all the way up the two staircases and pointed out the clumps of cat hairs I'd missed. So even though I worried about Gabriel downstairs (I couldn't hear a peep out of him, which was unusual) I had to take my time with the cleaning. The second staircase, narrow and twisty, darkened towards the door at the pinnacle. In the tower room on the top floor I moved to the window, letting go of the vacuum nozzle. I gazed out at the view over all the rooftops. Seeing the sea from this angle was something I looked forward to every time.

Even from that high I could see white horses galloping on the surface of the steel-grey sea. In my head I could hear the roar and boom of waves crashing over each other. Brought up in a seaside town, the sound was in my blood. Along with all the things I didn't know about my background, things I refused to let Geraldine tell me because of how it upset Mam…

I had a sudden urge to push open the dormer window and climb out onto the roof. *Imagine what it would be like to close my eyes, open my arms to the elements; my hair whipping about in the icy wind like angry sea serpents.* With my hand on the window catch, I came to with a shock. It was freezing out there, dangerous. What on earth was I thinking?

Every now and then I had these crazy thoughts. Much as I loved my life with Gabriel, sometimes the idea of freedom surged through my blood. The idea of being bodiless, uniting with the wind, soaring over the earth: it drew me so strongly I'd find myself shaking with desire.

"Mad girl," I told myself. "Just get on with your work." It made me a bit sad, like I was older than the actual years I'd lived. But I pushed the struggling feelings of freedom down inside me and locked them away. I had to. That kind of thing has no place in my life now I'm a mother.

When I'd finished my work, I made lunch for the three of us and we ate in front of the fire. I worried about Mrs Bingham, knew she normally kept warm by an electric heater in the back room. Most of her children popped in regularly but she still spent much of her days and evenings alone.

She asked me about the jewellery collection I was working on, and whether I thought attending the two day a week course at college was improving my techniques. She said she'd like to buy earrings or bracelets from me for her two daughters who both had upcoming birthdays. I asked her to tell us another story about her childhood in the house we were sitting in. Gabe and I loved to hear about how she had to hide under the table in the kitchen when the bomber planes came over in the war.

But Gabe wasn't listening today. Snuffling noisily in his sleep, he was unnaturally flushed.

Mrs Bingham and I studied him. We both knew our cosy afternoon was over. When the fire died down she'd go back to her electric heater in the small room off the kitchen. As for me, I had to recalculate my weekly finances and get a taxi home. My heart sank as she said it, even though I knew it was coming. "You'd better take him home, pet."

I'D MISSED MY afternoon shift at Mrs Riesling's house. I rang her at work, a thing she hated, to tell her I couldn't go in. As I expected, she got angry. When I explained it was because my little boy was ill she spat out, "You shouldn't have had children if you can't manage to look after them properly."

Thanks for that, Mrs Riesling. I didn't point out it was *because I was* looking after Gabriel that I couldn't clean her house. She said I'd ruined the dinner party she was having that evening and I should consider our conversation to be my final warning. *Final?*

"One more misdemeanour and I'll report you to the agency."

Not turning up *without* letting her know would have been a misdemeanour. I turned the key to her house over in my hand, considered throwing it off the balcony into the premature evening darkness, but didn't. I couldn't afford to get a bad reference. I worked hard on keeping my temper under control. Like Mam was always reminding me, I'd been a proper fiery redhead as a teenager, the beast inside me always ready to leap without looking first. I never listened to my parents' good advice. No wonder I ended up pregnant at seventeen.

Gabriel slept in his blue-papered bedroom, curtains pulled across the dark and the night lamp shining dimly. The phosphorescent stars on the ceiling glowed. My heart tugged. Crossing the floor, I stepped over his toy castle and picked up a tiny plastic pig from the rug, returned it to the farmyard his granddad made for his last birthday. Gabe's delight at the animals in their painted wooden barns and matchstick-fenced fields had been contagious, but as soon as Damon had turned up with a handheld gaming toy, all his other presents were temporarily forgotten.

Damon, discharged from the Army before seeing service because of a minor injury, was now intent on getting a recording contract for his band. They'd been together since they were at school. Since we were all at school together, in fact. We'd split up a long time ago, but I still missed him when something was wrong with Gabriel.

Gabe coughed in his sleep, throwing up a string of mucus which woke him and set off a screaming fit. Confusion and panic blazed in his eyes. Rocking my struggling, burning-up little boy I cried into his damp hair, lonely and frightened.

I needed help.

❧❧❧❋❦❦❦

"MAM; I CAN'T come home so soon after Christmas break, they're short-staffed as it is. And I don't want to miss college. Are you sure you can't come up here? I'm sorry to ask, but…"

"Pet, *I* can't just drop everything and go tootling up to Whitby." Mam worked in a supermarket. "But I'd be happy to help you look after him here at home. You could commute back to Whitby if you really can't take time off work, and you'd just have to miss college. You'll have to do that anyway if you stay up there on your own, won't you?"

Through my tears, I could hear her tutting. "Now stop crying, it's not going to help anything, is it? Is it the train fare you're worried about? I can sort that out for you."

"It's not that, Mam. It's just…it feels so hard when Gabe's ill. I'm scared here on my own. Sorry."

I took a break from struggling to speak through sobs and blew my nose. Wet, flat drops of rain plastered themselves against the uncurtained living room window. "I know, you warned me about this. But I don't know what to do now."

"Come on now, calm down a minute. There is a solution to all this. I could ask Geraldine to go up and stay with you for a few days if you think you could handle it. What do you say? I'm sure she would."

Mam knows I can cope with Aunty Geraldine in small doses. But I wasn't sure if I could put up with her for more than a night or two. On the other hand, what else could I do?

"There's something she wants to talk to you about anyway," Mam said. Her voice sounded sad. "We were on the phone earlier. You know, this could be beneficial to both of you. What do you say, love?"

I sniffed hard, my eyes throbbing with the weight of tears. My head ached. Maybe I was coming down with whatever Gabe had. Casting a glance around the flat at the strewn clothes and the pile of unwashed pots, I wondered what Aunty Geraldine wanted to talk to me about.

⤜⤜⤜⟫⟫⟫

SHE WAS A lot older than Mam, but they seemed to have a close relationship. On second thoughts, maybe not that exactly, but more a complicit acceptance of the other's role. Dad's words of a few years ago came back into my head as I pictured Mam and Aunty Geraldine circling around each other, testing their strength. *In. The. Contract.* I shivered, tugging the sleeves of my sweatshirt down over my hands.

As I grew up, Geraldine had engineered an intense relationship with me and I'd often found it puzzling seeing as she had two daughters of her own. I couldn't see why she needed me.

It all made sense now, though.

GERALDINE HAD DRIVEN straight over from Leeds as soon as Mam rang her. She entered the flat in her implacable way with food and hot water bottles and infant paracetamol. She filled a bowl with lukewarm water and set about cooling Gabriel down, then dressed him in a clean pair of pyjamas. Once he was settled on her lap she asked me to sit down because she had something very important to tell me.

It annoyed me, the way she still spoke to me as if I was a child.

And then it was like one of those films where it turns out that all the scenes leading up to this one have been a dream, or a different twist of fate than what you've been led to believe.

SHE DABBED HER red eyes and blew her nose yet again. I couldn't believe this was the cool, collected woman (the classy old bird) I'd always known. She looked wrung-out, but she couldn't have been half as exhausted and emotionally flayed as me. She'd been deceiving me my whole life. *Everybody* had. All making out that they were so open and honest. Sure, they told me about the adoption, but they left out the most important thing.

Until now.

I felt sick.

Mam had given me a strong sense of identity. She and Dad explained as soon as I was old enough that they'd been thrilled to get me because they couldn't have a child of their own. Mam and Dad were both from single-children families. Geraldine had been around since I was adopted, a cousin, but as close to Mam as a sister, because Mam didn't have any of those, either.

But now I'd discovered she'd actually been in my life even before Mam.

9

WHEN I CAME back from the bathroom Geraldine was still sitting in the armchair by the window with my fretful son in her lap.

Her great-grandson.

I couldn't get my head around it. Why hadn't they just told me from the beginning?

Both of us had been crying; something I did often, but I'd never seen Geraldine cry before. I'd had a long bath while she persuaded Gabriel to eat something and then read him a story. I'd tried to get it all straight in my head. Geraldine had held me soon after birth. She'd begged her daughter not to give me up for adoption. My mother's name was Marianne.

So Geraldine had a secret daughter. She'd never mentioned Marianne to me. The girl changed her name to Maria soon after she 'lost' me, Geraldine said. She only gave me up with the proviso that Geraldine would be able to stay in my life.

And so my grandmother became Aunty Geraldine, Mam's older cousin.

I wandered into the kitchen, opened the door onto the balcony despite the cold. I needed to feel air. The wet flakes still falling from the sky melted on my hot skin. Outside smelt of woody smoke and sea spray, and the harsh, biting scent of cold. When I came back in and sat down on a hard chair opposite Geraldine my hair was wet. I twisted a length of it between my fingers as she lifted her face from my son's head and looked me full in the eyes.

"Your mother never felt the cold either."

How *dare* she start referring to her daughter as my mother?

I changed the subject.

"What did Mam think about you being such a big part of my life?"

Geraldine tightened her arms around Gabriel. She sighed. "She had to accept it from the start. It was lucky for us that we became good friends. She doesn't have many relatives of her own, as you know. I really do think of Audrey as my cousin now."

"I feel *used*." I choked. "Like you all made decisions behind my back. I wish you'd never told me any of this, I was happy just being Mam and Dad's daughter. I don't want these other complications."

Now I knew who my birth mother was, the thought of meeting her terrified me. There would be pressure to get to know other members of Geraldine's family – my birth family. It was all too much. No wonder Geraldine had pressed me to accept contact so many times. *What a liar she is*. I wondered how much stress it had caused my poor Mam.

"I'm happy this way," I said with finality. "I know where I stand. I've chosen Mam and Dad now just as they chose me when I was a baby. I don't need anyone else."

Geraldine's face twisted slightly. Her teeth went over her bottom lip, stopping words which were obviously trying to burst out. Probably something pedantic like *they didn't actually choose you, Mariana; you were given to them, on your mother's say-so*. I hated it that the woman I'd thought so much about lately had turned out to be Geraldine's *daughter*. My relationship with Geraldine was irrevocably altered, with her now on the *other side*. The heavy atmosphere in the flat compressed me onto the hard chair. I was shrinking, losing control.

"Why do you have to be my grandmother?" I spluttered. "I preferred it when you were just Aunty Geraldine."

"Life is more complicated than you seem to imagine, Mariana."

She looked sad. *Bloody hell.* Moving slightly in the armchair, she gently eased Gabe into a more comfortable position on her arm. I focussed hard on the sleeping boy, on whom her claim was much stronger than I'd known. As was her claim on me. She kept looking at me until I met her eyes.

"The funny thing is, your mother won't…"

I had to interrupt. "If you're talking about your *daughter*, don't call her my mother. Mam's my mother, the only one I remember."

It was shocking that her eyes filled with tears again. Until this evening I'd never seen much emotion of any kind from her. It was hard to breathe. I wished I was back in Mrs Bingham's sitting room, in front of the log fire, listening to stories about her childhood during the war.

"*Maria* is your mother," Geraldine said. "She breastfed you for six months, I'll have you know."

"Shut up!" I'd shocked myself. I tensed, waiting for Geraldine's reaction. I wanted her to be angry. But she didn't flinch, just carried on speaking in a flat voice.

"It broke her heart to let you go and she never got over it. She did it for reasons you will never understand and I don't want to burden you with them."

"Stop it!"

My shriek startled Gabe. He coughed and whined miserably. I stood up, not knowing what to do. I didn't want Geraldine's daughter to take shape as a real person in my mind. I *couldn't* let that happen.

"Here," Geraldine stood up stiffly. She struggled under Gabriel's weight. It occurred to me she was probably the same age as many of my clients, the ones I helped look after. And she had come to look after me. The sort of thing a grandmother would do. "I'll get him some more paracetamol," she said quietly. "He's still very hot."

She handed me my son and I cuddled him in the armchair she'd vacated. I wished I could offer him the comfort of my breast as I had the first three months before 'getting on with my life' as my school friends encouraged me to. *She breastfed you for six months.* She did better than me. *No, I don't want to think about it.* Geraldine came back with the sachet of medicine snipped at one corner. I squeezed it onto Gabriel's tongue then offered him the water she passed over to me. He gulped thirstily, his small hand contracted around mine as he drained most of the mug. When he'd finished I placed the mug on the windowsill behind me. Gabe yawned, eyelids drooping. Letting out a small burp he stretched on my lap and laid his head on the chair arm. He whimpered slightly as he fell back to sleep. I stroked his hair, trailed a finger over his cheek, kept my eyes down. But I sensed Geraldine's intent gaze.

"Maria is as stubborn as you. She refuses to let me tell her anything about you until you're ready. It's the punishment she's allocated herself. She doesn't even know she has a grandson."

So what? It was none of my concern. I kept the barriers up. "In that case, she's never going to know. I'll never be ready. I'm sorry, Geraldine; I can't cope with any of this. She made her choices and I'm entitled to make mine. Gabe and I have our family now. It seems to me you're lucky to have the place in our lives that you do."

Geraldine, wedged into a corner of the sofa, straight-backed as usual, raised one leg and rested it over the other. She leaned forward, folded her hands neatly together around her knee.

"Not *lucky*," she said coldly. "My place in your life was a gift from your mother. I'm sorry if *you* don't like that term, my girl, but it's what she was then and still is now, even if she hasn't seen you since you were six months old."

I pictured the sea from the balcony at the top of Mrs Bingham's house. In my head I heard the cries of a seagull; imagined its wings skimming the tops of those white-tipped waves. What a mistake it had been to invite Geraldine here to my stuffy, increasingly oppressive flat.

"Will you listen to me?"

Slowly, I brought my eyes back into focus. Her nose was like a beak, continually jabbing at my weaknesses. Her eyes were beady, like a bird's.

"She gave you up for a heart-breaking reason," she said. "And she would like to explain it to you now. You're a mother, Mariana; would you deny your child the chance to understand choices you might have to make? You can never predict the things that are going to happen."

Just stop it. Leave me alone.

"If you'd told me all this when I was younger, before I had Gabriel," I said, "I might have been able to deal with it."

But not now…

In the pink-shaded lamp light she looked like a marble statue, her face carved and still. Her white hair swept into a coil at the back of her neck, enhancing her classic air. With her thin features and impeccable appearance, she'd always been such a physical contrast to my comfortable, down-dressed mam. I'd marvelled at their (non-existent) relatedness. I imagined Geraldine's daughter, the woman who'd given birth to me, looking similar to her. It gave me a cold, disgusted feeling.

I couldn't sit there with her piercing gaze on me any longer and I couldn't bear to hear any more of her story. It was unfair of her to bring all this up now, when Gabriel was ill and I felt vulnerable. It felt like some kind of pay-off for her offering to help out.

Sliding one arm carefully back under Gabriel's neck and tightening my other around his body, I braced myself. He was getting heavy. Again, Geraldine's strength amazed me.

"I'm going to put him to bed and see if he'll settle."

Her answering silence was unnerving. She seemed to be staring at nothing. I wanted my mam, tried to think what she might do in the circumstances. *Always be kind.*

"I'll make us a cup of tea and a snack afterwards, shall I?"

Shuffling past, I threw her a nervous glance. Her head moved slightly in my direction as the long cardigan I wore over my sweatshirt brushed her seventy-denier knees.

"I'll just go and put him in his bed," I said again.

Nudging open my child's bedroom door, the cooler air of his room was like a refreshing wash after the burn of Geraldine's intensity. All the years I'd known her she'd kept an emotional distance, managed nevertheless to demonstrate love in her cool way. She hadn't even been disapproving of my youthful pregnancy.

I wonder how old my real mother was when... I jammed on the brakes. *My real mother?*

Mam, she was my real mother.

Gabe let out a moan when I laid him on the bed, rubbed his face into the pillow before turning over and snuggling onto his side. Maybe he felt better already. Perhaps Geraldine would be able to go home tomorrow, or at least the next day. Things between us had changed forever. I wondered if we'd see each other less and less after she'd returned home. *Sad, but.*

I kissed Gabe, breathed in his hot scent, left the door ajar so we'd be able to hear him if he cried. Before I went back to the living area I changed the sheets on my bed for

Geraldine and dragged a fold-out mattress and a spare quilt from the hall cupboard to put in Gabriel's room later.

Geraldine hadn't moved since I left her.

"What would you like to eat?"

She didn't answer. Could she be sulking? I bustled about in the kitchen, toes curled inside my slippers. Tension pulled my shoulders up. I shouldn't have panicked and rung Mam; if I hadn't, then everything would have stayed the same. I brought the plates of pita bread and humus, olives, bananas and mugs of tea to the breakfast bar where Geraldine had repositioned herself with robotic movements. I'd never seen her this depressed. Then she roused herself.

"Thank you, dear." Her voice was crisp as ironed linen. "You're doing a good job with that little boy, you know, we're all very proud of you."

Her and Dad and Mam. Family.

Trouble was, I'd believed her to be *Mam's* family when in fact she was my own. We ate our meal awkwardly, the sound of our chewing and swallowing offending the impression of comfortable silence. When she spoke again the linen tone had creased. I was horrified to see yet more tears appear in her reddened eyes. Pressing a finger to my throat, I felt my pulse beat erratically. I felt trapped by emotion. I shuffled on my seat, forced to listen.

"I've been blessed with having a part in your life and in Gabriel's. But I largely hold myself to blame that you couldn't remain with your natural mother."

Oh, for God's sake. I didn't want an explanation. But she was dead set on giving me one.

"I was a terrible mother to Marianne, believe me. I

suffered from appalling post-natal depression after I had her, and it was a whole year before I even began to come out of it." She took a sip of tea, I watched her swallow. "I didn't want to be a mother; it wasn't what I'd planned for myself. Marianne was a mistake."

Like Gabriel. But I'd been lucky enough not to get post-natal depression.

"I won't… can't tell you the whole story about your mother, that's something I'm begging you to consider hearing from her own lips. Please believe me, she did the only thing she felt she could when she had you."

The kitchen light buzzed and I hoped the bulb wasn't about to pop; I didn't have any spares. I pulled my attention from it back to Geraldine. The evening had taken on the quality of a dream. I concentrated hard, but still her voice wavered half-in and half-out of my consciousness.

"She loved you beyond reason. Make no mistake about that."

My skin prickled. I wanted to break out, escape like steam into the cold night air outside the flat. I wanted snow to fall, and cover me.

The back of my neck felt hot, yet at the same time I shivered. I twisted my fingers together in my lap and took a shuddering breath. *Say something.*

"Why are you telling me all this now? I didn't ask to hear it. What happened between you and your daughter is nothing to do with me." When I saw her face I added, "Even though I'm sorry about it."

I didn't know what else to say. She looked deflated and I was exhausted. She hadn't been invited here for this conversation. I tried to make my tone gentle. "You sound like you had a bad time, I really am sorry. But let's just leave it now."

I jumped up and opened the fridge, fumbled about inside. More than anything, I wanted to stick my head in it. But I pulled out two pots of yogurt.

"Fancy a dessert?"

Geraldine reached over and took one from my hand, maintaining her steady, red-eyed gaze. She clearly planned to carry on talking whatever I did.

"There is a reason I brought all this up with you now, Mariana."

Oh, no. What now?

I interrupted her through a mouthful of yogurt. "Look, if you insist, I will talk about it with you another time, I promise. Did you just hear Gabriel crying? I'd better go and check on him…"

Geraldine's fingers closed over my wrist, stopping me in my tracks. I laid my pot of yogurt on the breakfast bar. Using my free hand I lifted the weight of hair from my neck. Then I twisted my body away, intent on escape.

"Stay where you are," she said. "We need to talk about this, now."

She let go. She reached over for the toilet roll on top of the bookshelf, tore a length off, folding it into her hand.

Oh no, don't cry again.

"Maria is not very well," she stated. "Meeting you could make all the difference to her recovery."

That's not fair.

10

Cal

"WHAT DO YOU mean?"

I only knew my mouth had fallen open because of the cold air hitting my tongue. The kitchen door stood ajar. I was by the table, which had been emptied of breakfast debris, cleaned and wiped. The place was deserted, apart from my dark-clad, dark-spirited daughter.

"Exactly what I said." Angel made an exasperated face. "She left about half an hour ago. Mum gave her a lift to Restingham 'cause she was going there to do some shopping anyway. Alice offered to drive her all the way back to... wherever it is she was going. But she said no."

Angel hunched over the breadboard, hacking off a portion of her staple diet. No wonder her complexion was sallow, her eyes dark-shadowed and listless. She only ever seemed to eat bread and butter. Masticating like a cow in a field.

She gave me one of her stares, loaded with indifference.

"Why do you care, anyway?"

Much as I hated *Maria*, I couldn't bear that she had gone. My hand missed how it had grasped her bone-thin arm. The feeling that I could have torn her apart was still eating me up. I missed the carved slopes of her face, simply because they were a focus for my hatred and frustration. I missed her amber eyes sliding from side to side, because I recognised them from so long ago. They were the eyes I'd seen from the moment I opened my own.

I *needed* her.

Those hours she'd been back in my house had disturbed the hungry beast always crouching inside me. I had to find her again. Get her back and finish the mess we'd made together.

"I… well, I just wasn't expecting her to leave without saying anything." I shot Angel a look of resentment. She had no right to make me feel so small.

"Well, she's not *your* friend, is she?"

My daughter flipped open the pedal bin, tossed her crusts inside. She turned back to me in her customary slouched-shouldered pose. "Although maybe she is. Apparently, she's both Alice's boss *and* a long-lost friend of Mum's. What's your connection with her?"

She sniggered. I could have put my hands around her neck.

How can you be a daughter of mine? But it was more than obvious; that was the problem.

There were moments when I almost connected with her, at my father's funeral, for example, just the day before Sarah and I saw that girl. Angel had sung a solo, her pure young voice rising into the rafters of the church. *Then* she'd been like my daughter, she'd reminded me of her aunt Marion, with her passion for music. But there hadn't been many such occasions. She seemed to spend her time simmering with umbrage, especially around me. I'd given up trying. Lisa was always trying to engineer circumstances in which Angel and I could 'relate' but they were seldom successful. Lisa must have been very disappointed in me as the father of her children.

A pool of light from the little window above the sink bathed my hand, spread on the table. It was the impossibly small aperture Marianne, *Maria*, had squeezed herself through the day she decided to ruin all our lives by painting our kitchen red with her blood. I looked down at my hand. Lit up, it seemed beatific; an agent of higher purpose than humanity was capable of.

Fear stirred in my gut. I whipped the hand away.

Angel's black cat pushed the door open even further, slipping into the kitchen. I went over and slammed the door shut after it and Angel rolled her eyes at me.

"That cat is perfectly capable of using the cat flap. That's what I put it in for, after all."

I couldn't help using an instructive voice on her, the same kind I'd hated as a teenager.

The animal ignored my agitation. It stalked across the floor towards Angel. She ignored me, too. She bent with a small cry to scoop her pet up in her arms and murmured endearments to it in a childlike voice. It patted her face gently, claws retracted. Utterly confident of her care.

There she was, the little girl Lisa had given birth to. I wished to God that Angel would wash the black out of her hair, take the horrible scowl off her face for me the way she did for her cat.

THERE WAS NOBODY left in the house. Angel had taken one of her loaves to Jim next door. She'd probably stay there a while; take the old pony out for a walk, as she sometimes did. I watched her leave by the back door, made sure she'd gone around the side of the house. Then I went into the office at the other end of the kitchen and peeped out the window which overlooked the front, and saw Angel turn into next door's drive. *Good.* I moved back into the kitchen and climbed the stairs. On the first floor landing, I opened the door at the bottom of the attic staircase and made my way up very slowly. I'd done this, alone, a million times over the past two decades, reliving the moment Sarah and me ascended to find Marianne standing frozen in the room at the top, drenched with sea water and as rigid as a marble statue after we had fruitlessly searched for her on the beach.

I never even thought about how Angel would feel if she caught me invading her privacy. The attic was completely different now, divided into two separate rooms, but I still remembered it as a vast, open space. It was the room Marianne, that innocent girl who had turned into the crone who now called herself Maria, had loved. I'd promised her she could stay there, but then I let her down.

>>>><<<<

ALICE WOULDN'T TELL me where Maria lived. I felt as helpless as I did when my nemesis tried to kill herself in our kitchen, and afterwards I hadn't known whether she was alive or dead. *If only she had died.*

"Cal, mate."

Alice was a plucky little kid back then. Seen death, as good as, in the kitchen where we now sat, nursing mugs of tea. New life had emerged in the kitchen a mere six months later, her brother Aiden born in a pool placed over the spot soaked by Marianne's blood. Lisa insisted it would override all the bad feelings.

But they still came back, again and again. I had to get rid of those feelings for good; I was missing my own life in the meantime. *So many years wasted. Marion, how could you have done this to me?*

Alice was the only one who could talk to me when the blackness descended. She touched my arm with her smooth hand. I glanced down. If I hadn't been consumed by the predator inside me I might have teased her like I often did about how her hands looked as if she'd never done a stroke of work in her life. But it wasn't true anyway. Her unsullied appearance merely reflected her happy-go-lucky personality. She took after her mother, though I feared I'd worn Lisa down prematurely. But then again, she'd known what she was taking on when she married me.

"Why don't you get back to your studio?" Alice said. "You produce some of your best work when you... you know."

She thought I was a pathetic wimp.

I pulled my arm away.

"I *do* apologise for being such a pain. I'll get out of your hair now. You shouldn't be worrying about me, anyway; it's not your job to do that."

Alice tutted. She picked up our mugs and carried them over to the sink. "I'm not falling for that 'poor me' attitude of yours. I was merely suggesting that you try and make use of the terrible feelings I know you're having right now."

She spoke calmly, but the shape of her shoulders showed her hurt. Funny how I shared this empathy with my step-daughter. My own children couldn't stand the sight of me. Aiden spent as little time in our home as possible.

"I can't work; I can't concentrate," I tried to explain. "If I was a painter I'd splash my anger on the canvas in hot, red colours. If I was a composer my music would be all cymbals and bass drums. Do you understand me?"

Alice pulled a face, but nodded slowly. She dried her hands on the tea towel and hung it back on its hook.

"I can't write about this," I said. "Not this time. She's really alive, Alice. I truly never thought she was. Her mother as good as told me she was dead after she... you know, did that terrible thing in our kitchen. *Je-sus*. The last few years, since I saw that girl in Scarborough, it's all been a lie. How do I deal with it?"

⇢⟫⟪⟪

IN THE MORNINGS, as Lisa returned to our bed from her nocturnal wanderings, I crawled out of it. White fog floated in front of my eyes; white noise constantly interrupted my hearing. A shadow crouched at the edge of my vision, but when I put out my hand to touch whatever was there, it shrank away. Lisa tried to pull me back in: to myself, to our marriage.

"Cal, honey, don't go out again at this time of the morning. It's still dark, and so cold you'll end up with frostbite. Darling, get back in here with me. It's lovely and warm."

As if I could be tempted by material comforts. By the body she was lifting the quilt up to show me. *Sometimes she's so naïve.*

She had no idea what I was going through. As far as she was concerned, Maria had shown up, the two of them made their peace, and now it was all okay. She expected me to feel the same as she did. But what about that girl I'd seen in the cafe?

None of this made sense. I had to connect the pieces of the puzzle. No, I couldn't go back to bed.

The savage pre-dawn feels like home now. Each day I leave the house wearing only a thin layer of clothes; my feet sockless, chilblained in boots that will take the top layer of flesh off. I want to be flayed.

WHEN I LOOKED at Lisa, it was like a ragged picture in a book with holes in the pages. I could see through each page to the one below, so the images were all jumbled up. Sometimes the ageing woman in my bed was as comforting as a blanket wrapped around me, at other times I felt frightened of her. In the past, her ordinariness had grounded me, the only thing that stopped me breaking into pieces, but now I wanted to shake her off. She insisted on keeping me warm, oppressing me, tried to null the sensations blossoming awake that I needed to notice. I didn't want anything to hold me down.

A familiar blackness had descended on me as soon as the *she-devil* left.

I'd seen the flaring up in her eyes. I knew Marion still dwelt in the faded relic of that girl, once called Marianne, now known as Maria.

11

Mariana, January 2013

I F I'D STILL been into writing poetry, the sight of Whitby would definitely have inspired it. The ancient ruins of the Abbey loom over the town and colourful, higgledy-piggledy terraces of houses and shops straggle the harbour. The atmosphere and history of the place got to me; you know, its association with Dracula, smuggling, and all that.

Words floated out of my head and dissipated in the veil of mist above the sea as I looked down from the top of the craggy cliffs, holding Gabriel's hand tightly. I wished I could rewrite the recent weeks of my life – finding out about Geraldine being my actual grandmother and the funny, mixed feelings I kept having about Mam. I couldn't help picturing the young girl that Geraldine said my birth mother was when she had to give me away, and wondering how she'd felt when she handed me over to Mam and Dad. Geraldine said she'd loved me. It was probably all in my imagination but I kept thinking I remembered things – like the sound of her voice. One that wasn't Mam's, anyway. Just this secure feeling of being in somebody's arms. But that was probably Mam.

It had taken Gabe a good week to get over his illness (Geraldine had left after the second day) and now he was full of renewed energy so I'd taken him for a long walk in the hopes of tiring him out. We climbed the one hundred and ninety-nine steps up to the ruins, and messed about with the interactive video displays in the museum. Then we ventured out amongst the wrecked stones and I told Gabe about the Abbey when it was made of wood, commissioned for a nun called St Hilda, in the Seventh Century. Then I had to explain what a nun was and what the Seventh Century meant. I read the information boards while Gabe played on the stones with his toy dinosaur.

Back down at the bottom of all the steps, Gabe wanted to go into the amusements. I checked my purse and found a few 2ps for the slots. I was staring out at the sea when I heard a crash of coins in the tray.

"Look, Mammy," Gabe squealed. "It gived me some more!" So I had to wait a bit longer, restlessness tingling through my muscles.

When the copper coins had run out we stood across the road at the railings, looking at the boats in the harbour. There weren't many people about and I imagined being alone in the middle of the sea. A good feeling. Then I noticed that Gabe was climbing on the bottom rung of the fence, his toy stuffed in his pocket. My heart thudded extra hard in my chest at the thought that I could have been staring off to sea, revelling in the idea of solitude, while my child was falling over, sinking below the surface of the green slime of the harbour. I grabbed his hood and pulled him down from the metal bar. He glared at me, opening his mouth to shout (hopefully not one of the obscenities he *may* have recently picked up from me). Instead only a sort of indignant howl came out, followed by. "It's not very nice to grab me like that."

"Sorry, but it's dangerous," I explained. Now I was looking at him properly I could see he was shivering, poor little man. "I don't want to lose you over the edge, do I? Anyway, how about we pick up the shopping and then go for a hot chocolate?"

It did the trick. He caught hold of my hand and started jumping up and down. "In our favourite café?"

"In our favourite café," I agreed. "Don't pull on me like that, Gabe, you'll have my arm off."

We were waiting to cross the road at the crossing by the railway station, shopping bags at my feet, when a guy on the other side took my attention. Wearing what looked like a black waxed jacket with the hood up, fair hair peeked out around the edges. I couldn't really see him properly above the two-way flow of rushing traffic, but in the gaps between it I could feel the intensity of his gaze; it kept pulling my eyes back in his direction. Something about him was familiar; I don't know whether it was the way he stood, his arms at his sides, somehow open and vulnerable – or whether my mind was playing tricks on me because I'd been trapped in the house too long. It made my skin prickle. Maybe I just needed a distraction from my everyday mundanity.

The lights changed. People on either side of me surged forward as I bent to pick up my bags. "Mammy," Gabe cried as I stepped forward, checking he was beside me. "My dinosaur, we dropped my dinosaur." I stepped back onto the path but I couldn't see anything because of the tramping feet in both directions. The beeping noise had already ended and the traffic had started to crawl forward again. "Damn, Gabe." I put the heavy bags back down on the pavement. "Where is it?" Tears welled up in his eyes; the stuffed dinosaur had been Damon's when he was a kid. It must have dropped out of the shopping bag. "Don't worry, we'll find it," I said, feeling more heat prickle under my leather jacket.

"Is this what you're looking for?" An old woman had leaned down towards Gabriel, holding out his toy. "It must have rolled all the way over there, behind the bin."

Or perhaps it had been kicked. "What do you say, Gabe?"

"Thank you." He gave her his sweet-little-boy grin, cuddling the toy against his chest.

I thanked her as well and she made some remark about how well-behaved my child was. When she moved away a brief image of the guy who'd been staring at me from the other side of the road flashed across my brain, but he was nowhere to be seen now. I decided not to bother going across to the newsagents to collect my jewellery-making magazine after all, I could always pick it up on Monday. I reached down to fold my fingers around the handles of my bags again. "Come on, Gaby, let's go and get that hot chocolate, shall we?"

>>>><<<<

QUITE A FEW people were walking around the edge of the harbour despite the weather. Others stood in a queue waiting for a boat to take them out, determined to carry on their holiday activities whatever the conditions – even the boat trips were on sale post-Christmas. Rain had started to soak into my hair; it'd take forever to dry. "Pull your hood up over your hat, Gabe," I said as we walked over the bridge that spanned the slimmest part of the harbour. "And put your gloves on, they're in your pocket, see." Taking a left, we turned down a narrow side street.

In the summer it would be so crowded down here that you'd have to shuffle along in formation. Now we walked briskly on the cobbles across the market square which in a few months' time would be filled with tables and chairs, a street entertainer performing under the old town hall which was raised on stone pillars. Now only a few people milled about, browsing the craft shops and art galleries round the edge of the square.

Our favourite café was in a Tudor building, painted cream and red. The small interior was full, probably of people escaping the rain.

"There are some tables upstairs, if you'd like to follow me," the young waitress said. Gabe trotted ahead while I banged the walls on either side of the narrow staircase with my shopping.

In the upstairs room the wooden tables and chairs were all painted in different colours. It looked full but the waitress led us on a crooked path between crowded tables to one by the window, with a great view of the square below. Gabe clambered onto a chair while I settled the bags around my feet.

"What can I get for you?"

"Waffles!" Gabe squealed. "With cream. Can we, Mammy?"

If we go without our special biscuits that we usually pick up from the corner shop on the way home. "I suppose so, just this once. And two hot chocolates, please."

The waitress grinned at Gabe. "Lucky boy." She smiled at me. "I'll leave you your bill now. You pay it on the way out."

"Thanks." I shrugged out of my jacket and arranged it on the back of my chair. I felt like wringing my hair out but it would look ostentatious and was probably unhygienic in here. Sometimes I considered having it cut. Imagine the freedom.

Gabe had already pulled off his hat and gloves and one of the gloves had fallen onto the floor. "Pick it up," I told him. "Remember our motto?"

"If you make a mess, you clean the mess up." He slid off his chair and crawled under the table to retrieve the glove. When he stood his strawberry blond hair had sprung up like a halo around his face. I stretched over the corner of the table to undo his coat but he wriggled away. "Help yourself a little bit, come on, son." Gabe flapped his hands as I dragged the coat off his arms. He was making his seagull noise. "Stop it, Gabe." Prickling heat broke out on my skin again. "If you can't behave yourself, we'll have to leave." It was stuffy in the café, I wished I could open a window. If we were at home I would have the balcony doors open so I could smell the rain and feel a hint of freedom.

"Don't be mean," Gabe said, eyes glittering. "You just maked some tears come in my eyes. I was only being a bird."

"I know you were, but it's not appropriate in here. You might knock something over." I gave his coat a little shake before reaching across to hang it on the back of his chair. Sure enough, as I straightened and Gabriel clambered back onto his chair he knocked the menu-stand over with his elbow. It fell off the edge of the table and onto the floor with a clatter. Some shopping fell out of one of the bags.

"It's all right," I said in a calm tone. Gabe's green eyes had turned a slightly darker colour and the skin of his face was flushed. *Time for a tantrum-diversion.* "I'll get it."

"Here," somebody interrupted. "Let me help you. You seem to have your hands full."

The prickling on my skin intensified. I felt overpowered by a flood of familiarity as the man knelt on the floor at my side and began replacing the items of shopping. The hair waving gently at the nape of his neck was exactly the same colour as Gabriel's. He wore a green knitted jumper and although, like me, he must have taken his jacket off to allow it to dry, I was sure it was the man from the other side of the crossing.

He tucked the carrier bag neatly back beside the others at my feet and straightened himself with the menu holder in his hand. Placing it on the table, he asked Gabriel, "Can you fix the menu back into its slot?"

Gabe appeared dumbstruck. He fixed serious green eyes on the guy while he completed the task. "There, well done," said the man – boy, really. About the same age as me, I imagined. A melting took place inside my stomach, like when you're about to go on a scary ride at the fair: excitement mixed with fear. At the same time I experienced a great sense of inevitability. "Thanks for that," I gave him a self-conscious smile.

"Your hair's amazing," he said. Then his face coloured a furious red. "Err, sorry about that. Not a very PC thing to say, I know. What I meant to say was, hi, I'm Aiden."

He put out his hand and I grasped it.

12

Mariana, February 2013

ON SATURDAY, GABE and I got up early to go shopping. He'd been so good I'd bought him a toy animal from the Early Learning Centre. This one was a tiger, to add to his large collection, currently spread out on the living room floor. I was supposed to be playing with him but I couldn't sit still, instead pacing backwards and forwards in the narrow space between the living and kitchen areas.

Aiden was coming to visit us at the flat for the first time, and had texted to say that he'd set off at nine o'clock from Newcastle, where he worked for an ecologically-aware firm of architects. It was pure chance that we'd met in a café in Whitby – Aiden had only been in the town for two nights, as part of a work trip with his colleagues. *Good job I'd felt such a strong need to escape on my own for a while,* he'd whispered against my ear the first – the only time yet – we'd kissed, last weekend. Otherwise I wouldn't be waiting for him now.

It was half past eleven. He'd be here soon. Sunshine shone on the glass of the balcony doors and I pushed them open to let more in. The morning seagull chorus, *earghh, earghh*, rang out over the rooftops and the snow had melted everywhere except in the dips where chimneys rose from the slate roofs.

I couldn't work out how I felt about Aiden. A strong compulsion to be together existed between us, but it was very different from the attraction I'd had to boys in the past. With Damon, for example, we hadn't been able to keep our hands off each other. But so far on the two weekends we'd met since that first time in the café, I'd let Aiden kiss me once and that was all. Maybe I was just being careful. Gabriel meant the world to me, but I didn't intend to get pregnant again for a long time.

I took the wrapping off the cafetiere I'd just bought, measured the correct amount of coffee into it, wanting to be ready for his arrival. I thought Aiden might appreciate something more sophisticated than my usual instant. Going to such trouble gave the situation enhanced importance, though, and that made me more nervous. That, and the fact I'd invited Aiden home at all.

"Mammy!" My son called from the balcony. "Aiden's here. Look, there's his car."

My heart pounded. What was I expecting to happen between us? I joined Gabe on the balcony to look down at Aiden's reddish gold hair, strangely similar to my boy's. I felt a good kind of nervous, but underneath bubbled a feeling of inevitability, almost a weight. My hands pressed my stomach, fingers interlinked.

"Hi," Aiden called up. He stood in the street behind our house. One hand lifted in a wave; the other shielded his eyes from the sun.

Gabe jumped up and down beside me.

"Careful," I warned. I waved to Aiden.

Still flipping back-and-forth between attraction and repulsion.

I disengaged Gabe's hands from the balcony fence and made him stand down from the raised edging. Turning back to give Aiden a smile I saw him walking back towards his car.

Gabe burst into tears. I nearly did too.

"He's not coming, Mammy, he's going away again. Tell him to come back."

Aiden must have heard Gabe's panic. He stopped and turned around. "It's ok," he called up, "I'm just going to fetch something."

Hot on the heels of relief, my heart tipped towards something resembling love. It plonked itself inside me like a sleepy cat. I just wanted all three of us to be cuddled together on my sofa. Maybe it was because I'd had Gabriel with me when I met Aiden that I felt we were in a three-way love affair. It was different from anything I'd ever experienced.

I went to put the kettle on. A short time afterwards the door buzzer went. Drying my hands after rinsing two mugs, I pressed 'open' for the door without saying anything. I didn't trust myself to speak yet. Gabe had the letterbox open and was peering through it.

"He's coming, Mammy."

The tiniest fluttering in my stomach. I pulled open the door and Aiden stepped inside and before I knew it I'd wound my arms around his waist. I hadn't meant to. Almost as tall as him, I pushed myself away. His blue-green eyes were so similar to my son's, anyone seeing us all together would be convinced he was Gabe's father. For a crazy moment I wondered whether somehow he *could* be, if in a parallel life we'd been together and that was why the relationship between the three of us felt so familiar.

"Me too," Gabe pestered, his arms upstretched. "Pick me up." We both bent our knees and we scooped him up between us.

Aiden presented me with a silver necklace, a small heart on a delicate chain.

"I wasn't sure if it was too much, so early on."

I stared at the intricate silverwork in my palm, recognising the techniques used by the artist.

"It's not too much. Thank you."

My chest had tightened. It *was* too much. My feelings started to disentangle again.

I watched him take a boxed action figure out of the bag and give it to my son. At first I was alarmed; I didn't let Gabriel play with guns or fighting toys. But as they extracted it from the packaging together I saw that the figure was dressed in rock climbing gear. It came complete with a rucksack, ropes and various other pieces of equipment.

"Look Mammy," Gabe was beside himself. "You can take off his boots and his helmet and you can… you can… oh, look, you can make his knees go up and down and you can make him climb up a pretend cliff, like the one on the picture."

"I'm glad you like him, Gabe. He's a rock-climber," Aiden said.

AIDEN PUT HIS arm around my waist again. I leaned into him, turned the necklace over and over in my hand. When he whispered something in my ear his breath tickled my neck. Part of me wanted to press further into him, another part wanted to break away. Responding to what he'd just told me, I moved apart from him and said, "You tell him, then."

He grinned, unfolding a leaflet from his pocket. He showed Gabriel. It was a brochure for a local climbing centre.

"What would you think about having a go at this, Gabe? You could be a climber too, just like your action man."

AIDEN WOULD STAY the night. We'd made the decision on the journey back from the climbing centre and now I felt relaxed about it. Mostly. I could imagine spending the night cuddling in bed with him but nothing beyond that. We cooked spaghetti bolognaise together while watching a family show on my small TV.

Gabe got down from his stool at the work surface and went back to playing at rock climbing up the front of the sofa with his action figure. (He'd named it Thomas, after his best friend at nursery.)

My mobile rang dimly somewhere. I washed my hands and went to search for it but by the time I realised it was still in my bag by the front door it had stopped ringing. For some reason I felt reprieved. I placed the mobile on the kitchen table and resumed stirring the sauce while Aiden drained the pasta. But the phone rang again and this time I answered it.

"Hello, dear," said Geraldine (I'd dropped the 'Aunty'). I cursed under my breath. I hadn't seen her since she pronounced herself my grandmother.

"I've been shopping in York," she spoke more stridently, as if the volume was being turned up. I held the phone slightly away from my ear. "I would like to pop over to see you, just for a short while. I have both yours and Gabriel's birthday presents with me."

My shoulders sagged. I raised my eyebrows at Aiden. He gave me a sympathetic smile. I couldn't really say no, so I said she was welcome to have a cup of tea and a rest before driving back to Scarborough, where she'd stay the night with Mam and Dad.

"She won't stay long," I promised Aiden. I embarked on an attempt to explain my complicated relationship with her. I hadn't planned on telling him I was adopted yet, but I decided to just come out with it.

"We haven't been getting on very well lately," I told him. "But she insists on bringing mine and Gabe's birthday presents."

"Is it your birthday soon? You should have told me." He twisted a hank of my hair around his wrist, lifting it away from my neck.

I stirred the bolognaise sauce.

"It's on the ninth of this month. Uhm, next week in fact. Gabriel's is on the sixteenth."

"What a coincidence." Aiden let go of my hair. He slid his hands around me from behind. I settled against him and we rocked gently from side to side. "You know, you and I are almost twins. My birthday is on the tenth."

➤➤➤➤◀◀◀◀

IF GERALDINE WAS surprised to find a man in my flat she took care not to show it. I thought I sensed a flicker of recognition crossing her face, but it must have been his similarity to Gabriel.

"I won't be staying long," she said stiffly as she hung up her coat. "I just wanted to bring you these." She placed a hessian bag on the floor. Wrapped presents were visible inside and the child in me wanted to know what they were but at the same time I didn't want Geraldine hanging around too long. Gabe came running out of the bathroom, the button on his jeans undone, and I asked if he'd washed his hands before I let him take his present. Geraldine chatted to him while I finished clearing the table.

"Sit down with us," I offered. "Have a cup of tea. Sorry about the mess, we've just had dinner."

She inclined her head in her usual gracious manner and moved Gabriel's fleece aside so she could seat herself in the armchair.

"Aunty Geraldine," Gabe panted. He'd struggled out of his sweatshirt and substituted it for the bright green dinosaur jumper Geraldine had given him, pulled on crookedly around his neck. Geraldine adjusted it for him. "We went rock climbing. I climbed really, really high didn't I, Aiden?"

Geraldine smiled at her great-grandson. She turned to look at Aiden, who was pouring hot water into three mugs.

"That sounds nice." She raised an eyebrow at me.

"I'm sorry," I jumped in, bringing over a plate of biscuits. "I ought to have introduced you both. This is our friend Aiden Wilde. We've all had a brilliant afternoon together. It was so good for Gabriel."

The rhythm of Geraldine's breathing changed. She studied Aiden carefully, while he lowered two mugs of tea onto the coffee table and went back for the third. In the kitchenette he peered into it, then poured some more milk in. As he replaced the milk in the fridge he glanced up at me and smiled.

A feeling of nausea hit me. Geraldine was staring at him with glittering eyes. She'd had the same look on her face when she admitted to me that she was my grandmother, not an aunt. The air held still.

Everyone in the room picked up on the atmosphere, even Gabe. He tapped his right hand anxiously against his thigh.

"Aiden Wilde, did you say?"

Her words fell into silence. She'd failed in any attempt she might be making to sound casual. Her eyes had gone hard, her body sat even straighter than usual in the chair. "Pleased to meet you."

She didn't *sound* it. But her elegant white hand went out, marred by only one or two liver spots. Aiden shook it.

He settled next to me on the sofa and I noticed his thumbs were tucked inside his curled hands. I pressed my shoulder against his, my hair spilling down his arm. Geraldine took in our positions with a cool gaze.

"Whereabouts are you from, Aiden?"

"Aiden lives in a new castle," Gabe put in hesitantly. He tightened his hands into fists. His gaze swivelled between us. "I am going to go and live there one day as well."

"I live in Newcastle now," Aiden explained.

Gabe moved across the floor to settle at Aiden's feet. Aiden ruffled Gabe's hair, reaching down to assist the ascent of Thomas up his trouser leg. "Here, make sure Thomas doesn't get caught up in the rope, won't you?"

"But originally?" Geraldine persisted. The air around her shimmered.

Aiden hesitated before answering. "Oh, just a tiny village about forty miles down the coast from here." He helped Thomas onto the summit, avoided Geraldine's probing eyes. "Pottersea, it's called. Nobody's ever heard of it." He continued winding the miniature rope around his finger. When he handed it back to Gabe his movements were slow and calculated. Because of his absorption he didn't notice the colour blanching out of Geraldine's face. But I did.

"Aunty..." I rescued the mug of hot tea from her shaking hand before it spilled everywhere. "What's wrong?"

Was she having a stroke, or a heart attack? Rushing around between Leeds and York, Whitby and Scarborough at her age, maybe it had taken its toll. Again I remembered that she was the same age as my clients, who needed so much help.

"Aunty… Geraldine?" But after a struggle with her demeanour, she steadied herself.

"Tell me your father's name, Aiden, his first name."

It was an odd thing to ask. My hand crept onto Aiden's knee, which Thomas had just vacated. Aiden paused, still occupying himself with Gabriel and the toy. I could feel his tension. He attempted a smile but his facial muscles didn't seem to work properly.

Geraldine's expression confirmed that something was badly wrong. A chill travelled from the back of my neck down my arm. Maybe Aiden felt it spreading into his leg because he placed his hand over mine, squeezed my fingers gently.

"Cal," he said. He cleared his throat. "My father's name is Callum Wilde. You might have heard of him because…"

Geraldine made a sound like a hiccup.

"Oh, I've certainly heard of him." Her voice cut sharply through his. "But not for the reason you're thinking."

Her face had set like stone. Aiden and I glanced at each other. Gabe swivelled his head back towards Geraldine, jiggling about on his knees on the carpet.

"Thomas needs the toilet," he said.

Nobody took any notice of him, or of Thomas, who was having his trousers pulled down by Gabriel. The action man took a piss against the front of the sofa. Gabe made a hissing sound between his teeth.

Without taking my eyes off Geraldine's face, I registered that Gabriel had pulled up Thomas's pants. He scrambled onto the sofa beside Aiden, his lower lip thrust forward, making a low, growling noise in his throat. Before long he would announce that he was a tiger and threaten to bite somebody, Geraldine, if the way he looked at her was any indication.

"What do you mean?"

"You two." Geraldine coughed. Her skin took on a waxy texture. "I don't know what's been going on between you both but I'm telling you now, it's not possible for you to be together."

13

AFTER HER ANNOUNCEMENT that Aiden and I were related – I couldn't even think the words brother and sister – Geraldine immediately resumed her dogged insistence that I should meet my mother. As if that mattered more.

At that point Aiden was still next to me on the sofa, Gabe on his other side. My boy had stopped making growling noises and when I leaned forward I saw that his eyelids had drooped and I imagined the adventurous dreams he'd be having. I wished they were mine. The weight of unwanted knowledge pressed down on me.

Out of nowhere, I started coughing. I shrugged away Aiden's tentative pat on the back, my throat dry and sore. Geraldine waited until I was quiet, then resumed speaking in a voice that sounded automated, on a slightly faster-than-comfortable speed.

"She's very ill, Mariana, I'm terribly afraid she's going to waste away without seeing you. Darling, that would break my heart, and yours in the long run, however much you deny it. A blood tie is a strong one."

Aiden and I couldn't help glancing at each other. I'd pressed my knees primly together and leaned away so as not to be touching him. I'd even moved my hair over my other shoulder. Strands of it still clung to him. Even as I withdrew my physical particles, I couldn't help thinking of our kiss, the way our lips had fitted together so simply, and how I would have liked to do that again.

"You know everything now," said Geraldine. "Please try to be adult and do this one thing for her?"

I coughed again into my sleeve. Realisations were dawning. I wondered why Fate had brought me together with Aiden; he didn't even live in Whitby, it'd been pure chance that we'd come across each other. Was it because I was *supposed* to end up meeting my family?

"What's wrong with her?" I asked grudgingly.

Geraldine moved her lips a few times before the words came out. "She has anorexia. She's suffered with it on and off since she was a teenager. I'm so afraid… I think it's going to beat her this time. She's given up, Mariana. I believe she's simply waiting to die."

I'd never understood the disease. A friend of mine, Juliet, suffered from it when we were at school. I thought it had to do with wanting to look like models in the magazines we all pored over. I'd teased her with food, flaunting it and thinking she was deliberately resisting, convinced she'd eventually fall prey to the temptation of the doughnuts, chocolate bars and hot dogs I ate lasciviously in front of her. I couldn't comprehend that she had a mental illness. Juliet masked her despair so carefully with her façade of control.

Until they announced one morning in assembly that she had died.

She'd been off school a long time and I hadn't visited her for a while, although I knew she'd been in hospital. Her single-mindedness had frightened me, given me a glimpse of the darkness beneath my cotton-wool existence. I couldn't take it and so I'd pretended we'd never been friends at all.

I wanted to bury my head in the same way now. I couldn't agree to see Maria under this kind of pressure; it'd be horrible. What would she be expecting from me? I didn't want my only memory of her to be death. I remembered how Juliet had looked the last time I saw her. Maybe I could just ask Geraldine to show me some photos of Maria one day when I'd got over the shock. I could come to terms with my past that way…

Geraldine stared at her folded hands. Aiden and I leaned so studiously away from each other we made a 'V' shape on the sofa. He carefully shifted Gabe into a more comfortable position. My boy sighed and snuggled into the cushions.

Aiden patted my leg and I only flinched slightly. It was probably all right for a brother to do that. He got up and went into the kitchen; filled the kettle with water and flicked the switch. When he moved back into the living area to gather the cups, Geraldine lifted her chin and gave him a puzzled look, as though wondering what he was still doing there.

The cups clinked together and Gabriel stretched and woke up. He made a whimpering noise, saw where Aiden had gone and scrambled off the sofa to follow him, rubbing his eyes with his knuckles. *His uncle.* It began to dawn on me that this wasn't just about me. Gabe might resent me one day if I cut him out of a whole branch of his family.

Aiden poured Gabriel a cup of juice.

"She wanted you to be an only child." Geraldine must have sensed me weakening. "She told the social worker that she wanted you to be your new parents' whole world. She didn't want them to have any other children. You've got to believe how much she loved you."

The air felt muggy. I got up slowly, letting the blood settle before taking a step towards the window. I pulled the curtain aside, lifted the catch; pushed the top pane open.

So many thoughts whirl-winded in my head. Aiden talked quietly in the kitchen to Gabe. I heard him say "…pyjamas on." Taking on a familial role. I saw him smooth Gabe's hair back, reach down to take the emptied juice cup and place it in the sink. While Gabriel went into his bedroom, Aiden came back to the sofa, two mugs held by their handles in one hand, the third in his other. He lowered them carefully to the table. I sat down again, moving further into the corner of the sofa.

"It's a horrible illness," Aiden said. "Anorexia."

Geraldine glanced at him with a different kind of surprise. He sat down on the sofa, a cushion between him and me. Picking up his mug, he held it beneath his chin. Steam coated his skin in a warm mist. I found myself mirroring his actions as cool air from the open window stirred loose strands on top of my head.

Geraldine sipped delicately at her tea, looking enquiringly at Aiden.

"I don't have any personal experience of it," he said. "But I've heard them talking about it at family gatherings."

Geraldine tensed, leaned forward slightly.

"And I've seen the photographs," Aiden continued. His knuckles whitened around the handle of his mug. "My father's sister."

In his room, Gabe was singing off-key, "*I just can't wait to be king...*" I pictured him half-undressed, stomping around on his blue carpet, doing his Lion King dance.

I should be in there, reading him a story.

"His twin sister, her name was Marion."

AT FIRST I wondered what the vibration was, travelling through the sofa. Then I thought it must be Aiden trembling. But when I checked he seemed calm. Geraldine, in the armchair, had gone white again. It was her shaking. This time she had the foresight to place her mug on the table.

"What is it?" I asked.

"She died of anorexia," said Aiden. Had he not noticed the effect his words were having on Geraldine? *My father's sister*, he'd said. So she was my aunt, too. The knowledge hit me like a wave.

Geraldine pushed herself out of her chair and headed for the bathroom. The horrible sound of vomiting echoed through the flat.

"Shit," Aiden said. "Maybe I shouldn't have told her that. I'm sorry, Mariana."

"It's not your fault," I mouthed.

"Mammy," Gabriel emerged from his bedroom. His

cheeks were flushed, his eyes unnaturally bright. He was on the verge of a fit of giggles, which before long would turn into an extended screaming episode. He looked around wildly, saw that Geraldine was no longer in her seat, padded over to me. "Mammy, Aunty Geraldine's being sick, isn't she?"

"I think she's got a bad tummy." I wrapped my arms around him, felt his hot face against my chest. "Remember when you had a tummy bug?" I held him tight, felt his little heart pounding. "It was horrible, being sick, wasn't it?" I rocked him on my lap. My boy.

Geraldine reappeared. She looked exhausted, much older than when she'd arrived. She bent down to collect her bags and went straight to the pegs for her coat. She wound a silk scarf around her neck and pulled on her leather gloves.

"I beg you to reconsider. That's the only thing I can do for my daughter." Her eyes flickered over the Madonna scene my child and I must have presented. "I know you would do anything for your son."

I felt sorry for her. It must be awful to watch your child die.

"I'M GABRIEL'S UNCLE."

I resented that Aiden wasn't more cut-up about the situation.

We had stood around in almost-silence for five minutes after Geraldine left. Gabriel had tottered straight into his bedroom after having a pee. He'd put himself to bed. The living room smelled of the dinner we'd eaten. It seemed strange that the aroma of our earlier expectations should remain in the air to remind us of what we'd lost, that everything should go on as normal.

"And I'm your brother, your half-brother. Look, you're almost my twin, just like I said. Can't you see how wonderful that is?"

Not to me.

It was too late in the day for him to drive back to Newcastle, so we decided that Aiden would sleep in Gabe's room, to the delight of his nephew, who was lying only half-awake in bed when we pulled the mattress in and started making it up. Since Aiden and I hadn't discussed the night's sleeping arrangements beforehand, we didn't have to give Gabe any complicated explanations. I slipped in a few 'uncle' references before kissing him goodnight, and let him see Aiden give me a sideways hug and a peck on the cheek before we closed the doors of our adjacent rooms.

Once inside mine, I pushed the window open wide and pulled my bed directly under it. Then I knelt at the head of the bed with my arms on the windowsill. I couldn't even call it crying, what I did. It felt more like turning myself inside-out, and it produced so much water that I had to change my pyjama top and pillowcase before I could go to sleep.

14

Three weeks later

D AMON DIDN'T MEET us at the station.

"Damn." I dug in my bag for my mobile, but there were no messages.

"Where's Daddy?" Gabe extracted a bright green lollipop from his mouth. "He's supposed to be here, isn't he?" He probed my expression intently, probably worrying I'd lose my temper. It wouldn't be the first time. I felt grumpy and irritable anyway. Two weeks before, I'd told Aiden over the phone that I wasn't interested in celebrating our birthdays together. I concocted a story about a girls' night out and said I would be too tired after that to see him at the weekend. I still felt guilty.

"What about my nephew?" he'd responded. "Surely you won't object to me coming over for Gabriel's birthday?" But I said no because we were going to Scarborough to Gabriel's grandparents, and then to Hull for Gabe to see his dad. At least that wasn't a lie, even if we were doing it a week late.

Before he went back to Newcastle, I'd persuaded Aiden not to tell the rest of his family about me yet. "Not even Angel?" he had a close relationship with his (*our*) younger sister.

"Nobody, not yet." I said. "I've got so much going on right now. Please let me deal with everything in my own way."

STANDING NOW IN Paragon Station, having established that I wasn't about to explode, Gabe dropped his eyes from my face. He gave the lolly a minute examination and sniffed it before popping it back between his lime-coloured lips. We were standing beside the statue of a hurrying Philip Larkin, and Gabe absent-mindedly stroked the eminent poet's bronze leg as he sucked.

"He's supposed to be here," I forced a smile as I internally seethed. "I don't know where he is, Sweetheart."

Bastard Damon. I had no energy left; it was hard always being the one in charge.

"Shall we go to his house and surprise him, like a birthday surprise?" Gabe said. He was a sensitive kid, I didn't want him to get hurt. But he tugged impatiently on my hand. "Come on." He crunched the lolly with his back teeth. "Let's go see Daddy. I'm tired of waiting."

"If that's what you want to do, baby."

We had to walk about a mile from the station to get to the house Damon shared with a couple of his band mates. We stopped at a small supermarket on the way for a drink for Gabe, and I bought a cake. I grabbed a packet of birthday candles at the last minute.

"Because Daddy will probably have forgotten, won't he?"

Yup.

The house was in a grove down a side street off the main road. Hull is like that, rows of houses tucked away in all sorts of unexpected places. The doorbell didn't work so I banged hard on the front door and Gabe added a few thumps of his own. He shouted through the letter box. Finally, we heard the bang of an interior door and footsteps thumping down the stairs.

Damon pulled the door open. His straw-like hair stuck out at all angles. He wore a grubby grey t-shirt and a pair of black jeans which looked as if he'd dragged them from the laundry basket. His feet were bare and he was unshaven, not artfully, just a mess. When he spotted Gabriel he gave a roar which would have frightened the wits out of any other kid, but Gabe was used to his dad. Gabe offered him a high five and he returned it. Then he bent his knees, scooped his son up, and swung him around. Unreliable as he was, he did love the boy. In the end I had to remember that.

Gabe shrieked, giggled when Damon put him down. Then his face settled into a careful expression. "You forgot I was coming, didn't you, Daddy?"

Damon put on a sorrowful face. He stuck out his bottom lip, making Gabe laugh again. But I was furious – I knew our kid would forgive Damon anything, and it wasn't fair. "Can't you just put him first for once?" I muttered.

He gave me an offended look. I pushed past him in the doorway, turning my head away from his armpit because he was standing with his hand above me on the doorframe.

"Hey, don't be like that, Babe."

Damon pulled the front door shut and tugged Gabe after him. I walked through a cramped middle room into the kitchen. Removing the cake from its box, I looked for a clean plate. In the sink, pots piled in oily water, soggy bread floating on top. Damon slithered into the kitchen behind me and reached up to the top shelf of a cupboard. I smelled sweat and a faint aroma of sex coming off him as he put a plate on the crowded worktop and took the cake from me. *I hope you've washed your hands.* Standing next to him I saw the two of us with objectivity – how much I'd aged in the years since I loved him so passionately, yet he'd managed to retain the air of a boy.

"Are we going to sing Happy Birthday?" Gabe piped up, jiggling on the spot. In the back of my mind I thought *I must get him to the toilet, he hasn't been for a while.* But a movement behind him distracted me. Someone appeared in the doorway. A grin spread across Damon's face.

"Hey, you."

The girl with (dyed) black hair stood there and examined a scratch on the side of her hand. When she faced Damon, her eyes blazed. "Who were you calling Babe? Coz it sure as hell wasn't me."

There was something unnerving about her. Ready to spring, she reminded me of Pris from *Bladerunner*. She had scary eyes, but she also looked familiar. A ripple ran through me.

"Come on, don't be like that," Damon said in a mewling voice. "You know me, just being friendly, that's all."

He nudged past his son to reach her but she leant away from him, dragging those horribly familiar eyes over Gabriel, and then me.

"So who are they?"

Damon sucked his bottom lip. I'd never seen him nervous around a girl before. Heaven knows he has enough experience of flirting with them.

"Ah, well here's the thing, Babe," he spluttered. "I forgot to tell you. This is my little lad, Gabriel. It was his birthday last week, wasn't it mate?" He put one of his hands out for another high five with Gabe.

"I'm four," our child said, uncertainly.

"Yeah, you are mate."

The girl pulled away. "You never effing told me you had a son."

Damon looked offended. He was good at that. "Why, does it matter?"

Damon can be so dim. Of course his girlfriend would want to know he has a son. I stared out of the kitchen window at the tiny back yard while they bickered, my hands either side of the plate with Gabe's birthday cake on. Damon and his girlfriend moved further away into the middle room, their voices rising. Damon and I had argued a lot too, when we were together. At my elbow Gabe fiddled with a brightly wrapped parcel which he'd found on a shelf below the worktop.

"Do you think this is for me?"

I glanced down. "Yes. Look, there's your name. It must be from Daddy."

"Can I open it now?"

"I don't see why not. Daddy seems busy at the moment."

My vision blurred as I stared out at the bare branches of a tree I remembered had purple leaves in the summer. Its skeletal tracery splayed above the garden wall. Behind it, old brick and rooftops stretched into infinity. At intervals a trail of smoke rose into the grey, heavy sky. I felt like crying. I had finally answered the phone to Aiden the previous evening so he could wish Gabriel a belated happy birthday, but it just made me regretful to hear his voice.

Without thinking what I was doing, my hands lifted the kettle and filled it. Gabe crouched on the floor with a toy tractor, making vroom-vroom sounds. The arguing voices in the other room went quiet and there were loud kissing noises. Damon came back to the doorway of the kitchen with the black-haired girl clinging to his arm. He slipped his arm free and knelt down near Gabe, while the girl stood stiffly above them.

"I see you've found your prezzie," Damon said. "Do you like it?"

"Yeah, I love it Daddy. Look, if you push it back like this, it can... it can zoom forward all by itself."

"Come over here then, and show it to Angie."

Gabe looked up at his dad. His skewed smile made my heart twist.

"Say hello to Angie," Damon told him. "She's my girlfriend, so you'll be seeing her again. Lots." He glanced at Angie and nodded enthusiastically, putting his hand out for Gabriel to take. Gabe scrambled to his feet, his head swivelling from Angie to me. I gave him a reassuring nod.

I turned to Damon. "I've put the kettle on. Shall I leave Gabe with you for a bit, so you can all spend some time together?"

Doubt shadowed the girl's face. She rolled her eyes. Damon shook his head, pursing his lips.

"Ah, Ba... Sorry. I forgot to tell you, I've got to get off to a rehearsal in about," he craned into the kitchen to see the clock on the wall. "Hang on a minute, in about half-an-hour." He pulled one of his goofy faces at Gabe. My son pulled his hand away. "Sorry Gabe, mate," Damon wheedled. "I only found out at short notice. Our band could really be going places," he said to me. "There's like, this new label starting up and they might be interested in us. We've got a gig next weekend and they're sending someone over to listen to us. I'm not being funny but I can't miss this practice, you understand that, don't you? Hey, Gabe," he ruffled his son's hair. "How proud would you be if your dad became a famous rock musician, eh?"

Gabe's eye-colour had darkened and I could see him clenching and unclenching his fists, his tractor tucked under one arm. *If we hadn't made our way here as soon as we got into Hull we'd have missed Damon altogether.* We'd have come all the way from Scarborough for nothing. All my frustration of the past few weeks boiled over, and even though I knew it wasn't true I shouted, "You bastard! You don't give a shit about him really, do you?"

"Hey now," soothed Damon. He came into the kitchen and fitted his arm loosely around my shoulders. Gabe unclenched his fists and tagged onto him, his hand in the back pocket of his dad's jeans. He ran the tractor up his father's leg while Damon tried one of his winning smiles on me. "Come on. Let's light the candles on Gabe's cake. It's for our boy's birthday, remember? Don't spoil it."

Me, spoil it? From the corner of my eye I saw the Pris-like girl stiffening. I had a vision of the film, when she leaps on Harrison Ford's shoulders and smashes his skull with her thighs. But it was me she came towards. She pushed me away from Damon.

"What the fuck are you doing, coming here and spoiling everything? If you insist on bringing your kid to see his dad, well… fucking next time text or ring first; and then just drop him off. Get it?"

"Don't you dare fucking push me," I found myself mirroring her language.

"Hey, Angie…"

Damon was silenced by a stabbing look from those Pris-eyes. Gabriel hopped from one foot to the other. "Daddy, I don't like Angie. And I need a wee. I need a wee, Daddy."

Damon gave a helpless shrug. He hesitated and then swivelled towards his girlfriend, patting her shoulders. He'd turned away from his son. I went hot all over, and then cold. *Putting her first.* Inside I screamed curses but my body managed to behave as if it was calm.

"Come on Gabe," I snapped. "We're going."

"But Mammy, I…" Gabe tugged at the zipper on my jacket, then I saw why. A puddle spread over the dirty brown lino, the hot scent of pee rising up.

"Oh shit, look at that." Angie leapt away. "He's pissed himself. For fuck's sake, Damon, I wish you'd warned me about this."

I ignored her. "I'm sorry I didn't listen to you," I crouched in front of Gabe. He squeezed his eyes shut, a thin noise coming from his throat. His face reddening; he held two handfuls of my hair, pulling my head down towards his. I felt sick with shame. "It's ok," I whispered, close to his face. "Damon," I said out the side of my mouth, "have you got any of his clothes here?"

From the corner of my eye I could see he had the grace to look mortified. "Yeah Babe, don't worry. You come with me Gabe. I reckon I've got your old Bertie Dinosaur upstairs as well. He can help you get changed, yeah? And Angie," he paused and gave her a fierce look. "Leave off, ok? I'll be down in a minute."

"Look at the trouble you've caused," Angie hissed at me after they'd left the room.

"Don't blame me." Any energy I'd had left was seeping into the pool on the lino. "This was all arranged beforehand, I can't help it if your boyfriend forgot." I looked around for somewhere to sit down, but there was nowhere in the kitchen. "Anyway," I told her. "It's you who's ruined it. Get out of my way."

She continued to block the kitchen doorway. My anger rose again. I squeezed my fingers into my palms, tried to cut the skin with my fingernails, anything to release the pressure, but the nails were bitten too short.

"Move."

"Why does he call you Babe, anyway? Still *fucking* him, are you?"

If I'd been paying attention I'd have noticed how hard

she gripped her forearms and that she was shaking, but I only realised afterwards when I'd had time to reflect on what happened. I was too mad not to stop my temper from taking over.

"Just move out of my way."

I leaned into her with my shoulder, but she kept stepping from side to side. So I gave her a push with the flat of my hand. She pushed me harder, so I pushed *her* harder back. That time she lost her balance. Her shoulder and then her head hit the doorframe. *Oh, God.* But her head also knocked the corner of the windowsill when she continued falling. She made a funny little grunt and kind of folded up on the floor, a stunned look on her face.

※≫≪※

DAMON HAD BRAZENLY gone off to his rehearsal after dropping Gabriel off at our school friend Kayla's on Newland Avenue. *Why is it* me *waiting in the A&E department of Hull Royal with Angie, not him?*

"Well, it was kind of your fault, Babe…"

Angie had a pad the triage nurse had given her pressed against the side of her head. She'd been too confused to complain when Damon dropped us off outside the hospital, Gabriel sitting in the front seat beside him. He'd at least had the grace to give me a fiver for a taxi back to Kayla's to pick our kid up whenever someone arrived to collect Angie.

She looked small sitting beside me. We both stared at a TV in the corner. Pope Benedict had retired and North Korea had detonated another nuclear bomb. I wanted to get back to Gabriel.

"Angie Butler?"

"I'm ok. I can go in by myself," she said as I stood up.

She was weaker than she thought. She made another attempt but her legs were shaking too much.

"You'd better come with your sister." The nurse gave me a quick smile. I felt too stunned by her assumption to argue with her and Angie didn't seem to have heard what she said. "We've called your parents, *Angie*." I wondered why she said it like that. "Someone's coming to collect you."

"Shit," she muttered.

⟩⟩⟩⟩✳⟨⟨⟨⟨

ANGIE ACTUALLY GRABBED my hand. Her yelps sounded like a younger girl and I realised she probably wasn't as old as I'd thought.

"I'd recognise that caterwauling anywhere." It was a man's deep voice. A flushed nurse pulled open the curtain and announced, "Here she is."

Angie and I looked up. "*Dad*. Fuck." Angie said. Half-obscured by the curtain, I could see him, but he couldn't see me.

"Angie Butler, eh? Disowning your father, are you, young lady?"

The tone was falsely jovial. He twisted his hands, a gesture somehow reflecting my state of mind. He hadn't seen me yet, but I dreaded the moment he did, because I had a feeling he'd start quoting Tennyson's *Mariana* at me.

Angel had shaken off my hand. I eyed the curtain on the

129

other side of the cubicle, decided to get out before he and I came face to face. I gathered my things quietly. Something slid to the floor but I didn't stop to find out what it was. As I broke free of the swinging plastic sheeting that seemed to want to hold me back, I heard an indrawn breath and the quick shuffle of footsteps. The man's surprised "Hey," was followed by the nurse's flustered "Mr Wilde, wait…"

15

Maria, March 2013

ALICE DROVE UP from London to visit me at my parents' house. My business partner had asked her to bring me some papers to sign and Alice passed on her good wishes and an update on the progress of the youth theatre group she had helped us build up. Alice had even brought some get well cards along from some of the younger members. I still thought of Alice as the young girl who'd presented herself at my theatre more than four and a half years ago, but it occurred to me that she must be thirty years old. (I could now picture the seven-year-old she had been, rubbing the toe of a grubby trainer up the back of one leg, tongue poking out the corner of her mouth while she thought up uncomfortable questions to ask the seventeen-year-old me.)

Alice sat on the edge of my bed and seemed to find it hard to look at me. From time to time I remembered how frightening my appearance must be to her. It had been a long time since I'd had a relapse as bad as this – long before Alice appeared in my life for the second time. She must not have bargained for any of this when she'd been so keen to come and work with me, back in the summer of 2008. As a relatively inexperienced actress back then, my partner in the theatre company and I had agreed to interview her on the recommendation of a colleague.

⫸⫸⫷⫷

ALICE TURNER HAD stood in our office clutching her CV and a bunch of references. She'd recently completed her Masters' Degree and had worked with a theatre group in Leicester for three years prior to that. She told me that she'd played the part of Esther in my play *The Old Pathway* while still at university. She said she'd long since wanted a chance to work with the actual writer of the play. She offered to teach our new intake of youth theatre students for nothing in exchange for acting masterclasses from my partner and me.

There was something very likeable about her, familiar, even. The guileless blue eyes, the particular shade of her blonde hair, but I couldn't put my finger on it.

"Where do you come from, originally?" I'd asked her.

"Oh, you know, tiny village, back of beyond." Alice, I remembered now, had spoken dismissively but there was something evasive in her reply. She had an indefinable accent; I remember pinpointing a northern bias, its edges smoothed.

"Which county?" I thought maybe I'd be able to work

out where, if anywhere, I might have seen her before.

"Lincolnshire," she told me. *So she had said Lincolnshire.* The cream walls of my cramped office had seemed to pulse as I scanned them. I remembered wiping a hand across my eyes, tugging at the polo neck of my top. Alice had raised her chin and smiled, somehow conveying a subtle message of reassurance. I think our friendship began right at that moment; I must have come across as different even then, but she'd never shown a flicker of distaste or fear at my odd ways.

Sitting behind my desk, I had hoped it wasn't the familiar tingling I sensed in my jaw. Surely it was only ordinary pins and needles stabbing my fingers, I simply needed more air. After this interview I would convince myself to eat something. I'd taken as much stale air into my lungs as I could and made an effort to glance over Alice's references. All the time I felt the concerned gaze of my business partner, Tamika, on me.

"You've some good credentials, really good; yes."

I passed the sheaf of papers to Tamika, who rolled towards me on her office chair. It was getting hotter in the office. I tried to stand up to open a window, my hands shaking. Then I felt the blood draining from my face and held Tamika's eyes, a mute plea she would recognise.

Tamika asked Alice to wait in another room. As soon as the door closed I sank back into my chair, jaw stiffening, eyes glazing over. I knew Tamika would be ready with a glass of water and one of my tablets when I came round from the fit.

Five months after that, Alice took the lead role in my

landmark play *The Time Has Come*. It was a brand new work, my tribute to my relinquished daughter. *The play I had hoped would change everything in my life.* My daughter had turned eighteen and I asked my mother to invite her to a performance of the play without telling her who the playwright was. If Mariana had agreed, I would have asked my mother to tell her the truth about who gave birth to her and say that I was ready to meet her.

Only later did I understand the extent of my naivety: the misplaced simplicity of my belief that the baby I'd given up for her own safety would have spent her life anticipating our eventual reunion. No. I'd done my job too well, Mariana was so safe and so happy that she didn't need me. Even now that I knew my mother had told Mariana about me, I still refused to be informed of her circumstances unless she would agree to see me.

Alice had been in the office the day my mother had rung to let me know of Mariana's rejection for the second time, and some instinct had prompted me to continue the conversation in Alice's presence, and go on to talk to her about it afterwards. *I have a secret daughter and she doesn't want to know me.* Alice witnessed me in the grip of catatonia for the first time after I told her.

⫸⫷

"MARIA, WE ALL miss you. When are you coming back?"

My room in the house on Cornfields Estate was as yellow as the day I brought Mariana home from the hospital. There were still spare cans of paint stored in the basement cupboards. My father, never the most imaginative of types, brought them out every few years for re-decorating.

The door from the music room to mine was boarded over. Justine had been a child with minor learning difficulties and was now an accomplished musician, married with two small children. She lived close to our parents' and still came over to play, as her family's small terraced house didn't have room for her large piano. I could hear the piano music as Alice asked me her question. Handel's *Largo*. My deadened heart swelled.

"I don't know, Alice."

I'd asked my mother to remove the mirror from the room, frightened of the cat eyes in the pared-down face that stared back at me. They were less and less my own. I was engaged in a permanent battle with *her*. She'd come back for me. I felt she wouldn't rest until she had me, and I hardly had the strength to resist, nor did I really want to. If Mariana didn't need me, then I didn't need myself.

"Lisa was asking about you," Alice spoke quietly. "Look, Maria, I know there are things between you two that go way back beyond my understanding. But *I* only know you as Maria, and that's who I want back. You're fading away. I'm sorry, but it's true."

Oh, I know that. If I could have summoned the energy I would have laughed at her indignant tone. 'Bullet from a gun' is how Tamika had described our protégée on their first meeting. But instead I let my head fall back on the pillow.

"Lisa was the best friend I had, once." I rolled my head from side-to-side on the crisp pillowcase. "I mean, the best friend *Marion* had."

Alice had told me that Lisa was lonely in her house out there in the back of beyond, lacking a close friend. I should have overridden my fear of the situation – not allowed Cal to win again. I could have been the friend to Lisa that she'd been to Marion when they were both young. *So many regrets I have...* Alice put her hand over mine on the quilt and I moved my fingers to acknowledge her touch. It was all I could do. I was so tired. The fits had worn me out and I was very afraid I wouldn't be able to hold on much longer. But I still hoped to see Mariana and make sense of this strange life I'd had.

16

Angel Wilde, March 2013

HER FATHER HAD actually gone mad. Seriously. He'd always seemed dangerous, with his unpredictable anger. The other side of his personality – vulnerability, was a trap you could fall into. Her mother and Alice had a technique of dealing with his fragile moods that Angel had never mastered and didn't care to. Why should she spend her whole life treading on eggshells?

You're supposed to be the one who looks after me, not the other way round... It wasn't fair.

When she made new friends Angel used her mother's maiden name and called herself Angie. No-one would mess with *her*. She didn't want anyone to know who her father was; the 'troubled genius' one newspaper had described him as. He'd been cautioned for harassing some young girl four years or so ago. That was *so* embarrassing. But a year later he insisted he'd been wrong about that girl when he came back from a visit to Scarborough with Aunty Sarah. "This time it was *really* her," Angel heard him roar behind her parents' closed bedroom door.

Really who?

The media knew about the tragic death of his twin when he was a teenager; they never stopped going on about it. The picture of Marion that'd been used on the covers of her two published novels was dug out and added to the regular articles that came out after the releases of his new books; the headline always something like '*Forever Searching for His Other Half.*'

"Wow, she looks just like you." Her school friends used to say. To them her father's situation was romantic and exciting. But Angel had dyed her hair black. She was suspended from school for it. In the end her mother got her a special dispensation to have black hair on the grounds of *emotional welfare*.

When she first saw that girl in Damon's house she felt sick. Long red hair and those eyes. Mariana looked just like the pictures of Marion. And she had a stupidly similar name. It completely threw her. Especially when it turned out Mariana was Damon's ex; the mother of a child she never knew he had. *What the fuck?*

Things had first got weird, *extra weird*, when that woman, Alice's boss; their mother's long-lost friend, whoever she was, arrived at Blackberry House in the New Year. She was *sure* she'd heard her dad saying, "You were supposed to be dead." For a minute she'd even wondered if Maria could be the lost twin but of course she was too young, and anyway, that idea was stupid.

Since then, Cal had started getting up earlier than ever, sometimes not going to bed at all. Lack of sleep made him even more foul-tempered. But there was more to it than that. He had a far-away look in his eyes. When anyone spoke to him he stared over their shoulder as if he could see something behind them. He kept going to the beach. He said he was sure *she* would come back.

When Cal arrived at the hospital a nurse had tried to get his autograph and he was flattered enough to have some of his ego back. But he saw Mariana just as she got up to leave. The frightening look came back into his eyes; he started to hurry after her but the nurses called him back. It was only then that her name connected in Angel's mind with the second incident involving her dad. He and Aunty Sarah had seen a girl called Mariana on a trip they took to scatter their father's ashes. *This time it was really her,* Angel's dad had said.

SHE STOOD BY the bread bin, tearing pieces off a loaf and spreading them with butter. She had a pan of water boiling on the stove ready for the eggs her mother was collecting from the hens. It'd been raining all morning and now the sun had come out, making prisms of bright drops of water sliding down the windowpane. English coursework lay neatly at one end of the kitchen table, thoughts for her planned essay ran through her head.

The kitchen door opened. She expected it to be her mum with the eggs, but instead she felt like a startled rabbit in the glare of her dad's eyes, blazing like an orange traffic light. That was exactly what he was, stuck forever on the waiting line. Sad, really. He carried on standing there, staring in Angel's direction but not looking at her. It was like being in the room with a ghost.

"Mum's gone out to collect the eggs," she tried. "Do you want some breakfast?"

It was a worse kind of uncomfortable than usual. His short, catchy breathing rasped across the room. He might be physically ill. His eyes moved slowly over her face, made an effort to focus.

"Your hair…"

"Uhm, yeah," she said. "What about it?"

"Your hair, why have you done that?"

He came closer and started to put a hand up towards her hair, which for once she had brushed straight and fastened back with two ruby coloured clips. But she moved away before he could touch it.

"Dad, do you mean like, I've straightened it?" She eyed the door nervously. *Where's Mum?*

He made a clicking sound with his tongue. "It's the wrong colour. You've changed." Water welled up in his eyes. She backed away further. Her voice came out thin.

"It's been like this for ages."

He continued moving forward on hesitant feet. Like a zombie. She slipped around the other side of the table. From that angle she noticed his hand was plunged into his coat pocket, moving as though turning something over. For a moment she panicked, *it's a lighter, he's planning to set the place on fire.* Then her mother came in, stamping her feet on the mat, brushing back her short silvery-blonde hair. She carried the basket of eggs in one arm. Angel felt a rush of love.

"Mum…"

Lisa had her back turned, removing eggs carefully from the basket, setting them in the china bowl on the worktop. She took a large spoon and transferred a few of them into the pan of boiling water.

"What is it, Pet?" She wiped her hands on the towel that hung beside the sink. "You haven't got the bread cut yet. Cal, are you having some breakfast, Love?"

Angel knew her mother missed the days of three children in the house; a dog bouncing around, a husband who felt like part of the family. Cal muttered to himself and Angel caught the flash in her mother's eyes: could've been anxiety or exasperation.

"I don't think he recognised me," Angel told her in a hushed voice. "It was weird."

Lisa met her eyes. She braced herself with her hands on the worktop, taking a deep breath.

"Cal, Love. Come and sit at the table. Let's get your coat off."

She moved to Cal and attempted to slide the coat from his shoulders but he clung on to it, one hand still jammed in his pocket. Lisa stopped, rested her head on his shoulder. She put her arms around him.

"You're cold. Come on, let's get you warmed up."

Biting her lip so hard she tasted blood, Angel pulled a chair from the table over to the woodstove and Lisa led her husband to it. His eyes glittered. Angel looked at her mother over her father's head.

"Pop some Rescue Remedy into a cup of hot water." Lisa said quietly, putting faith in her regular cure-all.

Angel flicked the switch on the kettle. Her mother huddled over Cal, talking in her most gentle voice, reminding Angel of childhood illness. Angel made the drink and carried it over, then went back to her breakfast preparations, a weighted feeling in her stomach.

Her mother managed to persuade Cal to take his coat off. She asked Angel to hang it up. Angel put it over her arm, warm and heavy, it smelt of *father*. She wanted to bury her nose in it. Glancing back as she carried it over the quarry tiles towards the pegs under the stairs, Angel felt in the pocket to find out what her father had been hanging onto so grimly. A mobile phone. It felt smaller than Cal's. Angel had a sudden vision of Mariana getting up quickly from her chair, something clattering to the floor. One eye on her father and one on the hurriedly retreating girl, Angel had registered somewhere in her brain that a shiny purple mobile phone lay under a trolley. But when she remembered to look for it later, the phone was gone, and she assumed one of the nurses had picked it up. It wasn't her problem.

WHY THE FUCK did Cal have Mariana's phone? Angel examined the photo gallery. There were the usual eyes-looking-up-into-the camera selfies and lots of pictures of the kid.

Her boyfriend's son. She'd still not got used to that.

But, what? Her mouth fell open. There, on Mariana's phone, was a picture of Aiden. Looking into the camera, blue sky filling the frame around him. Sunlight gave him a halo. And another of him, crouched in front of Mariana's son, placing a helmet of some kind on the child's head. Angel's heart thumped. *Gabriel could be Aiden's son.* Now she thought about it, the child didn't look anything like Damon. Had there been some kind of massive subterfuge to prevent Aiden's family knowing about his child? There was another picture of Aiden, half-way up a climbing wall with the little boy beside him. This was more than crazy. It was upside down.

Angel weighed up her discoveries and tried to make sense of them.

It was definitely Aiden on Mariana's phone. Mariana's son definitely looked like Aiden. And Mariana looked like Angel's dead Aunt Marion, not to mention Angel herself. Oh. And Angel's father had stolen Mariana's phone. He'd reacted with panic when he spotted Mariana apparently trying to escape from him in the hospital. Did he know something Angel was still trying to work out?

Angel added one further element to the bizarre series of events: that woman, Maria. Although very thin and getting old, she also bore a resemblance to Mariana and therefore, Angel concluded, to herself. Cal's stranger-than-usual behaviour had begun that very morning in January. He'd been having an argument with Maria, and Angel's sister and mother had each offered conflicting explanations of who Maria actually was.

Angel moved over to one of the dormer windows in her

attic room. She stared out across rain-sodden fields to the thin line of sea on the horizon. Light raindrops fell on the glass and blurred her view. The phone felt heavy in her hand. It was wrong that her father had taken it, and that she, Angel, had it now. *Fuck*, the whole thing felt sinister. She shuddered, frightened of what might happen when Cal discovered it was missing, remembering the way he'd refused to give up his coat, pressed his hand over the shape of the phone. She couldn't shake off the look in his eyes when he asked what she'd done to her hair. "You've changed," he'd said. Maybe he was mistaking her for someone else. She pressed a hand over her stomach to stifle the cold, sick feeling inside.

She got into bed. Plugging her iPod into her ears she selected shuffle. It felt less personal to be going through someone's text messages if you were tuned into your favourite music, letting it claim you emotionally. But she needed to find out why Mariana's phone meant so much to Cal.

The last couple of messages Mariana had sent were from when she was waiting with Angel at the hospital, to the friend looking after Gabriel.

A more recent message from someone called Geraldine begged, *Please visit before it's too late.* Mariana hadn't answered it, of course, because she didn't have the phone. Angel drew her knees up to her stomach. The sick feeling had changed to a wobbly one, like she'd been on a train too long. She felt weak at her core, wanted to fold up and protect herself. The message after that was from the same person. *You'll regret it if you don't go. You may not get another chance.*

A few were to and from Damon, arranging the visit with his son. *Damn him*, he'd not mentioned anything to Angel. There were a few from Aiden: arrangements for meeting up mostly, the later ones full of affection and hopeful anticipation. The final one from him confused Angel: *Don't let this ruin us. Yours in another way now, love xx*

She closed her eyes, giving all her attention to an Adele song pumping into her head. Just as the song ended the mobile buzzed in her hand. Another text message from Geraldine. *Been trying to ring you but you never answer. Your mother is DYING! Come before it's too late.*

Angel felt herself trembling. This was obviously a message Mariana needed to have. A few minutes later another text came through, from 'Mam': *Baby, I have to agree with Geraldine now. Maria may die. Why won't you answer your phone, love?*

Things began to fall into place. Mariana's 'mam' and the person Geraldine referred to as 'your mother' were two different people. And it seemed her mother was named Maria, and Maria was dying. The image of that woman's gaunt face at the kitchen table came into Angel's mind. And with it a pure and sharp conviction.

Angel had inadvertently become involved in a tangled web of lives, and *lies*, with her father, her boyfriend and her brother caught up in it as well. At the centre of any web was a spider. She shivered again with an intuition. *Cal.*

She ran her finger around the outer edge of the phone, thought about what to do. She pulled the earphones out of her ears and wound the wire neatly around, slipping her iPod into the drawer beside her bed. The sound of the now heavy rain clattering down on the windows filled her head. Damon would know another way of contacting Mariana. The beseeching nature of the messages weighed on Angel's mind. Taking a quick, decisive breath she called Damon from Mariana's phone. He would think it was his ex.

"Hey, Babe," Damon answered predictably, but Angel was too flustered to care. "Whassa matter, is Gaby all right?"

"It's me, Angie, not Mariana."

In the resulting silence, Angel suddenly felt hot, kicked the quilt off her legs. "She dropped her phone at the hospital," she said. Damon was still speechless. "I... it doesn't matter how I got it. But it wasn't me that took it, I found it on the floor..."

"Angie, Babe," Damon finally interrupted. "What the, well why are you calling me on it, shouldn't you be giving it back to her?"

Angel examined her purple painted fingernails. She bit down on her bottom lip. "I don't know how to contact her. Do you have any other number I can ring her on, or like, her Facebook. I mean, what's her surname? I can find her."

"Babe, why would you want to contact her yourself? Give the phone to me and I'll get it back to her. Don't worry."

Angel intuited that he wouldn't be sensitive enough to give Mariana the news about her birth mother properly. She remembered her grief when her grandfather had died, the sadness that she hadn't got to say goodbye. She wouldn't wish that on anyone, least of all a girl she was beginning to feel a connection with.

"Just give me her surname. I'll do it myself."

SHE'D LEFT HER laptop in the kitchen and was scared to go down in case Cal had discovered the phone was missing. But once at the bottom of her attic staircase she could hear her mother and father talking in the upstairs living room. She turned the phone over in the pocket of her hoody, as her father had done when it was in his coat. This little phone connected her to Mariana, to Damon, to Aiden – and all of them to Cal. And to a woman who was dying. The world rocked under her feet, the onus of responsibility to sort out the whole mess on her shoulders.

She crept down to the kitchen, slipped her laptop out of its case and took it into the office. She sat at the old oak desk, opened the laptop and connected to Facebook.

Amazingly, there was only one Mariana Rivers when she hit the search button. Angel was tempted to explore Mariana's history on the site, find out how much she'd communicated with Damon, but reminded herself her purpose had only been to track Mariana down. A woman could die at any time according to the text messages. She had trouble deciding what to put in her message on Facebook, but in the end she kept it simple and to the point.

'*This is Angel Wilde, you knew me as Angie Butler, my mother's maiden name. I have your phone, only just found it, sorry. You need to contact your mam or Geraldine. Sorry for reading but there are some messages which look really important. Oh yeah and we should maybe meet up so I can give you your phone. I have some questions for you as well. Sorry about, you know. Contact me on here. Angel.'*

When she'd sent the message she allowed herself a browse of Mariana's page. More pictures of Gabriel; one of him with his father – Angel found herself touching the pixels that made up Damon's face. There was a shakily taken one of Aiden with his arm around Mariana's waist. Mariana's long red hair reached down to his elbow. *I could have had mine like that*, Angel found herself thinking. She touched her own hair, wondering how it would feel to let it go back to its natural colour.

She hadn't wanted to look like her dead aunt. But Mariana did. The significance of the similar name was not lost on Angel either. *Marion. Maria. Mariana.* It was fucked up. There were secrets, deep as mud; that the chance meeting with Mariana had got her embroiled in. And with so many physical similarities between the various protagonists, it had to figure that the girl with the long red hair was somehow family…

Don't let this ruin us. Yours in another way now, love xx

Aiden wasn't Gabriel's father; the connection was a different familial one.

17

Maria, late March 2013

ALICE VISITED ME again. I wished my own girl would come.

Alice asked me to let Cal visit; for the sake of her mother, who didn't know what to do with him. I said I'd think about it, but my mind drifted away too quickly to make any plans.

I had more memories of my first life. A different mother and father, a baby sister who died. I remember being confused because I thought it was meant to be me. My mother was always sad. She became furious with me when I was a teenager.

As the fading Maria, I understood how that other mother must have felt when she lost her teenage daughter as well as the one she'd lost in infancy. Marion and Cal's mother would be an old woman by now, but her grief would be the same even though the son she was also soon to lose was in his fifties. She'd still be cheated by fate. But Cal's path was inevitable. I could see the outcome as clearly as on a screen before my eyes.

Cal and Marion needed to go back to the beginning.

"Tell him he can come."

Alice's eyes shone. "Are you sure?"

I could hardly keep mine open. "Yes. And ask Lisa to come too."

We'd stopped pretending I would get better.

From far back in that other life of mine, I remembered the night Marion died; a blackbird singing late in the darkness outside the window next to her bed. Her brother and sister and father close around her, but her mother refused to attend.

Alice watched as if reading my thoughts. She put her hand on my shoulder for a moment and I felt her warmth infiltrate my bones. For so many years I thought I'd made a success of the life I was in; but it had all been at too high a cost.

"Mum told me," Alice was saying, "all about you two. You know, before. She was sad that she wasn't allowed to see Marion at the end."

My eyes were closed but in my mind was a clear picture of the teenaged Lisa and Marion: one plump with thick blonde hair; the other thin with hair the colour of a conker. She wouldn't speak and Lisa kept teasing her.

Sometimes I longed for Marion's silence.

"OH LORD, MARIA."

I almost laughed. Layers of time shifted like superimposed transparencies, shuffled like a pack of cards. I could hardly see what was in front of my eyes any more. The present was tenuous, but she had always been there.

"Lisa."

My hand fumbled above the bedcovers, reached for one or other of what seemed to be two figures: the Lisa from this and my other life. The older Lisa grasped my hand, thumb brushing my wrist. Her shudder ran through me, but it wasn't me she was weeping for.

"Cal," she managed to get out. "Alice tried, but your mother…"

"I know." My voice whispered like a leaf on a breeze. At the mention of Cal I felt *her* stirring within me. Like an embryo I'd always carried, she stretched and made me shapeless. Her deliverance was impending. *I want my brother.*

"He loses his temper and then cries piteously. He keeps saying that he's got to find her. *Her*: that's you, Maria, everything you are. Marion's always haunted him. I don't know what he'll do when…"

"I know, I know."

Let me go.

My mother had never forgiven Cal for what he did to me. I'd heard Alice reasoning with her on Cal's behalf, but she said she would not allow him into the house. The night before, I'd sworn to myself that I heard his footsteps pacing the track between our garden and the open fields. I'd sensed him wearing a hollow in the earth, crouched nearby like a hare. Surely it had been the steam of his breath filtering into my room through the tiny crack at the window frame. He was *in* me, just as much as Marion was. The three of us spiralled inside my shell like effervescent spirits.

"He'll know what to do," I offered Lisa. *Was she still there?*

MY MOTHER CAME in later. Through superimposed visions like tattered veils, Geraldine smoothed back her impeccable hair. Her fingernails were painted blood red as always. Red jewels dangled from her ears like more drops of blood. I imagined she rued the day she gave birth to me.

"Maria," she said. "I'm not being cruel in denying Callum Wilde, please believe me. But there are things neither you nor he know, and I'm going to tell you what they are. It was better that I waited until you said goodbye to Lisa."

"Mum," I said tiredly. "You can't stop me seeing Cal. It'll happen whether you like it or not." My words slurred.

I couldn't make her believe me. She drew in a deep breath and I heard the slip of her skin as she rubbed her palms together.

"We'll talk about that later. Do you want me to tell you about your daughter or not? I should do it before it's too late." Her lips snapped shut.

It was a relief to know she'd accepted what was going to happen. I thought back to when Marion died, and how her mother Jane couldn't accept it. Unaccustomed love for Geraldine swamped me, flooding in and then receding like a wave. Nothing could be permanent. I'd continued to refuse all knowledge of Mariana; convinced she'd come to me of her own accord. But now I realised she probably wouldn't, and in the end it didn't matter. I had to remember that I'd fulfilled my goal of keeping her safe.

"Tell me, then."

The fibres of me reached out to absorb the snippets of knowledge Geraldine would offer. She lowered the angles of her body onto my bed. She took up a hairbrush, began brushing my hair. I sensed the ticking of her thoughts with each brush stroke. The soft bristles felt like pins on my scalp.

Geraldine's breath caught. I peered through mist to see her pulling more hair from the brush. She laid her hand on my head like a blessing and I felt the cool touch of her fingers.

"Your daughter is a beautiful young woman, and strong in mind and body. A tall girl with long red hair."

A character from a fairy tale. My mother paused and I pictured the wriggling baby who'd just learned to sit up when I let her go. "Her eyes are the same colour as yours," said Geraldine. "She's also very creative, like you. She makes jewellery, and she studies at college in Whitby. She plans to gain a degree in Applied Art." She paused again. "As well as all that, Mariana is a mother. She has a four-year old boy named Gabriel."

She sucked her breath in and held it a moment. I imagined the rise of her ribcage, the way her stomach would be taut while she tried to gauge my feelings. It would just complicate things if I told her I already knew about the child. *Gabriel.* My angel.

"What's he like, the little boy?"

A real, flesh-and-blood boy. Does he look like Cal? Who

would have thought that long-ago Marianne Fairchild, obtuse daughter of Geraldine, could have sown the seed of such a creature?

Geraldine's face softened, I'm sure it did.

"He's a sweet little boy, Maria, you wouldn't believe it." Her fingernail scratched the sheet near my head and the sound went through me. I wondered if she'd wished for a son of her own. As if to confirm my suspicion, she added, "He likes all the usual boy things; cars and motorbikes, football. He's recently been rock climbing for the first time."

It went quiet then; my mother apparently lost in her recollections. My vision blurred further. I felt Geraldine give herself a slight shake, stretch her back. She rested her hand gently on my shoulder. "I know it's hard for you, hearing all this from me. You've been deprived of those two precious people while I've had access to them all these years. But you brought so much joy into the world Maria, remember that. Your life *was* meaningful. I know you haven't always felt it."

I wished I could float away, see my daughter and her son without having to give explanations, use any words. Maybe it would happen… *after.*

"There's something else I need to tell you."

I strained to see her face through the detritus of two lives: figments and shreds, Marion here, myself there. It was all blending together and I found it hard to distinguish one life from another. My mother's hand remained on my arm, holding me in place. In a soft voice she used my former name, leaning over me so I'd be sure to hear.

"Marianne."

A cough rumbled in my chest, a well in danger of

bursting.

"Your daughter fell in love. But I had to give her some difficult news." Geraldine's voice lowered even further.

"The boy she met is her half-brother. His name is Aiden, and he's the son of Lisa and Cal Wilde."

My daughter fell in love with her brother, her twin.

"He seems to be a good boy though," said my mother. "Nothing happened between them."

Aiden, I tasted the name on my tongue. *The same age as Mariana, born the day before.* I was sorry that Mariana had been disappointed in love of one kind, but happy she'd found her twin. She'd never be alone now. I thought of Marion and Cal in their young days, how complete it felt to be one half of a whole.

"I need to see Cal, please, Mum."

But though Geraldine had proved her love for me over the years since Mariana was born, she refused to give way on this one matter.

IN INTERMITTENT FLASHES I glimpsed Justine's fingers running up and down the pale horizontal stripes on my bedspread, felt the gentle press of each movement as she practiced her scales. Justine was due to perform her first concert since the birth of her second child and I perceived her nervousness. Other people's lives still made sense, even if mine didn't.

A slant of sunlight fell on the bed through a gap in the curtains, kept closed because the brightness hurt my eyes.

"I want you to do something for me."

It took Justine a moment to realize I'd spoken. She leaned forward; her pale oval face angled intently, her grey-blue eyes solemn. I'd loved my little sister dearly as a child and now she was repaying me.

"What is it?" her tone was as hushed as my whisper had been.

"I have to see Cal. I'll need you to help me. Mum… she won't let him in the house. But he has to come. He'll be around, we just need an opportunity."

Justine fidgeted. "Oh, Maria, I don't know…"

I didn't have to say anything, only give her a direct gaze from my half-blind eyes. She couldn't know that I could barely see.

She pressed her forefingers beneath her eyes and I guessed that they were luminous with tears.

"Please," I said again. "I need your help."

⟫⟫✕⟪⟪

GUSTS OF AIR from the open window buffeted me. I was weightless; everything I'd always wanted to be. Someone nudged me from the inside. *All right, all right. It won't be long now.*

The other presence grew, rediscovering herself. I had become so tired and hollow that there was space for her at last.

"Soon. Now be quiet."

No need for Marion to be so impatient. I felt less bitter towards her than I had done for most of my life, because I

156

knew that our time to be together was coming.

ON MY BEHALF, Justine had construed a diversion for our mother. Justine didn't say what exactly, and I didn't ask, guessing it was to do with... *future arrangements*. Now Cal would climb in through the open window. I'd known he would come.

Geraldine had been into the room before she left and closed it; tutting about catching a chill, but Justine had reopened it for me. She popped in to check on me every quarter of an hour, as she had promised our mother. When Cal arrived there was a scrabbling sound, a heaving, and the thud of something heavy landing. My heart stirred painfully. The air altered and in my mind's eye the muslin curtain at the window blew inwards.

When he stumbled over to the bed I could see him, but not with my eyes. I visualized him twice his normal size, or maybe it was just that I'd become smaller.

Cal's head rested on the pillow beside mine and his heart beat out of rhythm. I kept my eyes closed, but I could still see clearly. I don't know whether or not I lifted my hand to stroke the wayward hair from his forehead, but I imagined I did. At any rate he relaxed. We settled against each other, returned to our proper places. We probably didn't use any actual words, but a conversation took place between us nevertheless.

Cal insisted on calling me Marion but I'd ceased to be bothered. Maria Child didn't need him to love her for the person she'd fought her whole life to become, and Marion only wanted closure.

There was music, an insistent guitar beat, harmonics; a voice like the cry of a gull. I stroked Cal's head; or I probably did.

"I couldn't accept you'd been alive all that time," he told me. "It was wrong of me. I knew it was you on the beach that day, but I wanted you to be young still. I'm sorry for letting you down."

It didn't matter. I continued stroking the thick hair that was no longer as silky and floppy as it had been. I could feel grey strands, wiry and abrasive.

"That girl, that other girl..." Cal shifted in the space we occupied together, either physical or spiritual, I couldn't tell.

"She was our daughter, Cal, my baby." A quarter of a century passed before I spoke again. "She's called Mariana."

His voice came back through time, quoting Tennyson in the garden of Blackberry House. I dropped away from the present, felt the tearing of thin membranes. But before I landed, I felt myself rising again. I flew into a black sky which masked my view of everything. I seemed to be caught up on seagulls' wings, heard their penetrating cries, snatching me back from oblivion. I swooped and hovered in the air above Cal. For a moment I thought he was going to be angry, but it was just a rogue wave approaching, froth-filled and earsplittingly loud. It crashed over us, flung us face down into the gravelly sand. Before long our private ocean lifted us up again, rocking us to sleep on its gentle swell. It reminded me of a time long, long before, when we had floated together in our private amniotic sea.

18

Mariana, April 2013

S O THAT WAS why the girl who'd been introduced to me as Angie had seemed familiar. Everything was falling into place, but at the same time it felt more confusing than ever. Aiden was my half-brother; Angie, or Angel as I'd had to learn to think of her since she sent me the first Facebook message, was my half-sister. And that crazy-eyed bear of a man I'd met twice in my life – he was my *father*.

Did he know who I was?

A rich tapestry of undiscovered relations flapped on a mental washing line at the back of my mind. I wanted to push through the images, examine each one. Before, I'd only wanted to be Mam and Dad's daughter, but now the curtain had been drawn back on my birth family, so to speak, I couldn't resist wanting to know more.

HAVING MADE ARRANGEMENTS to leave Gabriel with his

grandparents, I'd agreed to meet Angel at a seafront café the next Saturday. Scarborough was a short train ride from home for both of us, although to be fair to Angel she also had to undertake a long and boring bus ride from her home in a village 'at the end of the world', as she'd told me online. A small wave of false nostalgia washed over me at the thought of Pottersea, described to me by Aiden during the second weekend we spent together. We'd taken a boat ride to Seal Island with Gabriel; the three of us snuggled under a blanket Aiden had thoughtfully packed into his rucksack. I'd felt so safe. My feelings for Aiden, the ones I was still trying to block out, were deep and warm. It didn't seem possible to change them into the kind of taken-for-granted attitude other people had towards their siblings.

As far as I knew Angel was unaware we were half-sisters. I'd realised as soon as I learnt her real name, but she'd never heard of me.

The café was painted blue inside. I sat upstairs, watching white waves scrambling over each other far below in North Bay. Foam crashed over the sea wall. The tables in the café were dark wood, clean and polished. Woven placemats and cloth napkin-wrapped cutlery were already laid out. With its huge windows and sea vista, the café had been a favourite thinking place of mine when I was younger.

I didn't notice her arrival until the chair opposite scraped along the floor. Angel sat down, smelling of fresh air and vanilla. She looked different, younger with the scowl absent from her face, free now of powder. She wore only a trace of eyeliner, the fearsome Pris-eyes from Bladerunner gone. She had brushed her chin-length dark hair straight, clipped it back with plastic ornaments. I noticed the fresh scar at the edge of her forehead where her fringe had been blown to one side by the wind. I felt my face redden.

"Hi. Thanks for coming. Do you want a coffee, or a milkshake, or something?"

The scowl was back on her face. "Milkshake? I'm not a kid."

I shrugged, fiddling with a thick hank of hair hanging over my right shoulder. "No offence meant."

She looked embarrassed. "Sorry for sounding ungrateful."

In the pause, we both stared out the window. Then she laced her fingers together, making a wall on the table between us. "I had to look at your photos," she spoke sharply, as if I'd challenged her. "To find out who the phone belonged to." *She'll have seen the pictures of me and Aiden…*

She lifted her patterned rucksack onto the table and pulled out of it a folded jumper, a bottle of water and a tattered paperback copy of *The Time Traveller's Wife*. With her head bent, I saw the line of chestnut hair at her parting. A sisterly empathy, I *assume* it was that, took me by surprise. She probably resembled me more than I realised. I'd never expected to find lookalike relatives.

She passed my phone across the table. I turned it over, reacquainting it with my skin; then slipped it into the pocket of my jacket where I kept my hand on it for a while. The urge to examine the photos, to see an image of Aiden again, was strong. But it would be rude. And anyway I wanted to do it in private. I hated that somebody else had had access to it.

I must have been frowning.

"Are you all right?"

I withdrew my hand from my pocket. "Yes. Thanks, I appreciate you coming all this way to give it back to me. Where did you say you found it?"

Her face reddened. "I… Well, my dad picked it up at the hospital. You dropped it on the floor when you left in such a hurry…"

There's something she isn't telling me. "Let me get you a coffee." I took the chance to move away, breathe more easily. I went to the counter and ordered, dragging my feet on the way back.

We sat without speaking. Out the corner of my eye I watched her gazing at the horizon. When the waitress placed two mugs down, Angel met my eyes briefly. *My sister.* It made my heart flutter.

She traced a pattern in some sugar that had escaped from the teaspoonful she tipped into her coffee, then fiddled with the teaspoon in the small ceramic pot. The stripe of colour at her scalp repeatedly drew my eye. She already had a half-sister before she met me. That meant a new sister wouldn't be as exciting to her as it was to me, and I suddenly wanted to matter to her.

Cradling our mugs we both turned again to the window. A sea view is always compulsive. It was a bright, cold day with a sharp wind outside but inside Angel slid her arms out of her patchwork jacket. She slung it over the back of her chair. Turning back to me her face was flushed. I had to strain to make out the words she mumbled.

"There was something I wanted to talk to you about."

I tensed, wondering how much she knew. A seagull shrieked past the window, splattering the glass with a viscous green-and-white deposit. Angel's lips twitched in a smile and we caught each other's eyes. A minute later a tutting, uniformed waitress went out onto the wooden balcony with a cloth and a bowl of water.

"Erm, your phone," Angel said. "I saw the pictures of Aiden. Did you know he's my brother?"

This could get tricky; I sucked in my breath. "I didn't, before. Not until I learned your real name. Aiden talked about Angel, but when I met you I thought your name was, err, Angie."

"Oh yeah…" She took a gulp of coffee. Across the room, four people seated themselves at a table and I winced at the sound of chairs scraping over the wooden floor.

"So how well do you know Aiden anyway? Oops," she made an awkward display of feigning embarrassment. "That's probably a stupid question, isn't it? From the photos you seem quite close…"

She resumed drawing on the table with her finger. The waitress, moving back into the café with her bucket and cloth, gave Angel an annoyed look.

"There's something I want to tell you." I took a breath. "I met Aiden in Whitby, where I live. He was there on a trip with his work colleagues. We got friendly, you know, and he came to see me on a couple more weekends. I always had my son with me, so we all did fun stuff together, you know, going to the park and on picnics. We started liking each other in a different way, but then I found out…" I dabbed under my eyes with a napkin. "I suppose I'd better tell you this first… I'm adopted."

She looked blank. I guess my statement seemed totally out of context. "My parents aren't my birth parents." Which was quite obvious, I suppose. Angel leaned forward with her elbows on the table.

"Wha…what has that got to do with Aiden?"

You know, don't you? "This is such a mess, the whole thing. I'll try and start from the beginning. A few weeks ago I found out from a relative that *her* daughter was my birth mother. So that made Aunty Geraldine, the one who told me, my actual grandmother."

Angel fiddled with stuff on the table, accidentally on purpose spilling more sugar and pushing the salt and pepper pots around in it. I had a sudden flash of how it might feel to have a little sister and be left in charge of her for the first time. *The chance of all that was stolen from me.* The impact of the realisation stunned me. I tried to speak but found it hard to form the right words. Meanwhile Angel appeared to be getting restless.

"All this is relevant," I told her. "I promise."

"Erm, sorry but I'm hungry. Do you think we could get a sandwich?"

She'd dragged out a purse and was sorting through coins, apparently not very many of them. Once I'd calculated the cost of two (not inexpensive) lunches I decided it was worth sacrificing some treat or other next week at home. *For my sister.* After all, Gabe was currently being spoilt at his grandparents'. I realised how hungry I was – and the ritual of food would help me tell the story, *a win all around, then.* We took a reprieve from all the truth-telling while we chose and ordered sandwiches and fruit juice. Angel went to the toilet and I decided to go next.

In the tiled room I stood in front of a mirror and had a go at combing my tangled hair. Finding it impossible, I made a loop at the back of my head and pulled the hair into a loose knot. By the time we'd both sat down again I was wishing I'd remembered to check my phone messages. Mam had already told me about Maria, anyway – the dilemma over my birth mother was just another emotional plate I was balancing at the moment.

The waitress put the tray of sandwiches on one side and pointedly wiped the spilt sugar off the table before placing our plates in front of us. Angel and I exchanged a complicit glance. As we ate I noticed how Angel chewed each bite of bread for a long time, so I slowed in my eating in case I finished first and then had nothing to do with my hands. "Shall I go on talking while we're eating?" I asked between mouthfuls.

She nodded. "So," I said. "I found out that my birth mother was my so-called Aunty Geraldine's daughter. Her name, my birth mother's I mean, is Maria Child."

Angel gulped, apparently swallowing an unchewed mouthful of bread. It travelled visibly down her throat, reminding me of a heron I'd once seen swallowing a fish. She pressed her diaphragm while she took a sip of orange juice. Then she nodded. "Go on," flicking glances between me and her plate.

"Well. The last weekend I was with Aiden," my nose prickled unexpectedly, heat pushed at the insides of my eyes. I put my hand to my throat. "We took Gabriel rock climbing."

Angel dipped her chin, looking at me sideways. I remembered she would have seen the photos.

"It was great. We had such a good time. Your brother is very good with Gabriel. Afterwards, Aiden was planning to stay overnight at my flat for the first time. We were ready to, you know…"

She had a *TMI* expression on her face. Ah. I must have been overreaching the *brother* boundaries.

"Nothing happened. Geraldine turned up at my flat. She wanted to give me some news about my birth mother. She told me Maria is very ill and I should go and see her, but I didn't want to. I didn't feel ready." I imagined she would be thinking *what the hell has that got to do with me?* "There's a reason I'm telling you all this, don't worry."

I filled my fork with a piece of salmon from the sandwich and fragments of salad, munched a couple of crisps. Outside the sky was clouding over, white horses danced on waves far out to sea. A seagull, probably the one that had messed on the window, wheeled and swooped below the bulking clouds and I wished I could fly with it, be free. I fought the familiar feeling.

Angel looked up at me again. I gave myself a pinch on the arm, under my sleeve.

"I introduced Aiden to her and she asked where he came from."

The scent of the meal Aiden and I cooked together returned to my nostrils: tomatoes and basil. The tension of Geraldine's questions filled my head again. "He told her it was a place called Pottersea and said nobody had ever heard of it. That's when Geraldine turned white. She asked him what his father's name was – his first name."

Angel put down her knife and fork. She clasped her hands together. We met each other's gaze fully.

She whispered, "You're my sister, aren't you?"

I laid another crisp on my tongue like communion. The salt and vinegar seeped slowly onto my taste buds. An enormous anger flowered in my chest for the man who must have taken advantage of my mother. She was a vulnerable girl with anorexia, only seventeen when she got pregnant with me. So what if I got pregnant at the same age? I'd gone to school with Damon. It was different.

Cal Wilde must have been years older than Maria when he did that to her. I felt shivery. No point beating around the bush any longer. "Yes, we're half-sisters." I was shaking now. Angel tore shreds off a napkin, her breathing ragged.

"He must have always been a manipulative bastard, even then." Years of heartfelt history sounded in her voice.

>>>>><<<<<

"I'VE MET MARIA Child," Angel confessed as we walked along the sea front. We stopped to lean on the iron railings, *my sister and me.* Angel opened her mouth wide, tasting salt on her tongue. I used to do that.

"Where?" Wind whipped hair into our eyes. I wondered if she'd heard me. "Where have you met her?"

Suddenly I wanted my original mother. Even Angel had met her, but not me. The girl with anorexia breastfed me for six months. She gave me up because of her illness and now she was dying of it. And all she wanted was to see me. I could give her that small gift. I had to put her needs before Mam's now; I should take her grandson to see her before it was too late. I wanted to do it immediately – what if she died before I got there – *oh God*, I shouldn't have waited!

"I met her just after New Year," Angel was saying. "She came to our house with my sister Alice. Alice works with her in London. I know it's a coincidence," (she'd seen my face) "but it's true. It was her, your Maria Child. My dad went crazy when he saw her, he's been crazy ever since."

I gripped the railing harder, kicked at a paper cup blown up against my foot. I'd have chided Gabriel for sending it flying over the edge like I did.

"It's weird how everything's connected, isn't it?" Angel looked pale and exposed in the wind. "To think I've actually met your mother and you haven't."

No need to rub it in.

19

Angel

MARIANA HAD INVITED Angel back to her mam and dad's to meet Gabriel properly. She'd promised they would have crumpets and tea. Funny how Angel was already hungry again.

She huffed as she tried to keep up with Mariana; the other girl was much fitter. Angel created pictures in her mind of a cosy, functional family home as she walked slightly behind her new sister, up the twisty path through the park to the road behind it, where Mariana's mam and dad lived. Between breaths Angel punched out an occasional question which Mariana answered, but fell silent in between. She'd left school half way through sixth form and got a job cleaning offices. Then she'd saved a deposit on a rented place and moved into it with her baby. Angel admired that.

My nephew.

"This is it," Mariana said.

Angel was fully out of breath as they walked up a short driveway towards a glass-encased front porch. Inside, shoes and boots were arranged on a wooden rack. A concrete hare sat beside the doorstep. She imagined Mariana's parents bringing their new daughter home from the adoption agency or wherever you went to pick up a baby that'd suddenly become yours.

"They're going to get a surprise when they meet you, but don't worry, they'll be ok."

Did Mariana sound sure? Angel hadn't particularly worried up until then. Mariana bit her lip as she touched the porch door handle. She'd definitely been quieter since the seafront; probably worrying she might end up being too late to visit Maria.

The older girl put a key in the lock and turned it. In the hall a blast of warm air hit their faces. There was Gabriel, running to his mother, waving a toy figure around above his head.

"Thomas has missed you, Mammy!"

He launched himself upwards and Mariana scooped him up, tucking his legs under her arms. She kissed the top of his gold-auburn head. *His hair is like my brother's.*

"Gabriel, say hello to your aunty Angel." Mariana put him down. The child glared at Angel, tugging his mother's sleeve.

"That's not an angel." (He had a cute, high voice.) "You're telling a lie, Mammy. Her name's Angie, you *know* it is." He pressed his face into her leg. "I don't like her, she's horrible."

To be honest, Angel didn't know what she'd expected,

his only experience of her so far hadn't been a good one; she had to be fair. But now she knew he was her nephew it hurt to hear it. The child pushed away from Mariana, who mouthed "sorry," at Angel. He planted his bunched hands on his hips and stood with his legs wide apart, a proper little man. They stared at each other, aunty and nephew.

"Is that you, Mariana?"

A woman's voice from the other side of a closed door, indistinct over a blaring TV.

"Yeah it's me, Mam. Be in in a minute."

Mariana gestured Angel to get down to Gabriel's level. She knelt down as well.

"Listen, Scrappy-Doo," she pushed a finger into his tummy. He couldn't restrain a giggle. Angel envied her new sister. The child risked another glance at Angel and sucked his lips in, turning back to his mother.

"Her real name's Angel, honestly it is," Mariana said. "That's actually a great name, isn't it? Imagine if she really had wings, how cool would that be?"

Gabriel appeared to consider it. He turned his head shyly back towards Angel, looked her up and down. She attempted a smile, convinced he could see what a fraud she was. His bottom lip now poked forwards, the delicate flesh on the inside of it perfect and new. His hands were still clenched, one of them around the waist of the action man.

"You know something?"

The boy shook his head. Mariana took his chin in her hand and made sure he was looking at her. "It turns out, that Angel is my sister." She paused to let that sink in as well. "Wow," she gave him another tiny poke in the stomach. "I was so surprised to find that out. I bet you are, too."

Gabriel brought his bottom lip into his mouth. He looked cute with his small teeth pressing down. He glanced at Angel again and then quickly away. "So now you have an aunty of your own," said Mariana. "That's great news, isn't it?"

Gabriel subjected Angel to another, slightly less aggressive inspection. He unclenched his free hand and scratched his head. His hair being like Aiden's made Angel want to make friends with him. A frown appeared between his eyebrows as he continued to consider the information he'd been given.

"I do have an aunty already," he concluded, "Aunty Geraldine."

"Ah, but she's actually *my* aunty. She's your great-aunty. But Angel here is your very *own* aunty, because of being my sister."

The TV was turned off, creating a sharp burst of silence from the other room. Something, perhaps a newspaper, dropped to the floor. "Come on in then, Mariana," came the woman's voice. Somebody was pushing themselves up out of a leather chair, Angel deduced from the creaking noise.

Mariana shrugged off her coat and took Angel's thick jacket from her, hanging them both on a coat stand by the door. She pushed open the living room door and poked her head in.

"Hi Mam, we have a visitor." She moved fully into the room, beckoning Angel in behind her. Angel swallowed an excess of saliva. "This is Angel Wilde," Mariana said abruptly, stepping aside. She left a meaningful pause.

Mariana's mam was short, even Angel had to look down on her. Mariana didn't look anything like her. Overweight, the woman had bubbly blonde hair. There were dimples at the sides of her mouth, its corners turned upwards. She wore a thick red jumper: hand knitted, Angel judged, with neatly pressed blue jeans. On her feet were huge fluffy slippers.

"Angel, this is me mam," Mariana offered to Angel. "Mam, Angel."

Mariana's mam gripped the chair back, staring at Angel. She repeated Angel's name, her lips tightening into a bunched-up shape. Mariana did that gesture Angel had noticed repeatedly: sliding both hands under her heavy hair and dumping it behind her shoulders. When they were in the café she'd fastened it up somehow but it had worked loose from the knot during their windy walk. Angel began to be less envious of all that hair; it seemed like too much work. She decided she'd keep hers quite short, whatever her dad said.

Mrs Rivers ("Oh, just call me Audrey,") sank heavily into her leather armchair, causing it to make a noise like a fart. *Don't laugh*, Angel thought, quickly. Mrs Rivers didn't seem anything like the warm-hearted 'Mam' on Mariana's phone. She bent to collect fallen sheets of newspaper from the floor and resettled them into a neat pile on the coffee table, keeping her eyes on the task as if it was the only important thing.

On the mantelpiece a clock had little golden balls inside it that went around and around. It chimed the hour, three o'clock. Gabriel made vroom noises, played with a selection of toy cars on the floor, his action man propped in a climbing position against the end of the sofa.

"Angel Wilde," Mariana's mam said again as if she couldn't believe it. She shook her bouncing blonde curls and gave Mariana an accusing glance, completely ignoring Angel. "Your Aunty Geraldine told me about... but why?" Her mouth hung slightly open.

Angel and Mariana were still standing in the centre of the room. The older girl pulled Angel by the sleeve and made her sit beside her on the sofa.

"Yeah, Mam," Mariana glanced at Angel and then back at her mam. "I understand this is going to be a lot to take in but I think you might have guessed already. Angel is Cal Wilde's daughter."

Her natural father. Why didn't she say that? If natural was the right word to use about Cal. The fat woman tightened her mouth even more, her face turned red.

"God, Pet. What've you gone and done?" She flapped a hand in front of her face. "I feel right sorry for Geraldine, I do, I can imagine how awful it is for her to watch her child suffering because I know how I'd feel if it was you. So I've decided, I don't mind if you want to go and see Maria after all. But, well."

'Audrey' unfolded the newspaper again and wafted it in front of her face. Angel wondered if she was going through the menopause. "I didn't expect you to start unearthing the other side of your...your *birth* family as well." She flapped the paper more vigorously. "No offence to you, Love." She finally nodded at Angel.

"None taken." (There was).

Angel wrested her hands together. She'd been promised tea and crumpets, not a stuffy living room. Then as if her desire had conjured them up, noises erupted from somewhere – the kitchen – water running, a drawer opening and closing, the clink of pottery.

"Our Mariana's back, Love." Audrey's raised voice wavered. A door situated to the left of the armchair opened. It led into a dining room and beyond that, a brightly lit kitchen. Mariana's dad stood in the doorway.

"Well I'll be!"

He looked from one to the other of the two girls. "Your eyes," he said to Angel, "they're the spit of our Mariana's."

➤➤➤❃❃❃

MARIANA'S DAD WAS loads more laid back than his wife. He asked Angel to call him Rob, and said he was pleased Mariana wasn't an *only one* anymore.

She couldn't imagine her own dad being not at all bothered if she suddenly discovered a new family. He wasn't like other dads. Everyone, every*thing*, had to revolve around him. Mariana's dad seemed like the kind Angel had always wanted – someone who cared about *you* more than they did themselves.

It had been Rob who fed them with the promised crumpets. He who had kept the conversation going. He asked Angel questions about her family; fascinated to learn that her dad was a bestselling novelist, asked about his books. It didn't seem to occur to Rob it was also Mariana's father they were discussing. Angel felt uncomfortable, and she could tell Audrey did and even Mariana.

It took Audrey a while to get out of her chair but when she did she collected the tea things and carried them into the kitchen. Mariana followed her, and there was a low mutter of voices through the open door. Angel could feel how stiffly she was sitting on the sofa, wondering how to extricate herself from the situation made even more awkward because Rob didn't seem to know it *was*. Mariana shouldn't have left her alone in there.

Gabriel suddenly pushed himself up from the floor. He approached Angel with a sideways stepping motion, still clutching the same toy in his hand. Gabriel placed his action man on her knee.

"My Aiden brought him for me."

He gave her a sweet smile. She kept her eyes down because she might have cried if she looked at him. *My nephew.* She examined the figure, its camouflage trousers, miniature t-shirt and boots. It wore elbow and knee pads and a helmet, and various climbing implements were attached to its costume.

"Oh," she said lamely. "Aiden?"

She was disarmed by the way the kid leant against her, nodding. So trusting now he had watched her eat and make conversation with his grandparents. Her armour was gone, all of it. And she'd thought she was so tough. She whispered, "Aiden's your uncle, you know. He's my brother."

"So I have an aunty *and* an uncle?"

"Yes, you do."

He looked so much like family that Angel wanted to take him in her arms. Also, if things became more serious between Damon and her, Gabriel could end up being her stepson. (Ok, fairly unlikely but…) *Bloody hell.* It gave the kid a new aspect.

Rob smiled at her across the room. "He's a fine lad, isn't he?"

"He is."

She felt her lips stretching. Gabe had crawled away to behind the sofa. Angel felt something sharp at her shoulder. She turned; it was Thomas, the action man. The boy made strenuous noises as the figure climbed. Angel reached over, assisted the final ascent. The child's eyes fastened on her, underlined by the sofa-back.

"Did you do this?" she asked Gabriel.

The boy's head popped fully up. He sucked in his bottom lip, green-blue eyes solemn and still fixed on her. "Yes I did. I climbed a wall with Aiden. *Uncle* Aiden I mean. I climbed really high."

"I bet you did."

MARIANA RETURNED TO the room. She mouthed 'sorry' and Angel rose from the sofa. She told them she had to get to the station. That was when Rob insisted he'd drive her. Mariana gave Angel a brief, awkward hug. She said she'd be in touch in a few days. Angel wanted to hug the child as well but it might be a bit soon. Gabriel had turned shy again, clingy, demanding that his mother pick him up.

Mariana's mam only called goodbye from the kitchen. Angel sensed relief in the voice, recognised it because it washed over her too, as the front door closed behind her.

"Audrey will come round, you know," Rob said.

It didn't even matter; what was Audrey to her? They swung down the hill towards the station.

"We were lucky to get Mariana, and then Gabriel, what a gift that child was. We couldn't have been luckier. But I want you and your brother – Aiden, is it? I want you both to know you're welcome in our home. You're Mariana's family, just as we are."

As the heating kicked in, the car filled with the scent of plants and earth. Angel had noticed bags of compost in the back.

"I'm happy she's finally got siblings, honestly I am," Rob said.

Angel sneaked glances at his weather-beaten face. Mariana was the lucky one, landing a father like that in place of Cal. For some reason Angel's eyes were watering. Good job Rob had his attention focussed on the road.

They pulled in at the station. Rob double-checked the handbrake, then reached into the glove compartment and took out a business card and handed it over. *Rivers Gardening and Outdoor Furniture.* There was a line-drawing of trees with a bench underneath. "Just in case you ever need anything. You never know."

THEN ANGEL HAD to rush for her train while Rob wiped invisible smears off the inside of his windscreen. Angel was happy for her short experience of fatherly concern. She would store it up to think about later, after she had savoured the fact of her brand-new sisterhood.

>>>><<<<

ON THE TRAIN back to Hull she tried a few times to ring Damon, but only got voicemail; he must have been practicing. She'd hoped he'd call her back but he couldn't have heard his phone and she had to accept she wouldn't be staying at his place that night. *Damn.*

People in the other seats were looking at her, she was sure of it. Maybe feeling sorry for her because of the unanswered calls. Her reflection in the window showed a pale, young-looking girl with hardly any makeup on. It stared at her, blurred around the edges.

Checking the bus timetable on her phone, as she'd suspected, there were no buses going all the way out to Pottersea at this time of the evening and she knew the price of a taxi was way too expensive, so unless she was going to sleep rough, she'd have to call her mum.

"Oh, Angel, no." Lisa sounded exasperated. "I can't, I'm busy." She said Cal was already in town and it would have to be him that picked her up. Angel bit her nails. More reasons for the other passengers to pity her. She lowered her voice. "Mum, please, can't you do it?"

"Angel," Lisa sounded calm. "You've got to stop this thing with your father. I'm sorry he's not perfect but he's the only father you've got. If you want a lift home, I'll let him know he's to pick you up. End of subject."

The signal cut out. It was a few minutes before any bars reappeared on her phone and by then she was resigned. She'd talk to Cal as little as possible; avoid saying anything that might upset him.

When she got off the train a cold draught blew on her neck. She paused to pull her thick cotton scarf out of her rucksack and wound it several times around, tucking the ends into the neckline of her jacket.

➤➤➤✕◀◀◀

HER DAD WAS waiting under the high glass roof of the station atrium. Tall but hunched at the shoulders, he stood with his fists jammed under his arms. He had his ever-present frown between his eyes. She walked up to him, feeling the cold ground beneath her thin-soled boots as she settled each foot on the floor in turn.

"Dad." She tried a smile. Her dad responded with a quick flash of his teeth. His amber eyes, similar and yet inexpressibly different from her own, had always reminded her of a cat. A big cat. He studied her in the way she imagined a panther would have done.

"Had a good day?" An actual, normal-father question. *Whoopee-doo.* (How long would it last?) "Your mother told me to come and collect you. Where've you been, anyway?"

She hugged her bag against her chest, thinking of an answer. "I went to see a friend in, err, Bridlington. Fish and chips at the seaside and all that, you know." Something told her not to say Scarborough, one of the words that would cause an abrupt mood-change.

"Come on then," he said. "It's a good job I was in town. How did you think you were going to get back?"

"Uhm, I dunno." Angel shuffled her feet. She shifted the rucksack onto her shoulder as she followed him out of the station and into the car park. He scrutinized her under the lights in the station entrance. "Your hair, you know, you should let it go back to its normal colour. It would suit you natural."

Yeah, yeah.

She had a memory of how his eyes had widened when he spotted Mariana at the hospital. Angel still couldn't understand what he thought he was chasing. Was it the ghost of his dead sister? Or maybe he somehow *knew* Mariana was his daughter. He would surely be much more proud of Mariana as a daughter than of Angel. All that long red hair Mariana had, and her being like the mirror image of his long-ago twin, that was what he *really* wanted. It was exactly what Angel was determined not to be, and yet she felt jealous of Mariana for being it all the same.

In the car on the way back she felt suffocated. Her dad exuded an animal quality she couldn't correlate with fatherhood. He kept flicking his panther eyes over her whenever they stopped at traffic lights. At the junction in Ottringham he finally said what had obviously been on his mind.

"I lost something…" He tapped his fingers on the steering wheel, impatience, as Lisa often remarked, *his middle name.* "I… it was in the pocket of my coat, this coat."

He patted the heavy woollen garment as if reassuring himself of its presence. "Have you seen it?"

Before the lights changed Angel spotted the flash in his eyes. For a short while he'd appeared almost normal, picking her up at the station like any dad. But the crazy look remained just under the surface, never far away. She felt cold. She sat on her hands, pressing them into the warm seat of the car, feeling for the comfort of a familiar hole in the seat fabric.

"What was it?" *Try and sound innocent.*

He started the car again, roaring over the junction into the darkness of the unlit road. His fingers gripped the wheel so tightly she could see by the dashboard lights they were white. He glanced sideways at her, then back at the road.

"I'm not telling you what it is." His voice was definitely a growl. "I'm just telling you that I lost it. It was in the pocket of my coat, *this* coat."

20

Mariana, late April 2013

I T TAKES LONGER to die than you might think, unless you're, you know, *obliterated* instantly like in a car accident or something.

Don't even think things like that.

But illness, even when it's terminal, can drag on and on and the death can last for days – a bit like giving birth... *hmm.* Birth is an external thing though, a freshly-formed being emerging physically *into* a place. Whereas I guess death is the opposite – you leave your own body. The essence of you goes away. Yet this is really the bit that is the same (although the other way round, if you see what I mean?): at some point, whether it's at the moment of birth or when the baby's in the womb at whatever stage – consciousness has to arrive. And then it leaves again when you die; dissipates, or returns to wherever it came from.

My mind tangled itself in a web, attempting to work out

whether consciousness – arriving at some unspecified time while the foetus is in the womb – comes (and leaves) as an independent thing in itself, or whether it is created purely by the mechanical workings of the functioning body and thus ceases to exist when the body stops working… Maybe individual consciousness is simply an element of one *giant* consciousness, and is sucked back into the mass after the body expires… or maybe, *oh, I don't know.*

I hadn't experienced the death of anyone close to me before. (Not that my mother was actually close to me but, you know). Except the girl with anorexia at school, and I'd separated myself from her some months before. One of the reasons I'd agreed to meet my mother at such a late stage in her life, was because I'd suddenly become aware of how small my family was. Before Gabriel it had only been Mam, Dad and me, with 'Aunty' Geraldine as an add-on. That was it. It wasn't fair on Gabriel, was it? To deprive him of a family with so much family available.

We were sitting near the open windows of the balcony in my flat, the red cafetiere placed on the table between us. We were drinking from the rose-pattern china tea set I'd bought from a back-street antique shop in Whitby town. My former Aunty and I were having an in-depth conversation about my mother. Geraldine was explaining what I should expect to see when I met her for the first time, which I'd finally agreed to do. But it still made my skin prickle, setting off one of my shaking fits. The thought of coming face-to-face with the bedridden skeletal figure that Geraldine had described to me. She explained about my mother's illness, that her anorexia had progressed to a stage where Maria couldn't even eat if she wanted to, and her heart was about ready to fail.

Geraldine also told me that meeting Cal Wilde again in January had pushed Maria over the edge. I learned that since a few months after she got pregnant with me, my mother had avoided him. She'd even changed her name from Marianne Fairchild so he wouldn't discover her. Maria had eventually overcome the stranglehold of her demon friend Anorexia, and worked hard to build a new life. She stayed strong for hope of the day she might eventually meet *me* again.

Question: how awful did it make me feel, hearing that? *Answer*: about as unbearable as it could get. I dug my fingernails into the skin of my arms. I was culpable. I might have been able to make her well again once. But not now, apparently.

The balcony door let in fresh air and the intermittent sound of traffic. I wanted to stay where I was, keep everything simple, yet at the same time I wanted to rush to my mother's bedside immediately.

My heart thudded. I swallowed, hard. *Could it all be my fault?* I should try and make things better.

"Is there… uhm, if I… when she, you know, meets me and Gabriel, do you think there's a chance she could get better?"

I can't have left it too late. Suddenly I saw how my life could have been enriched by knowing my birth mother – having aunties, *proper* aunties, and cousins. Being *part* of a family and not the very epicentre of it – as I had been my whole life. *Don't upset your mam, love, she's done her very best for you, you know.* All the responsibility on me. All of their happiness: Mam, Dad and 'Aunty' Geraldine, had all seemed related to what *I* did. It wasn't fair. Mam should never have let me know how upset it made her when I ventured to mention I might want to be reconciled with my birth mother after all. Gabriel had been a few months old, it had felt like the right thing to do, but Mam had taken to bed with one of her headaches, and I thought I'd wait a few more months before mentioning it again. *And then a few more and a few more after that.*

I saw Geraldine's long fingers curl in on themselves. Her knuckles turned white. "It's my fault," she said. "It's too late, my dear. I messed the whole thing up, I can see that now."

"What do you mean?" My nose had become totally blocked. I tore off a strip of toilet roll and blew through my nostrils. "How is it your fault?"

"I should have told you the truth at the beginning. When you turned eighteen. Everything would have been so different if I had. Don't blame yourself, dear, but no. In answer to your question, it's too late for her to get better. All she wants is to see you."

I stood up quickly and paid a visit to the bathroom. I couldn't cope with any more of Geraldine's tears right now, I had my own to deal with. When I returned to the room I pulled the balcony doors closed.

Despite the sunshine it felt cold in the flat, especially with Geraldine sitting there like a marble statue. She looked out through the glass of the balcony doors, past the plane tree, the back gardens and the alley behind them. Like she was looking into the past.

"There's a very complicated background to all this that I'm not sure I want to tell you," she said, giving me an assessing look. "It is what Maria has spent her life trying to shield you from. But I think you should ask her about it. It can't hurt her now, but only she can decide whether it can hurt you."

How much more complicated can the background to my story be than it is already?

"Now, shall we have some lunch before we go and pick up Gabriel from nursery? My treat."

My knees felt like jelly when I stood up again. Geraldine would drive my son and me to Leeds. Waves of anticipation swelled and receded in my stomach. As I carried the tea set over to the kitchen sink a piercing cry – like that of a seagull – screeched through my head. I popped two paracetamol onto my tongue and swallowed them with a mouthful of cooling coffee.

❯❯❯❯❮❮❮❮

"I WANT YOU to know what kind of person she once was," Geraldine said as she lowered the tray containing our lunch salads onto the table while I distributed the knives and forks. "Not what you'll see on the bed when you go into her room. That's not the real Maria."

She gripped my hand, the first blood-relative I'd ever had. Her knuckles seemed to have swelled in the months since I really began noticing her.

"I never appreciated Marianne enough, until she had you. She was at her most vibrant, beautiful even, in the months of her pregnancy and after she had you. She loved you so much and… I'd learned to love her by then."

My stomach ached. But I still didn't feel ready for the great meeting – the resolution-to-be. The *Conclusion*. Geraldine dabbed her nose with a handkerchief, a proper one made of cotton.

"What was she like as a young girl?"

"She was an odd child. She felt different her whole life. I'm hoping she'll tell you the reason for that. But she never fitted in. And I didn't help; I never understood her. Our relationship was so difficult."

"Why was it difficult?"

I felt sorry for the little girl named Marianne, never at home with herself. I'd been a confident child, above anything else knowing I was loved. But Marianne – she must have felt so lonely outside her mother's approval. The one thing I could understand was her disconnection. I had it occasionally, the feeling I wanted to fly away. For the first time I sensed a thread connecting us.

"It was difficult because she never really felt like mine, like my child. And the truth is she never wanted to be, not when she was young."

What does that mean?

"It was… oh dear; her suicide attempts that made me realise how important she was to me. And then it turned out she was pregnant with you. Then we became closer and I did everything I could to help her."

"You said," I swallowed a horrible suspicion. But it continued to lodge somewhere between my throat and my stomach. "You said, *she turned out to be pregnant… do you* mean she tried to commit suicide while she was pregnant with me?"

Geraldine smoothed the front of her blouse with a trembling hand, slowly brought her eyes up to meet mine. Her tone was apologetic, as if she bore the blame.

"I'm afraid so. But she didn't know she was, I promise you that."

21

Angel, late April 2013

"HAS MUM RANG you yet?" Angel asked Aiden on the phone. It sounded like he was eating and she had to hold the phone away from her ear. It had a proper name, the aversion she suffered to hearing people eat, but she couldn't remember it at the moment.

"Er no," he said after a disgustingly audible swallow. "Should I be expecting her to?"

"Hmm. Well, maybe. She said she might. But I've got loads I want to talk to you about. It's all mixed up together; I don't know where to start."

"How about you start at the beginning?"

Now she had a line from *The Sound of Music* running annoyingly through her head. "Stop humming, Aiden," she protested. "It isn't funny. Dad's disappeared. Been gone a few days." She listened in case he wanted to respond but she could only hear him swallowing. "Anyway, well, he didn't come home one night last week as well, after I had a row with him. Mum was mental with worry, you know how she is, but then he came home the next day."

"What was the row about?"

"Well." Angel hesitated. "It was; uhm, about this girl. This girl I met at Damon's. I had a fight with her and I had to go to the hospital."

"*What?*"

"You know, like, just to get my head stitched. She had to stay with me until Dad arrived and when Dad saw her he turned weird. The same weird as when he saw that girl in Scarborough with Aunty Sarah, only I think," and here Angel paused, "it was the same girl." She shut up, took a few deep breaths. She could hear Aiden waiting, his breathing shallow. She gulped some water from a bottle; the plastic popped when she took it from her mouth. She resumed speaking.

"So, she dropped her phone, this girl, when she was running away…"

"Running away?" interrupted Aiden.

"Yeah, because of how weird Dad was being. Dad picked the phone up and put it in his pocket. He thought I didn't see. I was scared to say anything because he had to drive me home from the hospital. Then he went all dreamy for a couple of days. You know how he gets." Of course Aiden did, they hardly ever saw him at Blackberry House because of it. "I managed to get the phone out of his pocket," said Angel. "I wanted to return it to the girl." She breathed faster, concerned at how he'd react when he heard the next bit. "The girl's name is Mariana."

ANGEL SAT ON the stretch of carpet between her two rooms with her knees hunched up to her chest. Rain drummed on the window in the sloping roof. Aiden had sworn under his breath when she said Mariana's name and she couldn't be sure, but she thought he might have been, like, trying not to cry. *I know about you two*, she'd said, equally softly, after he'd blown his nose. *I know how you both had started to feel, Mariana told me. I'm sorry, Aiden. Yeah, ok, I'll go and get a drink and wait for you to call back.*

"Dad gave me a lift back home from the station the day I went to meet Mariana," she said now. "He had that mad look in his eyes, the one that's been getting worse lately. He asked about the thing missing from his pocket – the phone. I got frightened. So I waited 'til we got back to the house and then I said he should stop being so obsessed with Mariana. I said it was unnatural to feel that way about your own *daughter.*"

Silence after she spoke. She wondered what Aiden was doing.

"Didn't he know who she was already?"

"I guess he didn't. From the look on his face he couldn't have. He grabbed his head; like he was trying to pull it off. It was horrible. He got back in the car and drove away straight afterwards. But he came back the next day. This time he's been gone much longer and we don't know where he went."

><<

ANGEL WATCHED AIDEN run his hand along the grooved surface of the long table in the kitchen of Blackberry House.

This table had been here forever. She guessed he would be thinking about the time he ran into the corner of it as a small child, ending up with a black eye. Angel had been holding on to their mum's hand when the teacher at school asked Mum some awkward questions about her son's bruise. Angel also had a fuzzy memory of her dad plonking her down on the table while he pulled a new jumper over her head. She felt trapped inside the jumper for a long time until her head popped out and she could see again. She must have been tiny at the time, getting ready for a visit from her grandparents. Her mum, laying out the lunch, had shouted at her dad because of hygiene issues.

Yeah, and then there was the joint eighteenth-birthday party for Aiden and their cousin Connor – this table was so crowded with food that Connor's cake, wedged into a space at the edge by his mother, had got knocked off and Aunty Sarah had cried.

Mariana should have been at that party too. She was born the day before Aiden, and Connor was her cousin as well as theirs.

Instead of being envious of Mariana, for the long hair and the confidence she seemed to have, Angel now felt sad for her that she'd missed all of those family occasions.

Their mum finished laying logs in the woodstove. Rubbing her hands together, she stood up and gave Aiden another hug. He submitted to it with grace. Their mum shimmered as she moved away, wearing one of her long colourful skirts with little mirrors around the hem. She seemed calm about Cal's disappearance.

"It's good to see you, darling. I appreciate you coming,

but you needn't have. I told Angel, he finally answered his phone and he's ok. He just needs some time alone." She had a glint in her eyes. "He's probably staying with some obscure friend in town. He won't tell me. He came back last night to get the car," she added.

ANGEL'S CAT JUMPED up onto the table during lunch and was scolded and put down again by Mum. The big clock on the wall ticked happy minutes away. A rare feeling of *home* flooded Angel. Maybe because there was no tension, with her dad being absent. Sad but true. And Aiden was back. Alice had managed to get herself a weekend off, too. She'd collected Aiden from Hull station on her way up from London because his car was having some work done on it. But now she stood to collect her coat, obviously deciding it would be the best time to go and visit her friend and boss, Maria, in Leeds.

"GIVE HER MY love," her mother murmured. She closed the kitchen door behind Alice, pushing it shut abnormally carefully. Watching with interest, Angel saw that there were tears in her eyes. Angel was confused. Maria had got *pregnant* by her mother's man. It must have been literally within days, considering how close together Aiden's and Mariana's birthdays were.

"Did you know her, Mum? I mean well."

Lisa blinked back tears. She busied herself clearing the table, stacked dishes in the sink. "I did, a long time ago. It's not what you think, I... Oh it's very complicated, pet. We'll talk about it another time."

Angel caught sight of the flattened line of her mother's mouth as she suddenly dropped a plate in the sink (with a definite sound of breakage) and hurried away towards the downstairs cloakroom. By tacit agreement Angel and Aiden collected their coats from the pegs and decided to go out for a walk.

22

Mariana, late April 2013

"LOOK AT THAT big lorry. Mammy. It's a blue lorry. It's a BLUE lorry, isn't it, Mammy?"

We were sandwiched in the slow lane between the blue articulated lorry behind us and an equally long red one in front. Gabriel had already pointed out vehicles in every possible colour and description, insisting on confirmation of each pronouncement he made and I was weary of it by now.

"Yes, it is blue."

"Is it a light blue one or a dark blue one?"

"What do you think, Gabe?"

"I don't know, Mammy. *I don't know!* Is it a light blue one or a dark blue one? You tell me, go on, Mammy."

Ok. Damage limitation time. "It's a light blue lorry, sweetheart."

"Light blue, light blue, light blue." (And so on). I flipped the passenger mirror down and saw how flushed he'd become. He must have picked up on my nerves. I jolted when his feet kicked the back of my seat and my teeth clenched.

"Stop it."

He went ominously quiet for a matter of seconds, then, "I'm hungry. Can we stop and get something to eat?"

"We're not going to stop, Gabriel, we'll be at my house soon and when we're there I'll make you some pasta." That was Geraldine, in a sharp voice. *Don't mess with me.* For once I felt relieved to relinquish the discipline to her.

I was edgy about taking time off work. For once Mrs Riesling, whose home I should have been cleaning that afternoon, had been sympathetic. Her own mother had died the previous month. She'd even given me a packet of sweets for Gabe when I'd informed her the week before that I would be on compassionate leave. Geraldine had made a room up at her house for us but I wasn't sure if I'd be able to make myself stay there – already I felt trapped by our onward trajectory towards my mother.

"I feel sick."

Geraldine tutted. She glanced at me. "You're not going to be sick. Open the window."

AS WE DROVE into Leeds the feeling worsened. I heard the seagull again, though I don't know how, over the traffic; all mixed up with Gabe's chirpy voice, still going on and on. I wanted to slip out through the open window; rise on the seagull's wings above the traffic in this city in which my mother lay. It was too late to start a relationship with her now, I shouldn't have come.

"Not long now," Geraldine glanced at me again, switched her gaze back to the road. Afternoon sun shone on the back of her hands as they moved on the steering wheel, and from the corner of my eye I noticed more brown spots, stark against the rest of her extraordinarily white skin. I'd known her my whole life, and all that time she'd hidden a secret from me; hidden me from her daughter, at Maria's request. I felt like a helpless pawn in their story.

We were driving through a suburban area; clusters of houses now separated by stretches of farmland.

"Look, a tractor!" Gabe's excitement escalated as the farm machine he'd seen on a distant field was accosted by a cloud of white birds. Their piercing cries reached my brain. I felt faint and had to close my eyes.

"We're here."

Geraldine swung into a wide driveway leading to a double-fronted detached house with bay windows. She turned off the engine. Unfolding myself from the car, I stood on the gravel and examined the house in front of me. *My mother is in there.*

Geraldine unstrapped Gabe and guided him out of the car. "You're going to sleep up there," she pointed to one of the dormer windows.

"My husband and I compromised when we decided to live here," Geraldine explained as she ushered me forward, talking as though to a young child, in a calm tone. "I wanted to live in the town but Joseph preferred the countryside. Your Great-granddad Joseph used to be a farmer, you know," she had switched her attention to Gabriel. She helped him get his backpack out of the boot. I went over and lifted my own bag, still uncertain whether I would choose to enter the house or not.

"Great-granddad Joseph," Gabriel repeated. He'd taken his plethora of new relations in his stride. *Better than I have.* I'd never met my grandfather. His choosing not to have a part in my life because of my mother giving me up didn't make sense to me. Again, I was a piece in somebody else's game. *He couldn't have been that bothered.*

The sun was warm on my cheek. Spring had finally arrived, a time for new beginnings, but I didn't want mine. I longed to be back in my flat: the balcony door open, Gabe playing out there with his cars.

The door of the house had been opened. Gabe started to run towards it after Geraldine, but stopped and turned back to take hold of my hand. Geraldine beckoned us from where she now stood in the porch. To my surprise, two small children came running out, a little boy and a taller girl.

"Nana," the girl reached up to Geraldine. She had golden-brown curls and wore a cute denim pinafore with striped tights and soft brown boots. The little boy in his dungarees continued toddling out onto the drive and I felt compelled to catch him in case he ran into the road. As I lifted him up he laughed. He placed his hands on my shoulders, gripped me tightly.

"Babbababa?" he offered. Drool poured down his chin. Astonishment flooded me. Another relation of mine?

"William! Oh…"

A woman pushed past Geraldine into the sunshine and stopped when she saw me. A shy smile spread over her face. She moved forward. "I see you've met William. And this must be Gabriel." She knelt down to offer her hand to my son and he shook it solemnly.

"I'm Justine," she told him. "You can call me Aunty Justine if you want."

His eyes widened but he said nothing. She straightened and spoke to me, taking the baby from my arms. She had blonde hair, tied away from her pale face. There were dark hollows around her grey eyes. I judged her to be about thirty years old.

"I haven't seen you since you were much younger," she said, "I don't know if you remember me?"

"I… er…" *No.*

"I'm sorry I haven't seen you since then. I went away to college and, you know, had my family. But so did you. How lovely for Melissa and William to have a cousin around their own age. Gabriel, this is your cousin William."

She knelt again with the baby. He flapped his hands at Gabe, giving him the same greeting, *Babbabbbabbba.* My son looked slightly alarmed, stepped closer to me. I felt his warmth against my hip. I stroked his hair, thinking that actually, these two small children were *my* cousins. Justine was my aunt.

At a word from Geraldine the little girl came and stood in front of Gabriel. She was just a bit smaller than him. She tipped her head on one side, stuck a thumb in her mouth.

"This is your cousin Melissa." Justine smiled at Gabriel and then at me. "How lovely," she said again.

A BLANKET OF quiet shrouded the house. Justine had 'popped to the shops' with her children and I was informed that Maria's father (whom I would be introduced to later) was keeping an eye on his daughter. Gabriel and I had been shown all around the Fairchild home and Gabe had insisted on unpacking the contents of his rucksack into the empty drawer Geraldine allocated him in our bedroom at the top of the house.

I preferred to leave my clothes tucked away in my bag.

"Look," Geraldine said to Gabriel, bustling back into the room amidst a crinkling of cellophane. "I have a brand new pair of pyjamas for you to put on later. You'll be able to keep them here ready for the next time you come and stay with us."

Gabe reached out for them eagerly; they had a pattern of dinosaurs on a blue background. I felt the heat rise in my cheeks – she was hijacking my son – but I turned to the window and stood in the space of the wide bay of carpet, looking over the acres of neatly-positioned red brick houses. They stood on ample plots, some with green lawns out front and some with paved parking spaces instead of gardens. From where I stood I could see the back gardens of the houses opposite as well, bordered by arable fields. I pictured my mother, younger at the time than me, standing in this same position looking out at the view. Twenty-two years ago, she had her newborn baby in her arms. I continued to build up a mental picture from the photographs Geraldine had shown me until I almost felt Maria was standing beside me, the past becoming simultaneous with the present – me, both a tiny baby and an adult woman. At the same time I fought the tide of questions rising in my chest. Eventually I was compelled to break through Gabe's chatter and ask Geraldine if this had been my mother's room when she was young.

"No, dear." Geraldine said. "Your mother is in her own room, it's downstairs."

I gripped the back of a satin-covered armchair which stood to one side of the window, I'd almost forgotten Maria was at this moment in the very same house as me.

I'D RUN OUT of excuses. Geraldine had made me another cup of tea because I'd complained about my dry throat. At my insistence, she'd shown me more photographs of Maria from the time when she was Marianne Fairchild. She brought them upstairs and we both sat on the edge of the double bed Gabe and I would be sharing, photographs scattered around us. Geraldine was patient with me. I'd explained that I felt the need to get to know the person behind the concept of 'mother' before broaching a connection with a dying woman.

GABRIEL ALREADY SEEMED to be more a part of this family than I could make myself feel. He'd bonded with Melissa and taken a brotherly interest in the baby, quickly following Melissa's lead. Justine had by now taken all three children into the garden at the back of the house from where I could hear them laughing and shrieking excitedly. The garden sloped downwards from a huge sun-filled kitchen, one level below the ground floor.

"Come on. Don't put it off any longer."

Geraldine gestured me towards her as she came down the steps that led from the hallway into the kitchen where I'd been looking out the window. My child played happily on a swing set with his cousins.

"I've checked on her, she's awake," Geraldine said encouragingly. I seemed to be rooted to the spot. Geraldine beckoned again. "She's waiting for you, Mariana."

Oh no.

"Come on, you must." Geraldine sounded impatient now.

DID I HAVE a memory of this house, with its wooden-floored hallway running from one end to the other, cutting the house in half, or did I just imagine that? I seemed to see myself as a baby sitting in a high chair in this kitchen, watching a spoon loaded with something mushy coming towards my face, a pair of eyes dancing with a light that couldn't quite reach the shadows behind them, onto which I fastened my gaze.

I'd somehow got myself to Maria's door, the second one along the hallway. Geraldine pushed it open. My feet shuffled forward. Geraldine's hand planted itself firmly at the base of my spine and by then it was too late to turn back.

Jerkily, I crossed the room's threshold to the middle of a patterned rug and stood still. Half-pulled curtains darkened the room, but the window was open, air lifted the curtains and stirred the covers on the bed. It was a hospital bed, grey plastic with a mechanism for raising or lowering it. I shook so much my vision blurred.

One thing at a time… I managed to take in the catheter bag hanging at the side of the bed, the tube coming down from a bag of clear liquid on a pole to… to… a claw-like hand that rested on the striped bedcover. That hand had once bathed me, lifted me; caressed me. My body threatened to double up but I held it straight.

THE HAND ROSE from the bed and my gaze remained fixed on it. I didn't dare look up along the acres of covers towards the face…

No. I shouldn't have agreed to meet my mother for the first time like this. What a horrible memory it would be to take into the rest of my life. I should never have come. *Oh God, what have I done?*

I didn't know her. It would be different if I knew her, if I could have felt something other than terror. Love would have softened the blow, but this… it wasn't right, walking into a stranger's room like this. It was a mistake, I shouldn't have come. I wanted Mam, my real mother. *Don't make me…*

Then I heard something.

"Mariana."

A breeze came through the gap between the curtains, lifting them like a salute, and it was as if the voice, no more than a breath, had drifted in on that. I took a dreamlike step forward.

"You came."

The voice turned into a crow of pure joy, a baby's first, unformed word. Without even realising it, I was looking down at her face. And it wasn't so bad. The hair which I knew had once been the colour of mine had faded and thinned. The skin on the face was like paper, would tear if I touched it. But her guilelessness softened my perception. Her eyes, huge in the skeletal face, were full of light and warmth. There were no lies inside those eyes, just unfiltered truth. I was stripped bare, her baby again.

Geraldine pulled a chair close to the bed and pressed me down into it with a hand on my shoulder. The huge eyes on the bed stayed fixed on mine. Geraldine backed out of the room, mouthing "I'll be back soon," her face softening with a smile of encouragement.

The claw-like hand hovered above the bedspread, reached for something. Was it me she wanted?

I couldn't, not yet. I couldn't hold that hand, if that was what it was asking me to do.

I was in an underwater dream, moving my head or even my eyes took such effort, it seemed as if they were in the wrong element and didn't belong in my body at all. My tongue stuck to the roof of my mouth. I couldn't have spoken if I wanted to. I hadn't chosen this experience, didn't want this intensity of feeling. *Marianne... Maria. My mother.*

"Baby. My..." said the voice on the bed, making me jump.

I unstuck my mouth and tried a response. "Hello." That seemed pathetic. "Hello... it's good to..." but *what* was it good to? *Catch her before she dies?*

The eyes fought hard to hold onto mine, but my gaze struggled to slip away from hers. She seemed desperate for me to look at her, so I gave in. I let her hold me with her loving expression. And then it became like an embrace. She was transmitting warmth and knowledge into me. We stayed like that for a while.

Then she began to speak, her voice strengthening with each word.

"Tell you the truth…"

I leaned forward to hear better but had to draw back again, overwhelmed by the reek of her breath. After a few moments I adjusted to it and pulled my chair closer.

"So happy to see you again."

I nodded, calmer now. I had all the time in the world to listen. As she talked I started to see her as she once was. I mentally covered her bones with flesh, like on the photographs Geraldine had showed me: Maria with me as a baby. She'd had some colour in her cheeks then, her hair a rich copper. Like mine.

"The reason I gave you up…" she said. "Not the anorexia. I would *never* have. You made me *better.*"

Surprisingly, my fingers were creeping closer to hers on the striped bedspread. I left them there, our fingertips touching.

"…Something else. I was not myself. Not *only* myself. I was someone else."

Cliff-hanger pauses hung between every two words or so. What she said didn't make sense. Maybe she was confused – *she was not* only *herself, she was someone else.*

"Lived before… I couldn't live two lives."

Her eyes, huge and rounded, exposed by lack of flesh, searched mine desperately to see if she'd managed to make me understand. Then I put my hand over hers, for some reason shocked to feel it was warm. Alive.

"I don't know what you mean," I whispered, leaning forward.

She responded to my touch with a movement of her hand. It sent a ripple of connection through me. Her eyes widened even further. She dragged in a breath.

"Cal Wilde."

MY HEART THUMPED at the sound of his name. It signified danger every time I thought of it. He'd gone crazy, Angel said, after Maria Child visited their house. At exactly the same time, Maria had sunk into her final decline. She opened her mouth to make another effort at speech. "Cal Wilde, he was my twin brother... in *other* life."

What? Now she sounded crazy. Maybe an effect of being near the end. My hand whipped itself away of its own accord. I found my knuckles jammed against my teeth. What did she mean? Everything inside me seemed to stop for a moment. Then my heart started beating again.

"M...Marion Wilde," enunciated Maria so carefully. "Me, her... we were... the same person. Had to get away... had to give you up."

23

Mariana

GERALDINE BROUGHT GABE in while I was still sitting with Maria. I didn't know how much time had passed, but I saw now that it had got dark outside. Gabriel had his dinosaur pyjamas on and I focussed on the normality of it. Maria couldn't seem to see anymore, but with Geraldine's guidance she managed to lay a hand on my son's head. Gabe held himself very still: a child receiving a blessing. A glow emanated from Maria, she knew who he was, I was sure of it.

The sound of her breathing was detached from the person on the bed, it seemed as if all parts of Maria – her eyes, her voice, bird-like hands – were separate now. Her body occupied so little space it was hardly there.

Geraldine cuddled Gabriel, standing at Maria's side. He was quiet but his eyes took everything in.

"It won't be long now…" she mouthed to me.

GERALDINE'S EYES GLITTERED with the kind of fierceness I understood. That was her baby on the bed. I found my breathing echoing that of my disappearing mother. In my mind we were holding hands, but physically, I no longer touched her.

I heard Geraldine utter a minute sigh. She grunted slightly as she passed Gabriel to me and rubbed her hip when she had transferred him into my arms. I welcomed his weight on my lap. He patted my face, smiling sleepily.

Geraldine pulled a chair to the top end of the bed next to Maria's face. She placed her elbows in the space between the pillow and the edge of the mattress, before lowering her head into her hands. Soon she had adjusted herself until she was almost lying face to face with her daughter. As Gabriel opened his mouth to say something he caught my eyes and seemed to change his mind. He turned back to Geraldine and her daughter, gazed open-mouthed for a while, then sighed deeply and snuggled against my chest. It didn't take him long to fall asleep.

The atmosphere felt holy; I almost expected angels to sing.

Somewhere else in the house I heard a door open and close, running footsteps; the calls of small children.

It was intoxicatingly peaceful in the darkening room but by now I needed to get out. I needed the loo; I ought to put Gabriel to bed. Those other children were obviously used to staying up later than him.

Geraldine didn't move when I stood up slowly. My limbs had gone stiff but my arms were locked around my child. I backed towards the door, looking at my mother for the last time.

I would have felt self-conscious saying goodbye aloud.

OUTSIDE THE ROOM I backed into a grey-haired man that I recognized from photographs: Maria's father, my grandfather. His eyes were blue and watery.

"Eh, is that you love? Mariana, is it?"

The man gulped, his Adam's apple bobbing. Placing a hesitant hand on my arm he lightly stroked Gabriel's hair with his other.

"Great to see you lass. Thanks for coming… We'll talk later eh? You'd better get that young 'un to bed."

He edged into Maria's room, closing the door behind him.

I bumped into Justine at the top of the house. The little ones were tucked into the big double bed in the room behind her. Justine looked awful.

"Is she…?" Her grey eyes asked the question more eloquently than words.

I shook my head. "You could go down." I nodded at the children. "I'll stay up here and listen out for them. Your mum and dad are both in there."

"Are you sure? Oh I don't know, I want to… but shouldn't you be there…?"

You know her much better than I do. "It's all right," I shuffled my sleeping boy in my arms. "I've seen her. It's ok. You go down, honestly, I don't mind."

Justine rubbed the bridge of her nose with a forefinger. "Well if you're sure you don't mind. I feel…" She turned to check on the toddlers, fiddled with her tied-back hair. Then she gave me a quick peck on the cheek. "But I do want to see her. So thank you. I did ring Charissa you know, but she hasn't got here yet, I don't know. Oh dear, this is very sad. I'll er…"

She hurried off down the stairs, arguing with herself. I went into the other bedroom and laid Gabriel on the bed. On second thoughts, I lifted him up again. I tugged his pyjama pants down and held him over the toilet in the bathroom, which was between the two bedrooms. In his sleep, he emptied his bladder and I was satisfied I wouldn't wake up in a wet bed with him.

I DID INTEND to stay awake, listening out for the children, staying alert as I felt I should on such a solemn night, but I fell asleep. I came to in the glow of the dim bedside lamp sometime in the early hours of the morning. Something warm and light had brushed against my face. The warmth spread right through me and across the bed, Gabriel stirred in it too. Then I had the impression the draught left via the window, open just a crack. A feeling of joy lingered in the wake of the warm caress.

The feeling was still there when I woke again much later. Gabriel poked me in the ribs, giggling at the novelty of sharing a bed with me.

"Come on little man." My throat felt tight. "Let's go downstairs and see what the others are doing shall we?"

I'd much rather have stayed at the top of the house with him. I pressed my lips into his hair and he giggled a bit more, then stopped quite suddenly.

"Have you got two mothers, Mammy?"

I sat up and pulled him onto my lap, stroked the golden hair away from his forehead. "I suppose I have, Darling."

I wanted to add 'had'. Somebody would try to break the news when I went downstairs; I didn't want to hear it. I wanted to shout ahead that I already knew, for them just to be quiet and leave me alone.

Gabriel hopped off the bed. "I need a wee Mammy, where's the toilet?"

"You know where it is, Gabe." As he sucked in his lower lip I added, "But I'll take you if you like. You can have a wash as well." He was so young to have to deal with the pall of grief that would be over the house when we emerged from our cocoon in the turret.

Finally we left our secure den and went downstairs, Gabriel counting steps as we took them one at a time. In the lower corridor we passed Maria's bedroom. A wave of emptiness swept over me and I fought to hold on to the feeling of peace I'd had early that morning. Faces turned as I walked down the steps into the kitchen, Gabe suddenly shy, clinging onto my hand.

Baby William sat in a high chair at the head of the table, banging a spoon on the plastic tray. Melissa sat on Geraldine's lap on the chair nearest to me. Other seats were occupied by Maria's dad, Justine, and another woman who I didn't recognise. She had rich brown hair and was heavily made-up, but her mascara had streaked under her eyes. She reminded me strongly of Geraldine. I realised this must be the other daughter, Charissa, and I wondered when she'd arrived. Flicking my eyes to the clock on the wall above the fridge-freezer I saw it was nine o'clock.

They'd think I'd slept late – I must seem unconcerned about my mother.

The room had gone silent. Geraldine gave me a sad smile. My grandfather stood up with a scrape of his chair. "Come on in, lass."

He steered me towards an empty chair. Gabe held my arm with both hands, as if afraid he'd be torn away. When I sat down he climbed onto my lap, winding both arms around my neck.

"Before you say anything," I mumbled to the silent faces. "I know. You don't have to tell me."

Anything not to hear the words 'your mother is dead.'

I buried my lips in Gabe's hair, feeling the blush spread up my cheeks. Geraldine, sat next to me, touched my knee and I made sure to focus on Melissa's bare feet, tiny toenails painted with blue polish.

"It happened about 4am," Geraldine said. Without looking I knew she'd be giving me one of her contained little smiles. "Myself, her father, and Justine were with her. It was very quiet and peaceful. Your visit helped tremendously, she was happy to have seen you."

Heat flooded over me and then cold. A great, internal pit started to fill up with something. I was terrified it would flood out. I clutched Gabriel and he wriggled and protested, scrambling out of my tight grip. He stumbled as he slid down to the floor and let out a howl of frustration.

"I hurted my leg!" Gabriel wailed, "Kiss it better, Mammy."

I tended to my son and when I looked up again Maria's father was putting a fresh pot of tea on the table. He gave it a stir and then poured it.

"Here you are, lass."

I took the mug gratefully, letting the steam drift up against my skin.

Justine, pale and tight-faced, offered me scrambled eggs and toast, serving some up for Gabriel on a plastic plate featuring one of his favourite TV characters. He began an animated conversation with Melissa, his hurt leg forgotten. I wanted to eat and eat while their child voices filled my head with nonsense.

"Hi," someone hovered over me. It was the other sister, standing awkwardly close. "I'm Charissa. I haven't seen you since you were tiny. I'm glad you came to see Marianne – Maria I mean, before…"

I glanced at her quickly, wondering if she blamed me for not coming earlier.

➤➤➤◄◄◄

JUSTINE BUSIED HERSELF at the cooker and sink, as well as making sure her children were looked after and occupied, whereas Charissa spent the morning at the table being served tea. I offered Justine my assistance but she refused, thanking me with a warm smile.

"It helps to keep busy."

Geraldine had disappeared some time before, but now returned with a cardboard box, which she made space for on the table.

"Don't look at them right now," she instructed, "but these are your mother's notebooks, from when she was very young. She always wanted you to have them. They might help you to understand her better. They did me, eventually."

She seemed to surprise herself with a snort that escaped her self-containment. It turned into a series of hiccupping sobs. She swung quickly away, rushing up the steps that led out of the kitchen. At the top I saw her colliding with her husband, who had just closed the door on Maria's room. A shiver went through me with the sudden realisation that Maria must still be in there, dead and alone. For a moment I felt the floor swinging up towards me and I gripped the edge of the table with both hands.

Geraldine took her husband's place in Maria's room as he came down into the kitchen.

"Would you like to go in and see her, love?"

What would I be going in to see? Nothing more than an empty shell. There was hardly anything of her anyway. I wanted to remember her as the warm love that came brushing over me in the night. As my mother. I shook my head, mumbled "Sorry" and hoped again that the family didn't think me uncaring.

"Eh that's all right, chicken. It's good to have you back in the family. Welcome home."

A COLLEAGUE, APPARENTLY a dear friend of Maria's, had been scheduled beforehand to visit her that afternoon. She arrived as planned, a young woman probably in her late twenties or early thirties. She told me her name, Alice, and that she had taken the lead in Maria's autobiographical play,

The Time Has Come. The one about me.

I vaguely remembered Geraldine cutting out newspaper reviews and giving them to me when I'd just turned eighteen. At the time I'd wondered why she was making such a fuss. She'd tried so hard to persuade me to go on a trip to London with her to see the play, but of course I had a brand new baby and I thought she was mad for asking.

Now I understand why.

Maybe seeing the play would have encouraged me to accept contact from my birth mother. Maybe Geraldine would have broken her promise to Maria, seeing me moved by the play, confessed that Maria was my mother. This day of Maria's death might have been so different, or not occurred at all.

What if I hadn't come at all? I started thinking next. *What if she'd had to die thinking I didn't care?*

I didn't know how to control all the thoughts spilling out of me.

NOBODY HAD REMEMBERED to call Alice to inform her of Maria's passing, so she was shocked to find the house in a state of mourning. It seemed to be given to me to offer her tea and sympathy. I was relieved to have a role to play. Justine's husband had driven over in their big car and the two of them, along with Charissa, took all three children out for the afternoon. The undertaker's van arrived just after Alice. A blanket of solemnity enveloped us as we watched Maria being carried out. It felt surreal and impossible to be standing in a line with Geraldine, her husband, and Alice, our heads bowed in respectful silence.

My mother was leaving. A sick, cold feeling suffused me as the sombre men walked out through the door with their lightweight burden.

After the van drove away the oppression that had hung over us was lifted and we began to talk. Over yet another pot of tea I became aware that the two strands of my birth family were under the same roof with me for the second time.

My family… Alice's surname, Turner, had thrown me.

Geraldine sat down at the table with Alice and me. We chatted about Alice's life in the theatre with my mother. Apparently Maria had taken Alice under her wing, unusual for her, and they'd soon become friends. Alice knew all about me. She told me Maria had often spoken about her longing to see me again, but she'd also respected my privacy, Alice said. I tried to feel happy that I'd finally granted Maria's wish, rather than guilty I'd left it so long.

"Maria didn't have many friends, so Alice was very important to her." Geraldine leant across the table, steepling her fingers in a familiar way. "I only realised who Alice's stepfather was after Maria returned from her visit there in such a state," she explained. "Otherwise I would have strongly discouraged her from going."

Her eyes took on a glazed look and she began to laugh unnaturally. Her strained face twitched in an alarming way and the wild laughter soon mutated into tears.

"I'm sorry…" she struggled to get out. "This isn't like me at all. I do apologise." She let out another peal of hysterical giggles. "Please excuse me; I'm going to have a lie-down upstairs."

She pushed her chair away and hurried off, grabbing a

handful of tissues, heeled pumps clacking on the wooden floor. Alice and I looked at each other in shock.

"I'm sorry," Alice put a hand out and touched my arm. "I only found out recently myself. I mean that Cal, my stepfather, had another daughter and that she was – *you* were – the baby Maria gave away. I made the horrible mistake of bringing Maria to my family home. I had no idea until then."

The things Maria had told me raced around my head, things that still hadn't sunk in.

"Did she… was she upset when she saw him?"

Alice looked thoughtful. "To be honest she seemed more upset when she first saw my mother. Or no, actually. It started in the car when I told her where we were going. She had one of her fits."

"Fits?"

"Has nobody told you about that? She sometimes had these strange episodes. Absences. She couldn't move. Like she'd disappeared out of her own body. She had one when she found we were arriving at Pottersea, and then another early the next morning when she was talking to my mum in the kitchen." Alice breathed in sharply. She reached for the box of tissues somebody had thoughtfully placed in the centre of the table. Rivulets trickled off her chin and soaked into her blue jumper.

"I'm going to miss her so much."

I waited while she tidied her face. She swept up her honey-coloured hair, clinging in strands to her wet cheeks, fished in her bag for an elastic hair band.

"I phoned Maria's work partner," she said, sniffing. "To

let her know what's happened. She offered me a management position in the company. She says that's what Maria wanted. But at the moment I can't imagine carrying on without her."

I wished I'd known about Maria my whole life. She meant far more to other people than to me. They were wondering how they'd manage without her and I only felt empty.

"She told me something," I burst out without really meaning to.

As I stood up to put the kettle on yet again, a tall girl with pale face and long hair wavered in the darkening glass of the kitchen window, shoulders hunched. The eyes were deeply shadowed in the reflection, black holes; entrances to a vortex inside my head, spinning and swirling with incomprehensible knowledge.

Alice placed her palms flat on the table as if about to push herself up.

"What did she tell you?"

"She said... she said..." I twisted my hands together, watching the winking red light on the kettle. Alice looked at me with her kind blue eyes, patient, puzzled.

"Mariana?"

I twisted my fingers even more tightly. "Maria told me that she gave me up because... because she said she was not *only* herself. She said she couldn't live two lives. Cal Wilde, she told me... she said he was her twin brother, in... Well, I *think* she meant in another life. That's the only way I can interpret what she said."

I watched Alice's face to see if she thought I was mad.

But Alice half stood, and then sat down again. She closed her eyes for a second.

"Come and sit down, Mariana, this all makes sense."

I brought the refilled teapot over to the table and sat down opposite her.

"Pull a chair closer."

She looked much younger, wanting to tell me a secret. I moved around the table and sat on the chair next to hers. Our heads leaned close together and she began to speak in her low, husky voice. "When I was a little girl, only seven, my mum got together with Cal. She met him at a party one night and by the following week they were living together. They'd known each other since they were children. They were boyfriend and girlfriend when they were teenagers, so the speed of it wasn't as crazy as it sounds."

Her voice was mesmeric. But I wondered where my mother came into the story. Alice poured herself another mug of tea. I nodded when she proffered the pot towards me, watched the golden liquid trickle into the mug.

"At the time," she went on, "Cal lived with his sister Sarah in Blackberry House in Pottersea, where my family still live. But soon after Cal started dating Lisa again, Sarah and her boyfriend Mark decided to get married and went to live in Ireland."

It was still not a story about my mother. Alice took a few slow, deep breaths, carried on in the same low tone. "So the house was free to be made into a home for our new family. It's amazing how quickly I adapted to life with a stepfather, since it'd been Mum and me on our own for so long. I seemed to understand Cal from the start – his unpredictable moods, a peculiar vulnerable quality he has."

Alice was the first person who made my father seem half-human. She stopped speaking as we both heard a noise and looked up towards the ceiling. I checked my watch; Justine was bound to be back with the children soon. I desperately wanted to hear what Alice had to tell me, sensed it would change my view of everything. The footsteps moved from one side of the room to the other. Something creaked, and then it all went quiet.

Alice resumed speaking, telling a story that had not yet included the name Maria – or Marianne. "They made the attic into a bedroom for me. Two rooms actually – three if you count the bathroom. I loved it and was happy up there. But I used to see this girl…"

Her eyes clouded over. She gave a little shudder. "I forget about her for months, years at a time and then I remember. It was so weird… so weird it was easy to dismiss the memory in a way. And I was only seven when it happened."

When what happened? Tingling started all over my body. If my hair hadn't been so long it would have been standing straight up. I felt the roots prickling, like a thousand insects were running across my scalp. 'I used to see this girl…' Alice had said.

How come I knew what she was going to say next?

"She'd be standing stock-still, right under the first window in my bedroom. The same place every time. She stared straight ahead, eyes wide open. She never moved or spoke, she only stood there silently. And yet I wasn't really frightened of her, I called her the funny girl."

The funny girl. My mind said the words the same moment she spoke them.

I used to play a game called the funny girl when I was a child. I used to stand stock-still, just as Alice had described, in Mam and Dad's bedroom and when Mam started to get upset and told me to stop messing around I said I was playing at being the funny girl.

I tried not to let Alice see how sick I suddenly felt.

"She looked like... well, like you." Alice put her hand up to her mouth, trailing her fingers over her lips. "Like your mother, I mean, but like you look now. Then..." She shuddered. Poured more tea, proffering the pot again but I refused, arms folded tight across my stomach.

"Carry on, please?" I glanced at the front door. "What happened next?"

Alice took a sip of tea, placed the mug on the table. She looped her fingers through the handle and looked down at a placemat, lips pursed.

"I tried to tell Mum once or twice, but I guess she thought it was one of my stories. I suppose I was a creative child. Remember, I'd grown up on my own. And that was before she came to our house, you see."

"She?"

"Your mother. Three months after we moved into Blackberry House. We'd been for a picnic up on the Yorkshire Moors. We had my Labrador puppy, Bonzo, with us." Alice smiled, probably not even realising. I guessed she was remembering her dog. She took another sip of tea.

"We got back in the early evening, but it was summer and still light. And I saw through the glass in the door that the funny girl was sitting in our kitchen. For the first time I was scared; she was real that time. She had a stony look on her face. I could feel the anger coming off her as soon as I stepped into the kitchen. They called her Marianne, well Cal did, but my mum called her Marion at first. I clearly remember the distinction, because when Cal called out to her, Mum said something like, 'who is Mari*anne*?'"

Something tightened inside me, a screw that wouldn't fasten any deeper. Alice found my eyes with hers. "I don't know if you know this, but Cal's twin sister was called Marion. She died of anorexia, aged seventeen."

I nodded rhythmically, like one of those toys on the back seat of a car. Everything had begun to move in slow motion. The image of Geraldine rushing to the toilet to be sick when Aiden had informed her that his father's twin sister died of anorexia wavered in front of my eyes, like an old film.

"At the time Marianne – Maria as she became – sat in our kitchen, she must have been about that age. She must have…" Alice seemed to be doing some mental calculating, "she must have been born around the time Marion died."

We looked at each other without speaking. "That funny girl," Alice almost whispered. "That funny girl I saw in my bedroom… it might have been the ghost of Marion. Not Marianne at all. But when Marianne was in our kitchen I asked her why she acted so strangely when she was in my room."

She broke off as we both heard a car outside on the drive. Headlights filtered through the glass in the front door, reaching down the hallway almost as far as the top of the steps leading into the kitchen. From the room upstairs I heard the bed creak again, and footsteps cross the room. I needed to hear the rest of the story before the front door opened and my son rushed into the house, because when that happened I would have to give myself back to him.

"What did she do? Tell me." I grasped Alice's hands. She winced. Looking down, I uncurled my fingers one by one and sat back in the chair, gripping the wood instead.

"She started screaming." Alice's pulse raced in her throat, I could actually see it hammering there. "She started screaming at me that I was a liar, said I didn't know what I was talking about. She screeched that her sister said the same things about her, that she had stood like a statue with her eyes wide open and that if it was true then she must be a ghost."

We both tensed as car doors slammed and the front door rattled.

"Hurry," I hissed.

My nails dug into my palm. Alice's eyes filled with tears and she couldn't seem to speak.

"What happened next?" I insisted.

"And then," she said hoarsely, as the front door opened and voices echoed down the hall. "And then she threw herself across the room to the knives on the hooks above the sink, and she took one, and she slit both of her wrists before anyone could stop her."

24

Maria Child/Marion Wilde

Afterwards

*S*HE CAME TOWARDS *me through mist that swirled in front of my eyes. It was like looking at my mirror image, broken away from glass. I couldn't pull the curtain over her any longer, nor did I care to.*

My vision, which I had spent most of my life trying to focus outwards, had turned completely in, reaching far back across two lives. The last meaningful thing I did in the life of Maria Child was touch the head of my grandson. I felt his warm scalp beneath a layer of silken hair. When I rested my palm on his head my fingertips picked up the buzz of busy little cells fizzing inside him, growing and multiplying. I must have lit up from within. Light shone through my paper-thin skin, I somehow knew my daughter saw it. The existence of my daughter and grandson rendered every instant of Maria Child's life worthwhile.

I felt Marion should acknowledge that. But she tried to take the credit for that beautiful girl and boy being in the world. "You do realise, don't you, that if I hadn't lived and died, you would never have existed. Sure, some unmemorable child would have resulted from the copulation of your genetic mother and father, but it wouldn't have been you – in other words, me. You were me all along, really. Go on, admit it."

I strongly disputed her assertion. "You were the one who chose to die in the first place. The body I had was mine and mine alone. You know how hard I had to fight to maintain an identity of my own all those years. I had to give up my daughter for it, for Heaven's sake."

At that word Marion trilled with laughter. "Haha, do you think we'll go there? Anyway, if that body was so precious to you why did you abuse it – starve and disrespect it? Own up; you hated your body from the start, just like I did – yours, I mean."

If I'd still been a physical person my shoulders would have slumped at that. She was right. She'd held claim to me from the time I was in my mother's womb.

But I was the one who'd been able to have Cal in a way she never could, however briefly, and it was my genetic separateness that had enabled Mariana to be created, chromosomally pure. Everything was meant to have happened, right down to Cal impregnating Lisa with Aiden the night after he planted the seed of Mariana in me.

"Don't you get it?" I asked Marion, "Those two, Aiden and Mariana, are the new Cal and Marion, without all our hang-ups."

IT WAS TIME to stop fighting Marion. It didn't matter anymore. She was right: that beautiful girl, our daughter, would never have happened without both of us. It was Marion's spirit Cal had been connected to, and my body.

"It was never that I hated life, you know," Marion suddenly said. "I loved it. If anything I loved it too much. All those everyday things you have to do when you're a person, they all got in the way. I wanted to be spirit – to be free. I wanted to experience everything, not be confined by a stupid body. I was so mad when I got forced back inside one."

The mist had cleared and we sat together on a hill overlooking the sea. The grass an exquisitely vivid green, the patches of sky between startling white clouds were intensely blue. Marion beside me looked young, happy.

We tipped our heads back, imbibing the scents of nature: the flavour of that sharp green grass, a suggestion of the hides of animals, warmed by the sun. The salty tang of the sea below us coated the backs of our throats. Everything was pure and more real than it had ever seemed in my lifetime.

"I don't think we're going to be able to keep this up," said Marion. "That was the mistake I made last time, staying around too long. I've been trapped all these years, and it's so good to be part of The Everything again. You gave me a second chance. But we mustn't get trapped again."

"What do you mean?"

But a flock of seagulls swooped over suddenly and before I knew it we were plunging and diving over the sea, voicing piercing cries. We tore the shifting curtains of time apart.

WE TOOK AN amazing ride through both our lives on the wings of those seagulls. At the end of it we were back on the cliff. If anything the rays of sunshine were even more glorious than they had been before. A strong breeze rustled the long grass, and tingled right through me. Maybe that was because there was nothing to stop it; no skin, no bones. Still, I felt it lifting my hair up off my shoulders. Red wafted behind me like a banner.

"So here we are," said Marion.

We looked at each other; or rather I looked at myself.

"So here we are…"

I HEARD MUSIC that seemed both familiar and unfamiliar at the same time, the plaintive call of violins reaching higher and higher until I thought the notes would snap. Without the aid of any wings I found myself soaring up into the roof space of an old church. I looked behind me for Marion but she was inside me by now. No, not exactly – it was simply that we had never completely been two at all.

I looked down and saw them all in the pews below: her parents, Jane and George; then Cal, Sarah and Lisa, various aunts and cousins. Cal looked much younger than the last time I saw him.

Examining the congregation more closely it mutated. Now I spotted Geraldine and Joseph, Charissa, and Justine with her husband and children beside her. Justine, all grown up, my baby sister. Finally I saw my precious Mariana, her little boy in her arms. Her hair streamed down her back and she had a fierce expression on her face. She would be all right, my Mariana. On either side of her stood her half-siblings, Aiden and Angel. Alice, my dear friend, surrogate daughter, was there as well, next to *her mother. Where was Cal? I saw the others looking around as if they were searching for him too. The older Lisa was in pieces.*

I knew where I would find him.

"We can't stay out long," whispered an insistent voice in my head. For a moment I saw Marion beside me again. We were flying out over a city, and then over the sea.

"I know where he'll be."

We reached the beach where I'd invited the sea to take me, many years ago, before I had found my way back to the attic in Blackberry House. I still couldn't see him but I was confident he would come. Marion was getting anxious.

"Can't you hear it Marianne? The voices calling, the music. We can't stay out any longer. I'm not getting trapped again."

I found that I understood what she was saying, and I let go. As we watched, light filled everything. Something opened up in the sea below us, not really a hole. A hole epitomises emptiness. This was a space bursting with energy. It sounded like and tasted of and looked like and smelt of everything. It felt smooth and gritty and soft and strong all at the same time. It was light and dark. Sonorous chords reverberated through us. We peered into the glittering depths, which led upwards.

Marion and Marianne looked at each other.

"Come on," she said.

And we held hands and jumped.

25

Cal

FURY BOILED IN me, hot as a volcano. That *woman* had refused to let me see her daughter even though Alice had pleaded with her on my behalf. Alice informed me that Maria hadn't eaten for weeks. The whole thing was happening again.

Day after day we'd sat beside Marion's bed, apple blossom blowing onto her through the always-open window.

The scent of apple blossom still made me sick. When I first moved to Blackberry House there was an apple tree in the garden and I'd cut it down, hacking at it with an axe. I had to get a professional to help clear up my mess in the end. Sarah cried; she said it was a living thing and I'd killed it. Well. I was good at that.

"It wasn't about you," I insisted, pleading with Marion to change her mind once I realised what she was doing. I was only seventeen, couldn't be held responsible for my actions. How

could I ever have known writing that book would have such a devastating effect?

It wasn't my fault, Marion made her own decisions. She'd always liked to be in charge. *Didn't she understand I'd just wanted to do something for myself, by myself?* I don't know where the story for *The Shell* came from; it was so easy to write. It just sprang up inside me, fully formed.

"I forgive you," Marion communicated before she died. In a way that was even worse. If she'd raged at me, hated me for my betrayal, I could maybe have worked through the grief. I could have agreed with her that I was an utter shit. We could have had it out – 'I felt I needed to do this because…' But there was nothing to discuss. "I forgive you," Marion pronounced in her silent manner, condemning me with her magnanimity.

Now it was all happening again. I was a touchstone for death. Maria had kept herself safe from me for so long, and now she was about to die.

The sighting of that girl… Mariana, it had been a sign of what was to come. That things were about to change. I'd waited patiently for three years between seeing Mariana and Maria turning up. Things were becoming connected, I just needed to work out how. But it became complicated by my second sighting of the girl… And then what Angel said.

A GUST OF wind billowed my thick woollen coat around me. I paced up and down the cliff edge, looking out to sea. I pulled the hat tightly over my ears, pushed my fingers more deeply into my gloves. Over and over again I relived the night Sarah and I had come out here to search for Maria –

Marianne back then – after she disappeared from our house. I remembered how the dog, Jude, had gone running after a white-clad figure Sarah swore she spotted standing at the place where foam crashed onto the beach. But when I turned to hurry to the area she pointed out, there was nothing there. And yet we discovered Marianne, dripping wet in the attic on our return home.

I scrambled down the sticky sides of the cliff onto the beach below, the ridged soles of my boots filling with red clay. When I reached the bottom I hunkered partway back up again. I squatted under an overhanging ledge made of concrete. The sand usually remained dry at this point. But the coastline was unstable, shelves of concrete that used to belong to wartime bunkers or domestic dwellings working themselves loose and falling at any time. Just like the church of the original village in this place had done in the past. On a night of great storms the wind had ripped headstones from the graveyard, tipping the contents of coffins over the cliff. Villagers had searched for fragments of their relatives' remains on the beach.

It would be a fitting place for my bones to be found.

Far out on the ever-widening beach were huge lumps of broken architecture, half-buried in the sand. The cliffs were receding at breakneck speed. Up above, further along the coast where the cliffs rose higher, tattered polythene and long snakes of piping flapped and clattered in the wind, writhing out of the earth, exposed like the tissues and organs of a ripped-open body.

My body.

I used a flat piece of driftwood to dig myself a burrow in

which I planned to sleep. From here the sound of the sea was magnified, booming and crashing, resonating inside me. It echoed the beat of my blood, a sonorous pumping and swelling. I imagined saltwater sloshing into my eyes and ears, filling my mouth with grit and salt. I'd rung Lisa the day before to tell her I was all right, that I just needed time to get my head together, but I didn't know if I'd ever go back. What was the point? They'd all be better off without me. Alone I could spend long periods of time thinking nothing, and I was happy to remain empty a long time, with nobody to distract me or fuss over me or infuriate me. Marion's two years of silence made a lot of sense, I could see that now. I could just be me, whatever that was, absorbing and reflecting the rhythms of the sea, attaching my emotions and urges to the elements of nature.

Even that sounds like I was actually making an effort. I wasn't. My anger and grief had been carried away by the seagulls' wings. Occasional contentment crept over me in my aloneness. I found it in the rustling of wind in the grass on top of the cliffs. If I felt like becoming a body of movement, I would walk, even run along the sand. In moments of sudden vitality that contrasted with the flooding in of peace, I scrambled up the cliff and ran along the top, perilously close to the edge, arms outstretched. It simply didn't *matter* what happened to me; that was the beauty of my sojourn.

I realised that, towards the end of her life, Marion had shrugged off responsibility – all obligations to the expectations of human society. She simply was. And now I *was*, too.

I felt closer to Marion than I had done in the forty years since her death. In not eating, I empathised with her dedication to the craft of anorexia. In not having to think about where my next meal was coming from, or speak to anybody, I was free to pursue the pure art of being.

My muscles and bones were cold, my blood chilled, but I'd got used to it. Several days of hair growth covered my cheeks and jaws; from time to time I comforted myself by brushing a hand repeatedly over it. Once, I caught a glimpse of my reflection in a hubcap floating in a rock pool. I looked like a wild man, magnified by the curve of metal. If I gazed directly into the pool my eyes looked like glass beads, opaque and hard, unscratchable.

Those are pearls that were his eyes…

I felt invincible.

➤➤➤◄◄◄

THIS WAS MY second disappearance from home. Nobody knew where I was. The first time: *"You're a perv, Dad,"* was what Angel had said to me. *"Don't you know she's your daughter?"* I'd pushed her away from the car and got back in the driver's seat.

She'd shouted as I swung the car around on the gravel. The front door opened, Lisa appeared, the lights of the kitchen behind her. She was gesturing to Angel and our daughter shrugged her shoulders and threw up her hands, stamped into the house. I pulled the car out onto the road, foot on the accelerator. Off into the night I drove, not stopping to think. But halfway to Hull I turned down a long, desolate side road lined with trees and flat, black fields, nothing but dark emptiness stretched all around. I stopped the car and had a think.

I drove to Leeds, drawn back there as if by a magnet. I wouldn't return home until the next day. I would silence my daughter with a hate-filled stare – that black-haired daughter who haunted me like a shadow. She was as unfathomable to me as my own soul, a dark angel.

Mariana, the new daughter, was the one I now chose to contemplate as light and hope. The news of her parentage had shuddered through me at first, making me want to tear out my hair. I'd felt myself shaking like a tree torn up at the roots, but after the seizure I was left feeling cleansed. It all made sense; explained why Marianne – Maria – had hidden from me all those years.

But after I'd digested the news I hated myself for rejecting Maria when fate had thrown her back on my shore. I could never do anything right.

Two weeks earlier

I'D ACCOMPANIED ALICE and Lisa on their car journey to Maria's house, and that cow Geraldine had allowed Lisa in to say her goodbyes to her childhood friend but the door was barred to me. I felt like the baby Peter Pan in the story my mother used to read to Sarah and Marion and me when we were children. Peter had battered on the windows to be let in but nobody listened.

"I'm sorry, Cal," Alice said to me later. "I tried but nothing I said made any difference." Lisa was also sympathetic, but it hadn't done me any good, had it?

The address was imprinted on my brain and my body knew exactly the direction to take the car. Once I had driven through Leeds I found the lane which stretched away beyond the housing estate into dark countryside, parked my car in the shelter of a tall hedge. I watched the house which contained the woman who'd been a part of my life in some way or other forever.

From inside I heard the sound of a piano. It made my heart hurt in my chest; the music played so exquisitely. I sniffed like a dog in the night, scenting out the one to whom my soul was connected. By the time the car engine had cooled down I had left the vehicle. My eyes became accustomed to the dark in the lane beyond the houses. I followed a path that went up the side of the last house and doubled back behind the row. On the outer edge of the path were fields, a low mist lying over them. The bark of a fox rang out, answered by a dog in a garden somewhere to my right. Something fluttered in some bushes up ahead and then everything settled down again. I walked on, breathed in the sharp night air and blew it out again to form miniature crystals that coated the skin of my face.

The third house from the end was hers. The generous garden sloped down from the building to a fence which gave onto the path. A frost had settled on the earth by then and my feet crunched on the hard ground. I jammed my hands into the pockets of my coat, marched along the whole length of the path and back again, as far as the end house in the row. Soon I narrowed my trajectory to the width of Geraldine's garden. I still remembered the face of that woman from our single meeting years before, when she had warned me to stay away from her daughter.

I used all my senses to intuit when the house on the edge of farmland was settling down for the evening. After a long time I slipped my hand over the top of the gate, found the bolt. On the dark grass I made out the shapes of a squat plastic swing set and a small playhouse. My foot nudged a ball in a flower border on the way up the garden and I stumbled, froze for a few moments. I checked that my action didn't seem to have disturbed anyone. When I reached the building I crouched like a thief by the wall.

I could hear no sounds so I stood up to my full height and saw from the dim outlines through the French doors that the room was a kitchen. Keeping my shoulder against the bricks I shuffled around the corner and saw ahead of me in a side wing what I knew straight away was Maria's bedroom. White, wraith-like curtains wafted over the windowsill in the cool night air. A dim lamp illuminated the room. I edged closer.

Her voice called me in, though I wasn't sure if it was real or in my head. It was easy to push the window open further, climb over the windowsill, slip into the room behind the curtain. I did all that, yet it felt like a dream. I made no sound, not even footsteps on the wooden floor as I dropped down from the window, or the crash of the plastic feeder beaker, the kind you give a toddler, that I knocked over with my hand. It was all silent.

Someone came into the room to check on Maria but

they didn't notice me pressed against the wall by the window. Her mother, older of course than when I'd last seen her, now-silver hair drawn back as elegantly as ever, tapped across the room on low heels, a longish skirt swinging around her legs. The hairs on the back of my neck rose as I watched her, like the hackles of a dog.

"Sleep tight," she leant over Maria's bed. "I'll see you in the morning."

She tapped out of the room again, leaving the door open a crack. I wondered why she hadn't seen me, raising a hand in front of my face to check I was really there. It looked solid to me, the skin dry and weather-browned. The dim lamp on the table beyond Maria's bed created a halo of light around my hand; I was a visitor from another planet in a Sci-Fi film.

I paid no heed to the medical equipment in the room as I approached Maria, only wanting to get to the spirit of her. The closer I got the more I felt it. I wanted us to be together again; the physical body of her never had been important.

THAT NIGHT I turned her away from my bed in Blackberry House… The look in her amber eyes that were so similar to mine as I led her to the door at the bottom of the attic stairs and kissed her on the top of her head. She was so young then. I only vaguely remembered the sex we'd had earlier, feeling horror that I'd allowed it to happen. She'd bewitched me, I was convinced of it. I would never have allowed it to happen otherwise. Even then, it was not about the body of that barely-more-than-a-child creature that had wound her thin arms and legs around me, pulled me in. It was the voice of Marion hissing in my ear, entangling our spirits and bodies together again as they had been in the womb.

A kind of reverence effervesced in me as I looked at the ghost-like figure on the bed now. The sex that had tortured me with guilt all those years ago and made me hate her afterwards had produced Mariana. That must have been why she'd come back, my sister and soul mate. It was why she'd returned to starve herself to death all over again just as I'd feared she would, the night Sarah and I discussed the meaning of Marianne in the kitchen of Blackberry House.

IT WAS AFTER we'd found Marianne catatonic in the attic: frozen in the same pose as Sarah had once found Marion. The experience of seeing Marianne wake up and scream, the horror it induced in Sarah and me, galvanized us into an unspoken agreement to cut the ties we'd started to make with her. She was a different girl, not our sister at all. Trying to prove otherwise could only bring harm to all of us.

I CLIMBED ONTO the narrow bed beside the woman that young girl had become, or at least I think I did. It's what I choose to remember. My head lay on the pillow beside hers. Even though she didn't open her eyes I knew she could see me. I found myself weeping the way I'd wept on her thin body all those years ago. I don't know why, it was just the way we'd been created, but Marion had always comforted me, led and instructed me, never the other way round. I couldn't remember ever comforting her.

Her hand moved in my hair, stroking and soothing. I was almost asleep. I could have drifted off with her there and then. It would have been easier than facing the fact of her absence in this world.

I felt her dropping away from me momentarily, and then with a sudden swoop upwards she seemed to be high above the room. A piercing cry rent our joint consciousness. It seemed as though her wings were beating against my face. I reached out, trying to cling on to her.

"Don't go."

Then I felt a wave take us both, accelerating us in a hurtling trajectory towards the shore. After that I discovered that we were rocking together again in our once-familiar amniotic ocean.

I FOUND MYSELF out on the path behind the house again, shaking and cold. Crouched in the frozen earth at the bottom of a hedge, my gloved hands shoved inside my coat, chin buried in my collar. By the time I'd managed to unfold my stiff body, pain shot through my knees, shoulders and fingers. I took one stumbling step forward and then another. A fox barked far off and nearer by a dog gave an answering woof. I shook my head, in a moment of déjà vu. I found my way back to the car and slept the night in it, curled up and miserable. I presented myself sorrowfully back at home the following day.

26

Cal

O N THE BEACH under the overhanging rock I pushed myself up out of my hole. I looked out towards the grey sea and let a roar out into the wind. Nothing could assuage my frustration.

Could I have prevented Marion from choosing death over life? She was exceptionally talented, both as a musician and a writer; better by far than me. That was one of the reasons I'd written the book in secret and rushed to submit it before she could submit hers. But she'd been honest, unlike me. She'd never have believed I'd betray her the way I did.

I fumbled for matches in my pocket, thinking of lighting a fire but something stopped the efforts of my trembling hands. I heard a sound. It may have been carried on the wind or it might just have been inside my own head but anyway I heard it as a call, a cry to action. *Cal...Cal.*

I felt impelled to follow it.

I hadn't been home in two days but I had my wallet and car keys safe in my coat. I needed to get to Leeds again. My time in the wilderness was over. I had to be there at the end, even if only as a sentry in the street outside.

I rose from the edge of my burrow under the cliff, climbed up to the path that led through the caravan park, quiet at this time of year. I wobbled on my feet, was filthy and smelt bad, but if I risked going inside my house I wouldn't be able to get away again. Lisa would have me in a hot bath, try to moisturize and massage me. Calming was all she knew how to do. Then it would be too late. So I stumped on unfeeling feet along the road, turning the car keys over and over in my hand.

Blackberry House was quiet and dark when I reached it. I slipped into the car as quietly as I could. If the noise of the engine woke my family, at least they'd know I was still safe, maybe stop Lisa worrying about me.

I drove in a dream, lightheaded from lack of food and all the thoughts that had drifted unfettered in and out of my head over the preceding two days. I stopped at a service station on the motorway to Leeds, washed myself as best I could. Then I drank coffee, handed over by a suspicious assistant. I must have looked like a wild man.

After that I drove through the city, the lights of my car just one bead in a moving necklace dangling through the dark. Traffic was still busy on the inner-city roads. The lines of lampposts created a further string of lights, hung under the upturned bowl of night sky. Far above them a few stars were bright enough to twinkle through the orange glow that lay beneath the true dark of nothingness.

Driving out of the other side of Leeds my hands loosened their grip on the steering wheel. Relief washed over me as my car purred through the housing estate and pulled into the lane that led off through farmland. I parked in the same place under the tall hedge as I had before, to begin my vigil. Lights remained on in the house all night long.

Sometime before dawn a powerful feeling surged through me. I pushed open the car door and stamped my feet on the road. Looking behind me into the car I saw the red clay imprint of my form on the driver's seat. Tears burned my sore eyes. I wondered how much of an imprint Maria's fragile body would leave on the sheets once she was taken away.

You're leaving me.

On foot I negotiated the path behind the row of houses, and waited at the back of the Fairchild garden.

When it happened, I swear the house moved. The walls became invisible: I could see the colour of her spirit as it shifted out of the spent body, moved upwards through the house. It bathed the young woman and her little son in an amber glow, wrapping itself around them in their bed at the top of the house. I saw our daughter smile in her sleep, and the child wriggled pleasurably.

Then the walls closed up, and all I could see was faint, pinkish smoke seeping out of cracks between window frames and brick, out of air vents and chimneys. It spread out, into all the elements that made up the atmosphere.

I tasted it and smelt it, felt droplets touch my skin; heard a sigh as it drifted past my face.

My body ached as I watched the last pale strands of Marion dissipate into everything.

27

Mariana

M Y MOTHER'S DIARY collection dated from the time she was about sixteen. Since Geraldine had placed the box on the kitchen table I hadn't been able to keep my hands off the books, carrying one of them around with me all the time. I sneaked in the reading of a few lines between pushing Gabe on the swing in the garden (*Look at me, Mammy, stop looking at the book!*) and helping Justine prepare the children's tea. I read more while I was supposed to be watching a cartoon on television with him in the Fairchild's rarely-used living room (the family had gathered in the kitchen) and had another reading bout after he'd fallen asleep during his bedtime story.

Each time I opened Maria's diary I had to prepare myself for suffering, something I'd never really been required to do before. It had taken the death of my birth mother to make me realise how easy my life had always been. I felt so bad for resenting her as long as I had, for judging her all those years. As I read my heart broke for the girl she had been, how displaced she'd felt in her own life. I wanted to befriend her in retrospect, go back and make things better, say it would be all right in the end.

But now I was also grateful that she'd chosen to put me in a safe place. She'd made the biggest sacrifice. Her mind had been all over the place – split between two lives. She'd attempted suicide three times; not because she didn't want to be alive but because her body and mind were at odds with each other. She said in the book that she hadn't even known she was harming herself. I understood now why she'd had to cut all ties with her previous life, and that included me. In doing so she'd made our eventual connection possible. If only I'd been told the truth earlier.

When I lifted my head from her neatly-written pages I felt as if I'd stepped through the back of a wardrobe. I'd returned from the past. I felt as if I, not her father, had said goodbye to her at the railway station in Leeds when she set off for her new life in London. She'd been recovering from a relapse of anorexia at the time, having kissed her baby (me) goodbye three months earlier. She'd won a playwriting competition and was going to work in a theatre in London with a new name, a reinvented identity and a small suitcase: a now childless young woman. It must have been so hard to pretend.

READING LATE INTO the night, I also learned from Maria's journals how much she had wanted my father. Through her words I saw another side of Cal. Alice had given me hints of his gentler, sometimes even humorous nature but I hadn't been able to take it on board until I read Maria's diaries.

She'd felt a deep empathy for him, a connection beyond the obsession of a young girl for an older man. I read about the evening they'd met at a live recording of a TV show – how she'd been impelled to go there and attract his attention. I read about the recognition she'd registered on first sight of both him and Sarah, not understanding it was to do with a somehow shared past. Then I read something which made my heart pound so hard I thought I'd have a heart attack. In scrawled, partly-obliterated handwriting she'd recorded:

I remember the day he told us he'd had his novel accepted for publication. It was a total shock, he'd never said anything about this before; he'd never even told Sarah or me about this particular novel at all. He'd been working on it secretly, in his room at night, while all the time he and I were preparing our 'first' novels simultaneously in our office, with Sarah acting as editor. He looked at me sadly after he'd made his announcement to the family. He said he'd just wanted to do something for himself, and by himself, for the first time ever. Later on he brought the manuscript to my room for me to read. He seemed anxious, his hands fluttering like moths. He said I wasn't to take it personally and I thought he meant about going ahead without me, until I read the novel. And then I understood what he'd really meant by that.

The text was almost illegible in places, scribbled through. Underneath, in a different coloured pen the girl who was then called Marianne had etched deeply into the page in large letters I DON'T UNDERSTAND WHAT THIS

MEANS!! But I did. It was evidence of what Alice had implied when she'd recounted her visions of the 'funny girl'. And also what Maria herself had struggled to tell me – she *had* been Marion Wilde in another life. Renaming herself as Maria Child and cutting all ties with her previous life hadn't stopped it from affecting what I now understood to be her second existence.

I remained sitting in the hollowed centre of the quilt in the dormer bedroom for a long time, my mother's book on my lap. Gabriel snored lightly at the top of the bed. I kept smoothing the pages of the diary, as though rubbing a genie's lamp.

⟫⟫⟫⟪⟪⟪

THE NEXT MORNING, Alice asked me to go back to Blackberry House with her for a few days and Geraldine encouraged it.

"I don't want you to struggle with your identity the way your mother did," she said. "It's all in the open now. I'm sure Audrey won't mind, I'll speak to her about it. She and Robert will always be Mam and Dad to you, I understand that, but it's equally important to acknowledge where you came from."

What a change of tune. Alice had told me Geraldine had refused to let Maria see Cal even though she'd wanted to.

"You're different," Geraldine said. "The man's your father, and the children he has with Lisa are your siblings. You *should* get to know them." She half-closed her eyes in the morning sun. Then she added, "I liked Aiden."

Alice gave me a wry smile.

THE DAY AFTER my mother's death was full of sunshine. Alice had stayed overnight on a sofa in the living room and we now sat around a table on the paved area overlooking the lawn. We ate croissants and drank coffee and tea. Justine was upstairs packing her children's things into two large suitcases, and Gabe was helping her, perhaps sensing that another change was afoot. Justine's husband had already taken their children home.

"She's been a godsend, Justine has." Geraldine sipped her tea delicately and gazed out over the garden. "I don't know what I'd have done without her."

She threw her other daughter a disparaging look. Charissa sat alone at the breakfast bar inside, insisting it was too cold in the garden.

"I gave that one everything when she was a child," Geraldine leant towards Alice and me. "Took her everywhere with me. Marianne, I could never get on with, and there's no excuse for the way I neglected Justine. And yet she's the one I'm closest to now."

Alice waited a polite moment then cleared her throat. "So will you come over to Pottersea with me?" She pressed a hand over mine on the smooth glass table. "I'll bring you and Gabriel back to Leeds for the funeral."

We held a short silence. The funeral was already organised for the following week. I'd arranged to take time off until after then and asked my boss to inform all my clients for me. I'd also telephoned my tutor at college and she had agreed to an extension on some work that was due in.

I pictured Mam's pursed lips at the thought of me spending time with my other family but Geraldine was right, it was important for me and for Gabe to understand where we came from. And I liked having family of my own. I was grown up now; Mam would just have to accept it. I crushed the thought that if I hadn't let Mam's feelings get in the way in the first place, I might not be in a state of mourning now.

"If you're sure, err, Lisa won't mind. I'll ask Gabe. But he already knows Angel and he'd love to see..." My voice trailed off.

"Aiden arrived home yesterday so Gabriel will be able to see him as well." Alice gave me a gentle smile. She started to load our empty cups onto the tray. Geraldine had been quiet since the funeral was mentioned, staring at the garden, her eyes reddening. "Excuse me." She got up suddenly and carried the tray into the kitchen.

Alice and I watched her leave. My throat ached.

"It's time you and Aiden sorted things out." Alice said. "Geraldine told me what nearly happened, but you didn't know the truth then. Now you're one of the family and that's an end to it."

My eyes grew wet and heavy. It was true; I needed to make things right with Aiden but there was still a dragging feeling in my belly when I thought of him. I didn't want to end up spending my life like my mother had, forever hankering after someone I couldn't have.

IN THE CAR on the way to Leeds Alice told me that Cal had disappeared from home. "I didn't want to mention it in front of Geraldine," she said. "She's only just holding it together as it is. Cal's not her problem."

We'd just got onto the M62. Gabe was asleep in his seat in the back, worn out from his adventures with his cousins, and I was grateful for his lack of questions today. It seemed impossible that only two days before we'd been in Geraldine's car, travelling to meet my mother for the first time. I'd never expected things to happen so fast – surely years must have passed between that journey and this one?

"I spoke to Mum on the phone and he still hasn't turned up." Alice engaged the handbrake while we waited at a busy roundabout. "But she said the car disappeared yesterday and she's assuming he took it."

"Why did she think that?"

Releasing the brake, Alice launched us into the flow of traffic. "She's known him most of her life. She's one of the few people who really understands him."

"Who are the others?" I fiddled with the catch of the silver bracelet I wore, one I'd made myself. I was still wearing the heart Aiden had given me on his last visit too, somehow it had helped during the past few days. I kept it tucked under my clothes.

"Well, I guess I do." I could see the flush creeping up her neck and flooding her cream-skinned cheeks. "There's a certain way you have to act with him. But the sad thing is his children can't cope with him. Angel's angry all the time and Aiden's indifferent. He tends to come home as little as possible. Cal *is* hard to live with, I admit." She gave me a shy glance. "But I hope you'll give him a chance, Mariana."

I felt loaded with responsibilities – to Cal, to Aiden. I was going to a strange place to stay with people I hardly knew and, at the same time, I had to come to terms with the death of a mother I'd only just accepted.

I heard a seagull cry in my head and it made me shudder. It was as if I was vibrating, breaking apart. The sensation of losing my grip caused panic to flap in my chest. *Take deep breaths.*

Maybe it was just the change of road surface under the wheels of the car. I needed to get hold of myself. Even so, I found my hands grasping the seat so tightly I had to loosen my fingers one by one. With a big effort I gasped in a lungful of air.

"Do you mind if I open the window a bit? I feel hot all of a sudden. I think…"

A sob pushed out of my throat. Alice whistled through her teeth and threw me a sympathetic glance. "Oh damn. I'm sorry for being so bloody insensitive. You've just been through a terrible trauma. A lot of traumas really, what with meeting your whole family all at once like that. And now I'm expecting you to do it all over again. Lord, how stupid can I get?" With her eyes on the road she fumbled in the well under the dashboard but her hand came out empty. She tutted with frustration.

"There are some tissues somewhere. Try the glove compartment on your side and help yourself if you can find them."

I found them and blew my nose.

"Are you feeling better?"

I could imagine Alice as the child she'd been, charming Cal out of the bad moods that seemed to be his trademark characteristic. I returned her smile. We'd come onto the A63, swinging around the deep curve of road under the vastness of the Humber Bridge. The car turned dark as we went underneath it. My stomach fluttered.

"Last stretch now," said Alice. The anticipation made my heart beat irregularly. *Aiden.*

Gabriel had woken up. Small feet knocked the back of my seat as he stretched, twisting in his restraints. Turning my head I saw his flushed face ready to scrunch up into a scowl of protest, but when he saw me there, ready, his blue-green eyes lit up with pleasure instead.

"Mammy."

"Gaby-baby." I used his old pet name, the one my friend Kayla invented.

He asked, "Are we going to Aiden's castle now?"

WE ARRIVED AT Pottersea after a slow drive on winding roads that led to the place where the river met the sea. A broad beam of sunlight lit up Blackberry House, slicing through a bank of grey cloud. Aiden had described the white-painted house to me in so much detail that I recognised it straight away. Beyond the building I saw a silver ribbon of water preceded by an expanse of mud, slick and smooth, crisscrossed with deep gullies. The mud reminded me of the dark clay we used for making beads in one of my jewellery classes.

The house's black-painted front door opened onto a small porch which led into a huge kitchen.

The woman I guessed to be Lisa turned from the sink as we entered. Drying her hands she came over and welcomed me warmly. I felt her anxiety, guessed it was to do with the fact that her husband – my father – had still not turned up. But she hid it well.

"Welcome to the family." She pulled me in for a second hug. "I'm so sorry for your loss. You look just like your mother. I was very close to her in…" It was weird how I knew she was thinking of Marion, not Maria. I gave her a complicit smile, which she started to return, before my son took her attention. Her hand flew up to her mouth.

"Oh Lord, he looks just like Aiden at that age."

She opened her arms, made cooing noises, but Gabe hid behind me, hanging onto the hem of my jacket. Then Aiden appeared at the top of the stairs which ran down one side of the kitchen wall. My real heart thudded, the little silver one I wore ticked at my throat.

Stay strong.

I heard Aiden take a deep breath when he saw me. He moved quickly down the stairs and walked straight towards me, flexing his fingers. I knew what an effort it must have been for him to act as casual as he appeared.

"Aiden!" shouted Gabe, barrelling between us. Aiden's eyes caught mine before he scooped Gabriel up in his arms, the hair on their heads blending. I glanced at Lisa, imagined her mentally framing this picture of her husband's son and grandson.

"Hello mate, how're ya doing? I've missed you, little

man."

I stepped forward, bravely pecked the air in the vague vicinity of Aiden's cheek.

"It's good to see you."

How prissy and formal I sounded, but at least we'd broken the ice that'd formed between us since our last encounter. And just as I started to move away, Gabe grabbed both our necks and forced our faces together. Surprising, the strength in such a small child.

"Kiss properly!"

My lips banged against Aiden's. In my rush to get away I backed into Alice, who was carrying in our bags. She took in the situation, dropped the bags and grasped my arm, moved me around while she pointed out where everything was. With sudden clarity it came to me that this was the very kitchen in which my mother had slit her wrists. I could practically see Alice as a child, hunched at the top of those stairs, screaming.

Blood pooled around my mother where she lay on the tiles, me inside her.

I was here then, too. I clung to the edge of a long table, feeling dizzy.

A FRIENDLY ARGUMENT went on in the background. Gabe hung onto his uncle with his legs and arms, staring fiercely at Lisa who looked desperate to get her hands on him. I moved back in their direction. "He's met a lot of new relatives over the last few days, I don't think he understands who everyone is."

Aiden gave me a smile. He encouraged Gabe to slide

down his body onto the floor, then he grasped my son by the shoulders as Gabe leaned back against his legs.

"Gabes," he said. "This is Lisa, she's my mum. You know that I'm your uncle, right?"

Gabe nodded solemnly, still pressing himself hard against Aiden. I could see the strain in his small body. But he scowled at me when he saw me looking, so I made a point of slipping back behind the table, staying within earshot.

"Well," Aiden said. "That means Lisa is one of your grandmas."

It was clever of Aiden to say one of them. Gabe would get that you could have several.

Once he'd assimilated this new information he was prepared to at least allow Lisa to shake his hand and kiss him on the cheek, even if his wiping the kiss off with a coat-sleeved arm afterwards was less than covert.

"Lord, he's adorable." Lisa said; fingers on her chin. "Do you want me to help you take your coat off, pet? We have some coat hooks under the stairs there, look. There are some just the right height for you. They were Aiden's and Angel's when they were little."

At the mention of her name my half-sister appeared at the back door, carrying a black cat. Gabe saw what she held and made a mewing sound in his throat. He hurled his coat on the floor and rushed towards the furry prize in Angel's arms.

"Gabriel…" I moved forward to make him pick it up, but Lisa stopped me with a hand on my arm.

"It doesn't matter, does it? Just this once," she said. "Let's allow him to settle in."

>>>>><<<<<

IT WAS TEA time when we all heard the sound of car tyres on the gravel.

"That boiled egg you're eating was laid by one of our own hens," Angel had just told Gabriel. He'd been out in the garden with her most of the afternoon, and she'd taken him to the stables at the house next door where an old pony and a retired seaside donkey lived.

"Mr Jim said he's going to get the saddle out for me tomorrow," Gabriel gave me a direct look, after ignoring me since he'd been reunited with Aiden and Angel. He took his time licking golden yoke from the edge of his hand. "And Angel's going to take me for a ride on Dodger." There was a *so there* tone to his voice. The fickleness of children.

"She hasn't had this much fresh air since she was Gabriel's age," Lisa leaned towards me to murmur under her breath about Angel.

When we all heard the car pulling in front of the house, tension threaded from one to another around the table. Picking up on it, Gabe grabbed my arm, his newfound independence apparently forgotten. Needing reassurance as much as he did, I pulled him onto my lap, his boiled egg abandoned.

Aiden and Angel assessed each other's reactions to the engine sound. Alice only sighed.

Lisa got up, wringing her hands together, an imploring look on her face. *It could be anyone. It might not be Cal. It could be the Police.* There could be terrible news. All those thoughts would have run through my head if I'd had a husband missing for four unexplained days.

My own mind raced with fear. If it *was* Cal, I'd have to face him again. He might rush at me, quoting *'Mariana'.*

Cal knew who I was now, though. What would he think of his new daughter?

A car door slammed. Lisa hurried to the small window between the office and the front door.

"It's him," her voice was sing-song. "He's back. *Oh Lord.*"

She flung open the front door and then the outer door of the porch. Butterflies battled in my stomach. I clutched Gabe to me.

"Mammy, stop it, you're hurting me again." He struggled off my lap and went to Aiden. Looking to me for permission, my half-brother put his arms out, moved his chair away from the table and hauled the boy onto his knees.

"Right, Gabes, you're about to meet another relative," he mumbled into my son's hair. "This one is a new granddad for you."

A BUMPING SOUND as the door was nudged back and Lisa drew a shambling figure into the room. We all stared, bewildered. It didn't look like the man I thought I was going to see. The others around the table seemed to struggle to recognise Cal as well.

Lisa's cheeks were wet, her face blurred. She pressed herself against the tall man's coat, dirty as it was. I felt hot in my chest. Their moment was intensely private, yet exposed and raw, and we were all watching. Cal's hair was uncombed, the skin of his face greyed, but I saw the coals of his eyes and they were familiar. It *was* him. This man. My father.

He hadn't noticed anyone except the woman holding him up. He let his shaggy head drop onto her shoulder, his eyes half-closed.

"She's dead," he moaned. "Jesus Lisa, she's fucking dead." A groan came out of him and it twisted my stomach to hear it.

"I know, my love," she murmured, stroking his filthy hair. "I know, I know."

28

LISA TOOK HIM straight to the bathroom, her hands supporting his waist as he lumbered upstairs. The rest of us may as well have not been in the room.

"Gross," said Angel after a bit. But I could see tears in her eyes, her gaze roved repeatedly over the table.

Gabe snorted. "Ghost," he spluttered. "She said it was a ghost!"

"That's not what she said, Gabriel. He's a poorly man, that's all. Lisa's going to make him better." I twisted the edge of the tablecloth into a point, cut the air with it. I couldn't help noticing the reddish footprints on the antique rug over which the man had walked, trailing away up the stairs. The sight made me feel hollow. Aiden murmured something to Angel, who was now crying into her sleeve.

"Are you going to finish your egg, Gabriel?" Alice broke the carapace of shock we were all enclosed in. "It may have gone cold by now. I can make you another one if you want. And we'll all have some more tea." She smiled brightly around the table as she got up to put the kettle on.

Angel grew quiet, began eating again, chewing in the same methodical way I'd noticed in Scarborough. I watched her pull a hunk of bread apart, spread butter on each piece and pop them into her mouth one by one.

"Are you all right?" Aiden had come to sit in the empty chair beside me. A sweet sadness bubbled in my chest. For the first time that day I looked fully into his eyes. I didn't know how to make what I felt into an acceptable kind of love, so I pulled away and placed Gabriel on my chair instead of me. I went to help Alice in the kitchen. From there I watched the chaos of a family happening in front of my eyes.

I understood its normality: people were surrounded by dramas: by love, anger and bitterness. My life had been too sheltered – something my birth mother planned with my best interests at heart. The past few days had been a revelation in family life and I felt a constrained excitement bubbling below the surface of my skin.

I DIDN'T SEE Cal until the next day. Lisa had run him a bath the night before and later she reported that he'd fallen into a deep sleep.

Gabe had asked to sleep in 'a boy's room' with Aiden. I said it was ok provided Aiden was prepared to take him to the loo at night. I was in bed by nine o'clock. The emotion of two families had overwhelmed me. A slow tide of grief had begun to come in and I had a premonition that the flow would only get stronger. I wanted to be alone when it happened. Alice showed me to a small room at the end of a corridor on the first floor, with a tiny en suite bathroom and a single bed.

"This used to be Angel's room," she offered in explanation for the one black wall. The other three were badly over-painted in a peachy colour. "Maria slept in here when she visited."

My mother brushed her hair at this mirror; slept in this bed.

Alice's mouth crumpled downwards.

"If I hadn't brought her here she might still be alive."

I could just as easily be blamed, I should have listened to Geraldine, not Mam. Right now I wanted to make Alice feel better. She'd known my mother much better than I had. "You said she was depressed and not eating. Remember you brought her here to try and cheer her up."

Alice sank onto the bed, her shoulders hunched. I sat down beside her. "I'm glad she had you," I said. "You were probably everything to her that I should have been."

"I can't believe she only died yesterday."

※》》※《《※

"I'M A BIG boy now," Gabe burst into my room, followed by Aiden who carried a mug of tea. "I cooked you a drink."

My child climbed onto the bed and started to bounce around. "Whoa," I said, steadying him with a palm on his back. When he'd slid down the wall onto his bottom, half-crushing my thigh as he fell, I said, wincing, "You certainly are big." I mouthed my thanks to Aiden as he placed the tea on the little cabinet beside the bed and backed out of the room with a smile.

"See you downstairs."

I rubbed my thigh and pondered. Maybe we *could* make it work.

"Wait for me," Gabe slipped off the bed before I could grab him for a kiss. I'd had to learn to share him over the past few days and our slow separation now seemed inevitable. He wriggled away and ran after his uncle. I pulled open the curtains and gazed out, thinking how this had been the view my mother saw when she woke up in this room that January morning.

I pulled one of Maria's journals out of the duffel bag; a random selection, from 1996. An established playwright by that time, it gave me a thrill to realise that she was quite famous in her world. For some reason it hadn't struck home until now.

There were reviews of one of her plays, *The Old Pathway*. It touched me to think of her carefully cutting the criticisms and accolades out, preserving them for the future. I wondered if she'd thought of me when writing the diaries, knowing I'd read them one day. *She wanted you to have them.* I pressed the marble-papered book close to my heart. Her death had started to hurt more, and I was glad.

I MET CAL at the bottom of the garden. I was leaning on the broken wall, looking out over the river. The tide was in and the rhythmic sloshing against stones on the strip of beach had lulled me into a dreamlike state.

He came up behind me, his footfall heavy on the paved path. I felt a bump against my arm, as if he'd tripped, then another arm appeared next to mine on the wall.

"Almost thirty years, I've admired that view." His voice was deep, calm. Not what I expected at all. His hands were large, dangled over the edge of the wall. For a moment I thought I'd turned into my mother, compelled to be close to him. The feeling was the opposite of the desire I'd had to get away from him the last two times we met. I shifted my feet on the sandy earth at the foot of the wall, not daring to turn my head towards him. My hot cheeks were shielded by a wall of hair. I cleared my throat.

"Did you have a nice sleep?"

He nudged his arm very gently against mine. "Kind of you to ask. I did, thank you. Shit few days, y'know. You?"

"Uhm yeah." I scrabbled around for something else to say. "I could hear the river from that room. It's nice."

Ineffectual, I know, but a conversation of sorts. Brambles pushed their way over the wall from the rough ground on the other side. I had this crazy idea of plunging my hand into them; suddenly wanted to rip my skin open.

I had no warning for the bout of crying that raged through my body then. I'd waited for it to happen during the night but it never did, thoughts of the days with Maria's family going over and over in my head. And I'd relived seeing Aiden again, and Lisa bringing Cal into the house. All those things. But the tide of grief for my mother hadn't broken until now.

I sensed Lisa watching from the top of the garden but didn't turn around to look. She was an angel, guiding us together. Alice's gentleness had come from her.

My shoulders shook. Cal stayed there, keeping me solid. This was Alice's Cal, not Angel's. *My Cal.*

I still didn't meet his eyes but I could feel his warmth through the woollen jumper he wore, pressed against mine in my jacket. He smelt clean, and in some way familiar.

29

Angel

B Y THE END of the new sister's first day at Blackberry House, Angel couldn't help herself. She was sick of *The Princess*. She'd hoped there would be a special relationship between them, especially since it was Angel who'd been the one to kind of get them all together. She'd made the effort to give Mariana's phone back to her after all. It wasn't fair how Mariana now had everybody wrapped round her little finger (or more likely tangled up in that over-the-top hair). Aiden fawned all over her, made her constant cups of tea, and of course assumed the *Very Important* role of looking after Gabriel. Mum practically followed Mariana around carrying her bloody hair like a sycophantic bridesmaid. It was perverse: the girl was her husband's *bastard* daughter, for God's sake. Alice, well, she played her usual sweetness and light act, enough to rot her teeth; sugar and spice and all that.

Yeah, she knew she wasn't really being fair. When it came down to it, all Mariana had to do was exist. She hadn't begged anyone for their attention. *And she does have a cute kid.*

But still. To cap it all, Dad finally turned up when they were having tea, after Angel – yeah, *Angel*, had worried herself sick about him for four days. As if he'd only been waiting for Mariana to arrive to make it worth coming home.

Angel had *never* been good enough for him. Maybe she should have changed her name to a character in a poem, let her hair grow back natural. Turn herself into bloody Rapunzel for him. He'd have preferred her like that, if his attitude towards Mariana was anything to go by.

Cal had hardly spoken to his *real* daughter. He was strangely calm now, considering the state he was in when he arrived home the day before, but from past experience this could precede a storm. Angel watched, a hot tide washing through her, as her father walked down the garden to Mariana. *The Princess* stood at the back wall, hair hanging down like a cloak. Dad wore leather sandals over a thick pair of socks, his customary at-home winter and spring footwear. Angel clenched and unclenched her hands, wanting to resist the compulsion to stand there, being left out of everything as usual, but unable to move.

As he planted one foot firmly on the ground before lifting up the next, each step her dad took looked painful. He'd been out in the cold for three nights, Angel winced on his behalf. And yet she knew if he turned back to her now, said something nice to her, she'd probably only throw it back in his face. What was *wrong* with the two of them? No wonder her dad was giving Mariana a try. Angel had heard Mum encouraging him to start a conversation with his dream daughter. Maybe Lisa realised he'd do better with Mariana than with Angel. She wished she'd stuck by Mariana's side from the time she arrived, then she could have been part of the *great reunion* with Cal. But Alice had seemed to be the one Mariana trusted.

She watched as Dad reached the patch of gravel beside his studio. She saw him put his hands out in front of him as if he wanted to reach Mariana sooner than his feet would take him. Angel didn't see her half-sister turn to face Cal, but it looked as though they were having a conversation, something Angel wasn't much used to with her dad.

She finally made herself move and went upstairs to the little room that used to be hers, nervous in case Mariana would notice she'd been in there. The room housed a bookshelf full of her father's novels. She'd read many of them as a young teenager, when she was actually *interested* in his work, but one of them her mum had advised her not to. Angel had trusted Lisa's judgement at the time because she didn't usually censor her reading at all. But she picked up the book now.

The Shell, Cal's very first novel.

30

Cal

ALL MY SENSES had sharpened, feelings so jagged it hurt to put my feet on the ground. I felt in front of me as I reached the end of the garden. A strange, pinkish glow around the edges of my vision meant I couldn't see clearly anymore. The smoke or essence of Marion had insinuated herself inside me so we could look at Mariana together. She, Marion, had always wanted to be a part of what she called 'The Everything'. Now she was a part of me again.

I'd almost forgotten the girl was Maria's child, not Marion's. Maria/Marianne: she'd only ever been a conduit to the missing part of me. I stumbled, fell against the wall; straightened my body before leaning my arms on the bricks next to Mariana. Peace such as I hadn't known for a long time descended on me. The questions that had haunted me since Marianne slit her wrists, and the question from later, when I first spotted this girl who stood beside me now, had all been answered. The pieces had slotted neatly together and the mystery was solved. If I'd not been so exhausted I would have felt euphoric.

The girl started crying in an intense, held-in sort of way. I moved my elbow closer to hers on the wall but I didn't presume to touch her with my hands. Something sprinkled all around us, not wet or dry, neither cold nor warm. Invisible, just a feeling, but I was sure she could feel it too. We stood together a long time, hardly speaking.

31

Angel

SOMETHING BUGGED HER. In the early hours of the morning Angel descended the attic steps, quietly, so as not to wake Alice who slept in the library at the end of the attic corridor. Closing the door softly at the bottom, Angel moved along the landing until she was standing outside her parents' bedroom.

GABRIEL HAD HAD a massive tantrum the night before. Suddenly he hated Aiden and only wanted his mother. Angel couldn't help feeling smug at the sight of Aiden's face. That'd teach him to think he was *Mr Perfect* – (*Why are you being such a bitch, Angel?*)

After spending about an hour in the garden with Mariana the afternoon before, Dad had come back into the house. Angel had seen Mariana go out of the gate onto the river beach. She must have taken a long walk because Angel didn't see her again until that evening. Maybe that was why Gabriel had the tantrum, because his mother had deserted him.

Dad went straight upstairs after the garden encounter, acknowledging Angel only with a raised eyebrow. (She wished she'd offered him a smile in return, now.) He looked paler than she'd ever seen him, drained of himself. Her heart ached. *Dad.* She'd almost hoped he'd make one of his sarcastic comments about the fact she was taking another loaf of bread out of the oven. *"Are those the only two things you ever do; make bread and eat bread?"* he'd asked her once.

Angel saw how he dragged himself up the stairs, hanging onto the banister with both hands. She heard his bedroom door close with a soft thud. Shortly after that Mum came in through the front door with a bag of shopping from the village store, Gabriel trotting after her. She'd finally won the boy around.

"Take your coat off, pet." She seemed to have accepted him as her grandson. To Angel she said "Was that your father?"

"Yeah." Using a folded tea towel as an oven glove, Angel upturned the bread tin and tipped the loaf onto the board. She then turned to her mother and shuffled her feet on the tiles, her usual awkward self.

"Was he outside all that time? Did they…?"

"I don't *know* what they did, Mum. I wasn't just standing there watching them you know, I do have other things to do."

Lisa gave her a gentle smile. She lowered the shopping onto the table. "I'm sorry love. It's all a bit much, isn't it?

Thanks for making the bread. I don't know what I'd do without you. But you do need to get back to college tomorrow. Don't worry about anyone else."

Even Aiden had taken several days off work. Cal disappearing and Mariana arriving had altered the pattern of everything. This week had been a sort of limbo, leading to the funeral of Mariana's mother. Angel got the feeling the family had gathered around as sentinels, only she couldn't quite get in place.

For once they didn't all sit down together at the table for tea. Lisa laid out a buffet and everyone took what they wanted in dribs and drabs. Angel had to admit it was nice having all the people around. Mariana seemed to be making a point of praising Angel's bread, which she supposed was kind, since it wasn't her best effort.

A few of the family watched TV in the living room for a while during the evening. Gabriel, hiding himself behind the red velvet curtains at one of the tall windows, got excited at the view of the thin sliver of sea in the distance and Angel found herself offering to take him to the beach the next morning. She *would* go into college in the afternoon, hand in an essay that was overdue, she really must.

Then Gabriel got overtired and had his tantrum. After that everyone went to bed early.

Up in her room, Angel read all the way through *The Shell* and had managed only about an hour's sleep. When she woke up she felt disorientated for a minute. Confused about where she was. For the first time in about four years she no longer felt angry with her father.

Wow. It was a strange release, an actual, active feeling of

non-anger. It pressed painfully on her heart. She suddenly understood how alike they were, she and her dad, because she'd finally read his book, the first one he wrote. Written at such a young age, she could imagine herself having written something like that, so uncompromising it was chilling.

She thought of Dad standing at the bottom of the garden with Mariana, their two figures looking so comfortable together, and she realised that she and her dad repelled each other because they were identical poles of two magnets. Maybe Mariana was the opposite pole to both of them: the thing that could be their connecting point.

But why did she have such a bad feeling?

So ANGEL NOW stood outside her parents' bedroom door, bare feet curling into the thick carpet on the landing. She wanted to be close to her dad.

She sensed that time was running out.

32

Cal

I FELT AS if I'd slept for hours. That night Lisa didn't get up in the dark. Catering for all the extra people must have worn her out. She found it hard to admit age had started to take its toll on her, was happiest when surrounded by family. She loved having a thousand jobs to do. I was glad for her that our family had expanded; she'd have plenty to keep her mind busy.

I'd enjoyed the awareness of her body nestled against me through the fog of my dreams. When I did awake, her being there made it easy to sink back into sleep again. Once in the night a seagull's cry rang through the dark.

I knew I was being called.

The pink smoke still filled my head even as I buried myself in sleep. It hovered at the back of my nose, a sweet, burnt taste. Marion's insinuations flooded my dreams, reminded me of all my mistakes. But there was no need to fight the demons any longer.

I awoke again and sensed a presence in the hall outside my room.

Marion?

It all made sense, such perfect sense at last. Colours sparkled and fizzed in my brain, loose connections that had flapped around for years reattached themselves.

I found myself looking into a universe of wonder. Then, one by one, the intense colours died down. With a deep sense of calm I drifted back to sleep.

IT WAS STARTING to get light when I slipped out of bed.

All the fuss I'd made over the years, all the drama I'd created from insignificant incidents, the hard times I'd given my children, I carried it gently in my arms. I didn't want to leave it in the bed with Lisa.

My wife stretched and resettled into the space I'd vacated. She let out a soft grunt, then her breathing settled again into a peaceable snore. Peering through the early morning gloom into the scratched mirror on the wardrobe door I saw myself haloed in pinkish smoke, my arms full of nothing.

MY STOMACH ROILED and my head prickled. I tested my footsteps on the unstable floor, bent to pick Lisa's jumper up. I hugged it for a moment before pulling it on over the long-sleeved t-shirt I'd gone to bed in the afternoon before.

It was fitting that I should be wearing her jumper. *Take her with me.* My jeans were half-under the bed; I extracted them as quietly as I could. Lisa seemed to be in a deep sleep.

I ignored the pain in my chest and gathered my thick socks, collected my wool jacket from the back of a chair.

I allowed myself a final, lingering glance at my wife; then I left the room.

THE JANUARY MORNING that had started all this… I'd left the house in the biting cold, pulled towards the beach by my compulsion to find my own soul; pulled apart inside by myriad emotions. It was Maria I'd discovered at the end of my walk. That seemed a lifetime ago now. But I'd had too many chapters in my life, and I was tired. At last the pieces had been laid end to end; there were no gaping holes anymore.

I LEFT BLACKBERRY House through the front door. Crossing the road I couldn't resist looking up at the building that had sheltered me for twenty-eight years. …And I saw Angel in one of the living room windows, looking down at me; her hands on the glass. Funny that she should have been the one to see me off.

My heart wanted to swoop up to her. Vague memories intruded into my present: I'd arrived home to find Lisa had given birth to her in my absence, midwives buzzing around; the hurt look from my wife at me not being there, an alien baby in her arms.

I should have been there for you. For both of them. But I wouldn't allow the impulse to translate into emotion. Instead I lifted my hand and gave Angel a wave, an apology of sorts. *She'd understand.*

I knew that, suddenly.

Sure enough, she waved back. I couldn't see the expression on her face through the dark of the morning and all that pink smoke, but I understood what she was doing. My little girl, the one with a soul as dark as mine, was bearing witness as I walked away from our home for the last time.

33

Mariana

FUNNY HOW SOMEONE so small could take up so much room in the single bed with me. Gabe wriggled like a mole in a tunnel. He made a loud yawning noise, exposing the pink inside of his mouth.

"I'm ready to get up, Mammy."

He pushed open the curtains and gave me a running commentary on everything he could see. Then he stopped to take a noisy breath and let it back out again. "What's for breakfast?" he wanted to know next.

"I don't know," I said. "Toast…Or maybe porridge."

He let out a bellow of laughter, as if I'd made the funniest joke. "Silly Mammy, you know I hate porridge." It was news to me; he hadn't the week before.

I wanted him to put his slippers on but he refused. Bouncing down the corridor in front of me as I stumbled, rubbing my eyes, he decided he was no longer hungry and asked if he could watch TV instead. Wearily, I pushed open the living room door and he jumped in before me. Light from the two tall windows hit me in the face and I stood, dazzled. It took me a moment to realise Angel was in there, hunched in an armchair, listing slightly to one side. In her greyish nighty she looked inanimate. Gabriel said, "Aunty!"

He trotted over and leaned against her knees, drawn up in the chair. Her hand moved up and down his arm but she didn't look at him, or at me. Gabe didn't seem to care. His hair stood up in clumps and his soft white belly showed between his pyjama top and bottoms. My stomach clenched, he seemed the only safe thing left. The haloed figures of my son and my half-sister created a silhouetted tableau as I stared at them. I'd drifted into a reverie, caught in the spell of their inaction. But Angel broke it.

"He's gone."

Her breath disturbed dust-motes, they danced in the rays of light.

"Pardon?"

She pushed the fringe off her face and revealed reddened eyes, blew her nose. My heart sank. *What now?*

"I've been up for about four hours already."

Don't give me that helpless look.

The carved wooden clock on the mantelpiece said it was eight o'clock. *Damn*, I wished I'd stayed in bed. I hovered at the door while Angel busied herself with scrunching up a sorry-looking tissue in one hand. She used her other to wipe her nose again. *Go and wash your hands*, I'd have said if she'd been Gabe. *And put some clothes on.* She looked a mess. Still, she *was* my younger sister. "You've been up since four?"

"Yeah. I couldn't sleep, and then…"

And then nothing, apparently. Glass rattled in the windows. Across the road a line of trees bent and dipped, a wind was getting up. My back ached. Gabe came towards me and grabbed my hand, pulling me down onto the sofa beside him. He'd found the remote control and worked out how to put the TV on.

Angel was giving me a pathetic stare, so eventually I had to give in and ask, "Are you ok?"

"Not really."

So what did she want me to do about it? Without makeup she looked vulnerable. I felt a bit sick, I didn't want her neediness; I was tired as it was. *My* mother had died, I needed comfort more than Angel. But she didn't seem to think so.

"…I saw Dad going out early this morning and I didn't do anything and now I feel guilty. I've got this … this really horrible feeling."

"What about?"

It was Aiden, leaning against the doorframe, scratching his chest. His mouth opened in a yawn that made me look away. He wore grey jogging bottoms and a white t-shirt, and his feet were bare. Angel pushed herself out of the chair.

"Aiden, oh, shit…"

He glanced at me with what I interpreted as a smug look and dangled his arm around Angel in such a casual way it made my sinuses prickle. They *knew* how to *be* together, it wasn't fair. I sat on my own and they moved together to the window and stood looking out.

Gabe's attention was fixed on the TV so I focussed my

gaze on the soft curve of his cheek, staring out the threat of tears.

"What's up, chuck?" I heard Aiden say in a growly voice.

Through a lot of sniffs and sobs, Angel eventually revealed that she'd seen Cal leaving the house. She was convinced he wasn't coming back. She'd been afraid to wake her mother because that would have made it *real*, the fact she was never going to see him again.

It all sounded rather melodramatic. But Aiden took it in. He tightened his arm around her and murmured sweet platitudes.

GABE SUDDENLY ANNOUNCED (again) that he was hungry. I wondered if I could possibly summon up the energy to stir myself and sort him out with breakfast. He tapped my arm repeatedly with the remote control and it wouldn't be long before I lost my temper. Aiden turned from the window, his arm slipping off Angel's shoulder.

"Hey, Gabe," he said. "D'you fancy helping me make some pancakes?"

Gabriel gave me a mean look which I knew wasn't his fault, he'd been so messed-about the previous few days, but it still hurt. He jumped off the sofa straight away and ran over to Aiden.

It isn't too late to build a proper family relationship, I thought. We'd only kissed, me and Aiden, just the once. Maybe the attraction, that spark that'd passed between us the first time we met was because we should always have known each other. I tried the concept again in my head, *he's my brother.*

Angel's face brightened as well. She wiped her nose with the same tatty piece of tissue. "I love pancakes."

Aiden and I glanced at each other. Angel had a red nose, last night's mascara smeared all over her face but at least she was looking more cheerful. "I know you do," Aiden said, winking at me. "Apart from *bread* they're your favourite food, aren't they?"

"Fuck off about the bread," Angel said. "You sound like Dad." Her eyes flickered to Gabriel. "Shit, I shouldn't have sworn, should I?"

"Angel *swore*, Mammy." Gabe jumped up and down, chuckling hysterically. That got a smile out of me at last. "Go on, you," I said. "Go and help Uncle Aiden make the pancakes. I'll see you in the kitchen, yeah?"

➤➤➤✦◀◀◀

WHY HADN'T MY half-brother and sister always been in my life? Maybe my mother should have handed me over to Cal if she couldn't cope. Then I pictured Lisa dealing with two tiny babies, one of them not her own. She probably wouldn't have appreciated the gift. But I wished things had been different, somehow. If I could have had my *real* family as well as Mam and Dad.

Now I felt my cheeks burn with guilt.

In the kitchen, Gabe laughed as he broke eggs with Aiden. I wondered if Aiden had ever done anything like that with our father. I watched my son and my brother tip mixture into the pan, place the finished pancakes under the grill to keep warm. Gabe's face was flushed and he kept giggling, but through the glaze of fun I spotted bleakness in his eyes. There would be a backlash for all the disruption he'd endured over the past few days and I hoped I wasn't going to be on my own with him when it happened. Yet I couldn't imagine being back at the house in Scarborough where I'd been raised with Mam and Dad either. It all seemed so far away.

We heard Angel clattering down the stairs. She'd made an attempt to drag a comb through her hair and had put on jeans and a long black jumper with a bee on the front, stretched out of shape either by years of wear or the way she kept rolling the bottom of it up over her pointy elbows. She stood next to Aiden, still with faint mascara stains under her eyes, and a needy air. When she asked Gabe for a hug he was reluctant. Finally he allowed her to put her arms around him but he kept his body stiff and appeared relieved when she let him go.

"Shall I get some more plates out now, Aiden?" He'd attached himself to his uncle; maybe because he didn't have many day-to-day male role models in his life.

"Sure thing, mate, but be careful with them, yeah? We don't want any breakages, do we?"

My little boy responded with another peal of slightly hysterical giggles. Aiden wiped his hands on a tea towel before going over to the laundry shelves under the stairs. Finding a face flannel, he handed it to Angel, mimed wiping it under his eyes. "The panda look," he explained. "It went out in the sixties."

Angel mimed "Eff off!" but her lips twisted in a small

grin. She moved to the sink and turned on the hot tap, squeezed the flannel under it and rubbed beneath her eyes. "Seriously, Aid," she said, (I pulled my eyes away from the blackened flannel she'd left at the side of the sink). "I'm really, really worried about Dad. I can't explain this feeling I got when I saw him walking away earlier. But I *know* he's not coming back." She turned to give me a pleading look as well as Aiden. "You've got to listen to me."

Her face was raw. I got a twinge of fear in my stomach. What if my newfound father had really disappeared for good this time?

34

Angel

S HE COULDN'T SHAKE off the feeling it was her fault. Yet she'd seen the look in her dad's eyes when he glanced up at her, as if to say *don't tell anyone*; a special moment between them. Then he just turned and walked away.

I ought to have woken Mum. Made her get up, made her stop Dad from leaving. Mum is the only person he would've listened to.

It's not fair. Angel had been Cal's daughter her *whole* life, but he'd been indifferent to her and she'd been horrible to him the past few years. But now that she'd read *The Shell*, she understood him better. *The Princess* might have the long red hair and look just like Marion, but Angel was *truly* like *him*, they were the same inside. She blinked back tears.

ANGEL PICKED AT the knotted woollen feelers of the bumblebee on her jumper. She'd had it, like, forever. She'd first worn it to a reading of her dad's single attempt at teen fiction, at the library in Hull a couple of years back. Angel had attended with her class from school, and was embarrassed because it was her dad. She'd begged Lisa to write her an absence note (Lisa had refused). But it turned out she enjoyed the attention from the other students afterwards, asking if she could get them Cal's autograph and stuff like that. It had been fascinating to see *Callum Wilde* through the eyes of other people for a change. For the first time she clearly saw the disparity between what people thought he was and his real battle with self-doubt and depression.

AFTER THEY'D HAD pancakes, Gabe asked if he could go outside in his pyjamas and look at the chickens and Angel had said he could as long as he was careful not to startle them; they wouldn't lay if he did. The little monkey danced about all over the place while Mariana tried to wipe the syrup off his face. The chickens would just be waking up, Angel explained. She told him that later, they'd let the chickens out into the garden. But she had a bad feeling all the time she was saying it, as if it wasn't really going to happen.

Once Gabe had gone outside (walking with exaggerated tip-toe steps), Mariana asked Angel what they should do about him. The three of them planned to go out and get Cal back before it was too late. Maria, the woman who'd been making Dad crazy, she was dead now, so if they could find him, her dad could finally let go of his obsession. They could all settle down into being a family.

Maybe it was normal to be jealous of your more confident big sister.

"What do you mean?"

"I don't want to take him out with us. I don't want him to pick up on our panic."

Panic… So Angel wasn't alone in feeling that way.

FOR SOME REASON Lisa had slept in much later than usual that morning.

"Don't wake her," Alice said. She'd come into the kitchen while Angel and Mariana were sitting there, elbows on the table, worrying. Gabe had come back in and run upstairs to Aiden. "She's been looking exhausted lately. Cal's shenanigans have really taken it out of her. Let her sleep as long as she wants to." Alice fetched herself a mug from the cupboard above the fridge. The branches of the mug tree on the table were empty, all the crockery languishing in the sink. "Has Cal come back from his walk, yet? I heard a noise early this morning and I assume it was him going out." She took the empty milk jug from the table and refilled it from the bottle in the fridge. "Cat got your tongues, you two?"

A blackbird sang loudly in the garden. Angel looked up to see it hopping down to the ground outside the open back door. It cocked its head and peered in, then stabbed the ground with its beak, took off again, wings flapping, a thick worm dangling. Its shadow trailed the ground in the wake of its flight. When Angel brought her gaze back into the room she caught Mariana's eye.

"What?" Alice held the milk jug aloft. She frowned and sat down at the table next to Mariana. "What are you two plotting?" She laughed as if everything was normal. "So this is what it's like to have a pair of little sisters. Ganging up on me, are you both?"

The blackbird chattered angrily from a tree. Maybe another bird had stolen its worm. An MOD Land Rover sped past the front of the house. Angel tensed, but it was heading away from the sea, not towards.

"No, really," Alice persisted. "What's the matter?"

"Will you look after Gabriel for a bit?" Angel said.

"Why? What's the matter?"

"Nothing," Angel said, pulling the bumblebee feelers straight. "Mariana and me and Aiden, we're just going off to explore, that's all. We want to show Mariana around. Might be a bit far for Gabriel." Her voice trembled. "He likes the chickens." She tried to keep her hands still. Mariana had got up to do some washing up, clinking mugs on the draining board. Alice's frown deepened.

"Well you're obviously keeping something from me, but if you want me to look after Gabriel, I will. Is that what you want, Mariana?"

"I would appreciate it," Mariana said from the sink. "Thank you." Angel caught the glance she threw her. Small feet thudded down the kitchen stairs. Gabe appeared wearing jeans and a long-sleeved t-shirt and his plimsolls with Velcro fasteners. "I got dressed quicker than Aiden," he announced. Everyone looked at him. It made him curl in on himself. Angel watched him sidle over to Mariana and press himself against her legs until she dried her hands and picked him up. "You are quick, aren't you?" She nodded at Alice who was pouring coffee. "Alice said she'll look after you while Mammy goes out and does some things with Aiden and Angel. That's nice of her, isn't it?"

It was sweet how she leaned her cheek against the boy's face. Gabe clutched her tighter. "I don't want you to go out without me."

⇥⟫⟫⟪⟪⇤

CHILDREN ARE SO helpless, they don't really have a say in anything.

"I know you don't, honey," Mariana says. "But it won't be for long."

Gabe whines and tangles his hands in his mother's hair. His wet mouth is poised against her neck but he stops just short of biting. "Ouch!" yells Mariana. "Don't do that…" She grasps his fingers and unclenches them from her hair, pushes his face gently away from her neck with the palm of her hand. He goes limp and sinks against her.

"You're always leaving me," he says. His face is wet. Tears bloom in Mariana's eyes and I feel sorry for her.

"Gabriel," Alice says softly. She approaches from behind Mariana's shoulder, facing the boy. "Would you like to come out and collect eggs with me? You have to hold them ever so carefully so they don't break. They'll be lovely and warm from the chickens' cosy bedrooms. Do you think you can be careful enough?"

His eyes open wide then narrow slyly. Slowly, he lets go of his mum. He kicks his legs slightly and she lets him slide to the floor. Alice gets him to take her proffered hand. He looks back up at his mother, rubbing his eyes with his spare fist.

"You can go," he says coldly to her. "I'm going to collect eggs with Alice." His fierce expression says 'I don't need you after all'.

It must be horrible to be torn apart by a whole load of different feelings for your child. I feel I ought to comfort Mariana, somehow.

35

Mariana

THERE'S A STRONG breeze out here, but even then it barely lifts the weight of my hair. I might have it cut. Imagine the lightness I'd feel. I don't know why I've held on to this burden for so long. I'm not my hair. I don't need that definition any more.

I'm a girl, a woman, a mother, a *sister*. I'm a daughter, twice over. My hair is not *me*. I'm not Rapunzel, needing hair to reel in a prince.

I'm not a princess.

I toss my head as much as I can with the heaviness dragging me down. We walk quickly, Angel, Aiden and I, in step with one another. Without Gabe clinging to my hand I feel like the child I never got the chance to be with my siblings. I'm no longer alone, an 'only one'. I miss Gabe but I also feel lighter without him.

Angel keeps sniffing.

Aiden glances between us. The intensity of the feelings I had for him have turned into another kind of bond that Angel makes possible. I'm one of three.

Our footsteps play different tones on the uneven tarmac. Angel's wearing heavy boots that announce themselves emphatically each time they hit the pavement. I'm wearing lightweight ankle boots that make an apologetic tapping sound. Aiden's rubber-soled deck shoes suck away from the ground each time he lifts his feet. Every sound and sensation is sharpened. We've been walking the same stretch of path forever.

At an L-bend in the road we all pause.

A narrow stretch of mudflats shines in the intermittent morning sun. The tide's coming in. Soon the rest of the mud will be covered in water. Further to our right are the sea-marshes. A path winds through them, eventually leading over a high bank to the edge of a low cliff. Beyond that is the beach. I know because I took that path yesterday, after I'd had my first conversation with my father. I wanted to visit the place where Alice told me he discovered Maria early one morning in January.

I made a pathetic cairn there with thick grey pebbles.

Angel and Aiden look at each other and then at me. "What do you think?" asks Aiden. At the same time Angel says, "Which way do you want to go?"

I don't know.

Cal Wilde left his home of almost thirty years this morning and he's never coming back, I feel it now as strongly as Angel.

My mouth feels dry. Without even realising I'm about to, I link my arm through Angel's. She gives me a hint of a smile but she pulls away, loosening her arm. I let go. She gets one of her tattered tissues from the sleeve of her incongruous jumper and blows her nose. When she's finished she stuffs the damp tissue back up her sleeve and gestures with a long-fingered hand. "Let's go down to the beach that way, to start with."

We're taking the road route. She marches ahead. Aiden and I fall into step beside each other. "Thanks for being kind to Angel," he whispers. I feel my first sense of entitlement. I'm not doing it as a favour to him. *She's my sister, too.*

I think he senses my indignation, because he nudges me as we walk. I recognise his playful behaviour from the days we spent getting to know each other, but I push aside those memories. I don't feel playful right now. I fix my eyes on the bee-stripes on the back of Angel's jumper. Pressure builds up, tightens my breathing. I've got a familiar prickling under my skin, something to do with the two seagulls flying overhead. They soar above us and my skin stretches, threatens to burst open, to release my pounding heart.

"Are you all right?" Aiden asks. I count breaths slowly. My vision's jagged around the edges. Angel hesitates in front of me and I almost trip up. She mutters an apology.

We pass a tiny church on our left. A sign by the gate informs us that services are no longer held. The hedge is overgrown and thorny; I spot a small brown animal disappearing into a minute tunnel in the straggling grass at the bottom. I imagine the safe, dark space it's entering and wish I could go there. Catching Angel's eye as she turns her head I think she's seen the little creature, too. We're all aware that the three of us are entering a different kind of tunnel and I can't picture what's going to be at the other end. I believe her, now.

"Come on," says Aiden. "What are you two waiting for?"

Fields spread out on our left behind the hedge and on the other side of the road too. Angel pulls back so that we can walk alongside each other. Aiden steps onto the road because the path isn't wide enough for all three of us. Our breath puffs into the air, Angel's the loudest. I don't think she's used to walking the distances I am, and Aiden goes to the gym regularly. An MOD car appears from nowhere and rushes past, headlights blazing even though it's broad daylight. "What the…?"

"The Ministry of Defence has got a base on the point," Aiden explains. "They're always rushing around like that. Think they're in an action film or something."

The sense of foreboding I've picked up from Angel grows.

At the crossroads, the entrance to the caravan park is on our left. The road that leads up the spit of land dividing the river from the sea is on our right. Straight ahead is the sea. I tilt my head. The sonic boom of waves crashes in my brain. The ground rocks. But Angel and Aiden have already crossed the road and they're making for the beach. I follow them, unsteadily.

Angel's straggly black hair whips against her cheeks, caught by the sea breeze. She looks pale and scared. We all pause, acknowledging what we're here for. *To search for our father.*

"Come on," Aiden says.

He walks in front of us, and we follow him to the edge of the sea.

36

Angel

THE THREE OF us spread out along the beach, Mariana to my right and Aiden to the left. I feel safe with them both here. Waves hurtle on the shore, greedy; they want feeding. I scan the beach. *Please* – nothing, no human presence apart from me and my siblings. Where does Dad go on his walks? We've *always* been the ones to worry about him, never the other way round – I think.

We keep walking up and down, glancing repeatedly at the swirling brown water, and further out, the turquoise waves that keep crashing inwards, dumping cream-coloured froth on the beach. Shells and pebbles glisten along the waterline. The breeze strengthens. I jam my hands under my arms; turn one way to locate Mariana and the other to see Aiden. They're both wandering as aimlessly as me. This is getting us nowhere. The sun comes out suddenly and a shadow trails across the sand, two shadows, separating for half a second before joining together again. A cry rings out, haunting and spectral. The seagulls dip to the surface of the sea, twist around each other, flying apart but always re-joining. I start shivering.

HE'S NOT HERE. *Fuck and damn*. I wasn't stupid enough to think it'd be easy but I was hoping, just hoping Dad might have been mooching along the beach, shoulders hunched against the breeze, hands shoved in his pockets. He'd be muttering, or maybe humming some tune he's obsessed with. That's how I've seen him before when I've watched him leave the house – but I can't see him anywhere now. There aren't any footprints either, apart from ours, though they could've been washed away before we arrived. I should have followed him. Whatever happens… it'll be my fault. *Oh, God*.

The sun glitters on the waves as they rush in, hurling themselves on the gritty sand. They lay their leopard-patterned foam in front of us like a welcome carpet. *No*. I turn the other way, examine the crumbling cliffs. Their concrete innards have tumbled onto the dry sand at the top of the beach. The cliffs have no more secrets to give up. *Where is he?*

The sea voices bellow then whisper, shushing their own noise. They fizzle to silence before starting all over again.

Dad's gone, I just know it.

37

Mariana

THE HORIZON IS blurred and hazy, with hardly any definition between sea and sky. A small boat rocks and sways on the undulating surface of the ocean, it seems to have come from the mouth of the river, probably belongs to a fisherman. I saw a few similar boats out on the river during my walk yesterday.

I walk up and down at the water's edge. The sea is like boiling soup, glittering salt-crystals on the waves. I put up my hand to shield my eyes. I can't see the boat anymore, it must have drifted too far out, obscured by the rising humps of water, the dark shadows that precede them; the shimmering, sparkling light. It dazzles me so that I don't know what I'm looking for.

I don't know what else we're supposed to do. He could be anywhere. I feel as if I've let Angel down. A voice shouts. I turn and see Aiden waving his arms, gesturing for us to

305

gather together. I think we're going back to the house.

WE WALK BACK home along the beach, past the part where the old road ends. Giant hunks of concrete form castles on the sand and if I'd been their childhood sister we would probably have played in them together. We find the place where the cliffs are low enough to climb up. I spot my cairn from the corner of my eye and wonder if I'll have to add to it.

The clay's too slippery and red stains my jeans as I try to climb up. Angel and Aiden are better at it than me. Angel reaches down to help me and Aiden pushes the base of my back. From the top we look out to sea again and I think I can see the boat I spotted earlier. The distant waves gather in a high bank before crashing down. They begin with a dark line on the water and I'm not sure if the rocking horizontal shape, much further out than it appeared to be before, is just the beginning of a wave. I start to say something but my tongue sticks to the roof of my mouth.

"Let's go back," Aiden says. "You never know, he might be at the house, drinking coffee."

"Being fussed over by Mum. *As usual*," says Angel, but she sounds unhappy and I don't think she believes it. We all pretend to laugh. *You never know. How funny that we were out here searching.* We descend the spongy bank of marsh grass and follow a barely-visible path winding across boggy fields. Something bursts up from the grass at the edge of the path. It's an owl, an unexpected sight in the middle of the morning. It grasps a wriggling shape in its beak.

A dead hare lies half-submerged in grainy black water in a dip at the side of the track; I spot maggots in a gaping wound on its side. We climb a style and cross a drainage ditch to get back to the narrow road.

Birdwatchers hunker in a hut at the side of the road, binoculars slung around their necks, cameras and tripods in their hands. They regard us warily. None of us speak as we pass.

We cross the narrow road, our feet resuming their pattern of mismatched footsteps; the sound deadening as we descend back onto the marsh path. We bump into each other and slip and slide on seaweed-covered rocks. Silver mirrors of still water reflect flashes of colour from our clothes. The sun has emerged fully from its nest of clouds. I raise my face to it. A flock of silver birds swoops by in one fluid movement and then seems to disappear into thin air. I look around but can't see where they've gone.

Concentrate on not slipping.

We come out of the sea marshes and onto the river beach. The water covers the mud completely now, a shimmering band of light. Soon we'll arrive at the back of Blackberry House. My stomach tightens. I picture the creaking wooden gate hanging off its hinges. Already it seems familiar.

We walk in silence, the sound of our breathing becoming laboured. Images from the previous week float in front of me, red-edged like a strip of burning film.

My mother's eyes, huge in her stripped-away face.

My father's eyes as Lisa led him into the house.

Bile churns in my stomach.

38

Angel

J IM FROM NEXT door is hanging over the fence at the bottom of his garden. *He's* what I imagine a father should be. (Or Mariana's dad). I used to have a massive crush on Jim's son when I was younger, but we hardly ever see Henry now. Jim opens his gate and picks his way across the pebbles towards us, doffing a pretend hat. He used to be such a joker. He's got stubble on his cheeks and his eyes seem to have sunk into his head since he's been on his own. Mum and me try and ensure he keeps eating properly but you can't take the place of a person who's gone.

He nods at us. "Morning." His eyes run over Mariana with a flash of interest.

"This is our half-sister, Mariana," I say. He offers a hand for her to shake, then nods at Aiden. "All right, lad?" but doesn't wait for an answer. "Odd thing," he says next.

"What is, Jim?"

"Boat's gone missing." He fumbles in his pocket, comes out with a pouch of tobacco. It takes a moment for his words to sink in. I look around. Jim's boat is usually propped up against his fence, but it's not here now.

Aiden and I look at each other and then at Mariana. Something catches in her eyes and she chews a fingernail. We all look at Jim. "When did you last see it?" Aiden asks. Jim says he used the boat yesterday afternoon for crabbing on the river. It had been leaning against the fence when he turned in for the evening; he went for a walk before bed and he saw it there then. Mariana keeps biting her nails.

"I saw a boat out at sea when we were looking for him," she says.

"Who were you looking for?" Jim asks.

"Dad," I put in. "He's gone missing."

39

Mariana

W E'VE BEEN ON the beach, on and off, most of the day. I've got sand in my hair, in my clothes and even between my teeth because of the wind. Their neighbour who's boat's gone missing rang the coastguard when we realised Cal might have taken it.

When we opened the kitchen door of Blackberry House, Gabe was standing on a chair beside the sink, helping Lisa wash potatoes. A licked-out bowl of cake mix was on the table and he had a smear of it on his upper lip. Lisa had a smudge of flour on her cheek. They both looked happy.

That moment is frozen in my memory and I keep returning to it. The moment before Lisa's face collapsed.

We've been taking it in turns to keep vigil on the beach.

The local newspaper has got hold of the story: a van with a satellite dish on top is parked in the seafront car park. The fish and chip shop on the caravan site is doing well for itself, thank you very much, and the corner shop has stayed open later than usual.

As the sun goes down the search and rescue man comes over and tells us they're calling off the search for the night. He advises us to go home and get some rest. Lisa refuses, and Alice says she'll go back to the house and fetch blankets and things. She'll bring them back in the car and spend the night on the beach with her mother. An old woman from the village has organised a collection of hot food and candles which are being distributed amongst the gathering crowd.

Cal would hate it, Angel says. Her eyes are red from crying. *He'd think it was a bloody circus.*

"You three go home and get some sleep," Alice tells us. "You've been searching all day as it is. You can take over in the morning."

In the morning. No-one's expecting him to come home.

"Take Gabe home, Mariana," she urges when we say nothing. "He needs you."

Bossy older sister. But she's right of course. My son needs me more than the absent father I never knew. Angel and Aiden don't need much persuading either. We're all exhausted.

I don't feel anything much, except tired.

THERE WERE NO phone calls in the night; no joyous returns.

I'm an orphan, is the first thing I think when I wake up. But I still feel calm. Questions I never even knew I've been asking have been answered. I know who I am now.

I look at my watch. 5:20am and fully light. Gabe sleeps, back wedged against the wall, his mouth open. His eyes flicker beneath almost-transparent lids, the blue veins in them delicate lines on tracing paper. When I push myself into a sitting position his hand reaches out and grasps my hair. It runs through his fingers as I start to get out of the bed. "Don't leave me, Mammy," his voice is thick with sleep.

"I won't," I promise. "Mammy has to go out, but you can come too."

I rifle in the bag beneath the bed and bundle him into some clothes. He slumps against me, warm and heavy. I realise that like me, Gabe comes from the blood and bones of Cal and Maria. I hold him tightly, then lay him down again while I dress.

Having dragged jeans over the shorts I was wearing for bed, I zip a thick hooded jacket over my t-shirt. A part of me decrees that I ought to choose my clothes carefully for this auspicious first day of my orphan-hood. The other part tells me not to be stupid.

"Come on, Gabe," I brush the back of my hand over his soft cheek to wake him again. He's curled up like he must have been when he was inside me. "Wake up, it's time to go."

I'll make us a couple of sandwiches before we head out to the beach, feeling compelled to be there as soon as possible. But Aiden and Angel are already in the kitchen when we get down, packing food into an insulated bag. The smell of bacon floods my nostrils.

"We were going to wake you, I promise," Angel says.

We're a team now, the three of us. Angel places a large flask into a cloth bag and manages to fit in a picnic blanket as well. Aiden turns from packing a final foil-wrapped sandwich and gives me a smile, but his eyes are sad. He puts his arms out for my son and Gabe climbs into them.

"I'll carry him." Aiden rests his cheek on Gabe's hair a moment. "It'll be quicker."

OUTSIDE THE SUN hovers over the fields. I spot a hare running along the ridge.

"Look, rabbit," Gabe says, sleepily lifting his head from his uncle's shoulder. He starts to wake up as he glances around him. I'm carrying the bag with the bacon sandwiches and Angel has the strap of the cloth bag over her shoulder.

"I'm sorry," Aiden says, looking at Angel. "About yesterday. I didn't really think there was anything wrong. Maybe things would have been different if I'd taken it more seriously."

Angel has tears in her eyes. She dips her chin and looks at the ground. I touch Aiden on the arm, but Gabe kicks out at my hand.

"*My* Aiden."

"You did take Angel's concerns seriously." I tell Aiden. "If we hadn't gone out to look for him, we might not have known about the boat going missing. Jim might just have called the police and not told us."

We repeat yesterday's walk. As we round the corner towards the sea, the fields surrounding us come alive with birdsong. Skylarks hover, their trill striking a chord inside me. A buried memory works its way to the surface of my consciousness. *I'm a baby, lying in a pram in a garden that backs on to fields. A woman, a girl really, with copper hair, leans over me, rocking the pram.* I'm remembering the skylark theme-tune of my infancy.

"I want to get down, please," Gabriel says.

Aiden lets him go and he runs ahead of us down the path to the sea. The car park at the side of the road is full of vehicles, a few MOD Land Rovers amongst them. A helicopter is already circling. The TV van is still there, or has returned from the night before. I see Alice's car, the one that carried Gabe and me into the heart of our new family.

Alice and Lisa must be worn out. I hope they'll go back to the house and get some rest.

I HAVE A song running through my head. It's weird because this song came out before I had even been born, yet it's playing on a loop in my mind right now; I think it's by U2. Damon's band used to play it. Then I realise how horrible it is that I'm thinking the lyrics of a song about a drowning man.

I wonder what it would have been like if I'd had the chance to get to know Cal.

The sea is angry and brown. The sky has clouded over and we've been told that if visibility worsens the search and rescue team are going to have to give up. No-one has much hope of finding him alive now anyway.

The empty boat, its oars gone, was discovered early this

morning, just after we arrived on the beach. It washed up on the shore when the tide came in. Alice persuaded Lisa to go home with her after that and they took Gabriel with them, since he was bored by then anyway. I was grateful they didn't expect me to go back as well, I wanted to finish this thing I started with Aiden and Angel.

I glance behind me. Most of the people who gathered to watch the search and rescue team have gone away now, just a huddle left standing at the edge of the car park. The empty rowing boat is loaded onto a trailer. A team of forensic experts in white coveralls have been working on it for the past couple of hours. The news crew appear to have been in consultation with search and rescue and it looks as though they're packing up their gear in preparation for leaving. We had to give them a few words – a 'quote' – earlier on and I was glad nobody asked me how long I'd been in the family.

The leader of the lifeboat team walks towards Aiden, Angel and me, shaking his head, sadly.

The helicopter whirred away some time ago.

WE'RE GOING TO be left alone, here on the beach, keeping vigil for our disappeared father.

DUSK FALLS AND we link arms, staring out to sea. We know it's useless to stay here any longer. The coastguard told us in the gentlest possible way that if something has happened to Cal, he might not be found in this area anyway. A flock of seagulls bobs on the surface of the grey waves. Earlier I saw a seal, its dog-shaped head popped up to peer curiously at us, its eyes brimming with tears. The seal disappeared but re-emerged even closer to shore, still staring intently at the three human watchers.

Go home, it was saying, *give us back our element. There's nothing to see here.*

But I couldn't stop staring outward. I don't know what I imagined I'd see; a waving arm?

Cal wanted to drown, we all know it. Lisa, the calmest of us after her initial outpouring of grief, she's the one who seems to have accepted it most easily. Alice had been the most distraught when the boat came in.

The three of us, alone on the beach, have become like one entity. *Neither Angel nor Aiden had an easy relationship with their father, and I never had the chance of one at all.*

Two of the seagulls rise on flapping wings and soar into the sky, screaming.

I SEE SOMETHING out the corner of my eye, further along the beach. The figures are hard to make out because of the falling blanket of dusk but it seems to be a boy and a girl. They're dressed in thin clothes and I wonder if they're cold.

"Look," I say softly, but the others don't seem to have heard me. After some discussion with Aiden, Angel's already turning to walk away up the beach but I pull back. Aiden, starting to follow her, hangs back as well.

"Come on, Sis," he says in a gentle voice. "It's over. Let's go home and get warm."

The words 'Sis' and 'home' leave a warm feeling in my tummy, but something else is distracting me.

"No, wait…"

The figures are walking towards us, looming through the weird, intense light that always precedes darkness. Aiden tugs at my sleeve.

"Can't you see them?" I ask.

Aiden looks around and shakes his head. "See who?"

I DON'T KNOW why he can't see them, but they are here. They look like characters on a screen, oddly contrasted against the falling dark. I can see them as clear as day, hear them talking but not what they're saying. The girl laughs, tosses back her hair which is the same colour as mine, and his.

As they get closer I see that she's wearing a long, lightweight skirt and what looks like a cheesecloth blouse. Her arm is linked with the boy's. He looks strikingly similar to her. I imagine that I can see the colour of their eyes, and that they're the same colour as mine.

The two of them walk along the edge of the sea, barefoot. As they pass Aiden and me the girl turns towards me and smiles. Something breaks open in my heart and at the same time a shiver runs through me.

I look away for a moment as Aiden pulls at my arm again. Glancing sideways I see that Angel's retreating figure is disappearing into the outlines of the cliffs at the top of the beach.

"Come on, Sis," Aiden says for the second time.

But I don't move. Instead I glance back and forth along the shoreline. Maybe twilight has given way to dark sooner than I realised, because I can no longer see the young couple at the water's edge, either.

Acknowledgements

The raw, wild coastline of East and North Yorkshire, from Kilnsea at the base of Spurn Point to Whitby, dominated by the bones of the Abbey and its associations with Dracula. The sea, always the sea with its symphonic choruses and mournful whispers.

My past, the particular affinity I felt with the under-pulse of nature and the call of 'The Everything'. How I always perceived myself to be to some extent apart.

The books I read as a child, as a teenager, as a young woman, stories that have stayed with me: *A Dream in The House*, *Wuthering Heights*; *Brother of the More Famous Jack*. The Brontë family for inspiring the Wilde family in my books. Jane Austen for her writerly investigation of the minutiae of relationships. *Heathcliff* for the character of Cal; *Marianne* in *Sense and Sensibility* for her name, planted in my literary aspirations when I was eighteen.

Sara-Jayne Slack and Fiona Thomas of Inspired Quill Publishing for their excellent editing services – the reason I returned for the third time to be published by Inspired Quill.

Fran Macilvey, Lynn Michell, Rhiannon Carmichael and Katrina Soper for reading and commenting on the manuscript, particularly Fran who gave me a basic edit of the whole book and Lynn who treated me to an edit of the first couple of chapters.

Phil for joining me in my newest literary and publishing adventures with Wild Pressed Books – something we can do together as we travel and explore as much of the world as we are able to reach in our bus-with-a-woodstove.

The people I gave birth to: Felix, Ruben, Zak and Faye, for being my constant inspiration and my reason to work harder and in turn be an inspiration to them.

The memory of Alice, her loss informs the mothers' griefs in my books.

La Leche League (GB) and League Family Camp, for showing me that 'family' need not only consist of genetics, blood and bones. Family is where you fit in.

And finally, R.I.P our beautiful Labrador, Riley Scott-Townsend, who accompanied us on all our travels.

About the Author

Tracey Scott-Townsend is the author of uncompromising family dramas which delve into often uncomfortable aspects of relationships of all kinds, but motherhood is frequently at the heart of her stories. Sense of place is also important. Three of her books feature the Humber Estuary in East Yorkshire, where she lived for a year when she was young.

Tracey writes in her shed in the garden, warmed by the wood stove. She and her husband frequently take to the road in a van which also has a wood stove. They go to wild places. Tracey's favourite is the Outer Hebrides, the setting for a future novel.

Tracey is the mother of four grown children. She is also editorial director of Wild Pressed Books, a small publishing company she runs with her husband Phil Scott-Townsend. They published their first three books in 2016, one of which is Tracey's third novel, The Eliza Doll.

Of His Bones, her fourth, marks a return to publication with Inspired Quill.

Find the author via her website:
traceyscotttownsend.com

Or tweet at her:
@authortrace

More From This Author

The Last Time We Saw Marion

When Cal and his older sister Sarah spot Marianne in the audience of a TV show that Cal is recording, they are stunned by her uncanny resemblance to Marion. They have to find out who she is, but they both soon come to regret the decision to draw her into their lives. Events spiral out of control for all of them, but whilst Cal and Sarah each manage to find a way to move on, Marianne is forced to relinquish the one precious thing that could have given her life some meaning.

The book is set in a haunting estuary landscape of mudflats, marshes and the constant resonance of the sea.

The Last Time We Saw Marion is the story of two families – but the horrible truth is that two into one won't go…

Paperback ISBN: 978-1-908600-26-4
eBook ISBN: 978-1-908600-27-1

Another Rebecca

Rebecca Grey can't shake off the hallucination she had while in hospital, but her alcoholic mother Bex is too wrapped up in the 'Great Grief' of her youth to notice her daughter's struggles to define dream from reality.

After lurching from one poverty-stricken situation to another, and ghosts from the past are disturbed, Rebecca's dream comes alive. Why does the old woman who left them a sudden inheritance believe she is Rebecca's grandmother, and why did Bex swear to stop living when she was only nineteen?

The setting of the novel transitions between the flat seascape of Skegness, the fields of Lincolnshire, the mountains of Ireland and the rolling hills of Leicestershire.

Another Rebecca is a family story of secrets, interdependency and obsessive love.

Paperback ISBN: 978-1-908600-43-1
eBook ISBN: 978-1-908600-44-8

Available from all major online and offline outlets.